CONSPIRACY OF SILENCE

CONSPIRACY
of Silence
—— A NOVEL ——

GLEDÉ BROWNE KABONGO

iUniverse, Inc.
Bloomington

Conspiracy of Silence
A Novel

iUniverse books may be ordered through booksellers or by contacting:

iUniverse
1663 Liberty Drive
Bloomington, IN 47403
www.iuniverse.com
1-800-Authors (1-800-288-4677)

ISBN: 978-1-4759-4567-6 (sc)
ISBN: 978-1-4759-4569-0 (hc)
ISBN: 978-1-4759-4568-3 (e)

Library of Congress Control Number: 2012915328

1. Middleclass/upper middleclass women—United States—Fiction
2. Marketing executive—United States—Fiction 3. Childhood trauma—United States—Fiction 4. Criminal trial—United States—Fiction 5. Infertility—United States—Fiction 6. Boston landmarks—United States—Fiction

Printed in the United States of America

iUniverse rev. date: 08/30/2012

Dedication

To my husband Donat, my first reader whose support and endless patience made this book possible. Thank you for lifting me up when I was drowning in self-doubt.

CHAPTER ONE

W hen Nina Kasai was a little girl, she learned how to deceive. As an adult, she never revealed to her husband the reason her father wasn't invited to their wedding; he didn't know why she turned down academic scholarships from Harvard, Princeton and Columbia, and chose instead to attend college on the West Coast. And he didn't know why she secretly despised her looks and the attention her beauty brought.

Lately, she'd been receiving a lot of attention. Nina felt as giddy as a schoolgirl as she sat in her office on the twenty-eighth floor of One International Place in Boston's financial district. At thirty-five, she was the youngest executive to appear on the cover of *Executive Insider*, a high-profile national business magazine. She kept reading and rereading the cover story as if they were talking about someone else. The almost life-sized congratulatory bouquet of flowers from Marc filled the air with an array of sweet-smelling fragrances that seduced the senses, bringing a dimpled smile to her face.

Phillip Copeland was on edge as he sat in a small conference room three doors down from his target. The source of his discomfort was the image on the cover of *Executive Insider*. Although he'd been secretly keeping tabs on her, this was the first time in over a decade they would meet face-to-face. Once he discovered she was an executive at Baseline Technologies, the rest was easy—he simply placed a call to his buddy, Baseline CEO Jack Kendall, so they could "catch up."

Baseline's PR agency was discussing media placement opportunities with Nina on their weekly conference call. They had just landed her the keynote address at the annual Marketing Executives International Conference, along with interviews with several traditional and online media outlets. She was about to wrap up the call when she heard a knock on the door.

"Come in," Nina said airily.

"That's the best invitation I've had all week."

Nina's heart fell to her stomach, or so it seemed. She clutched the receiver too tightly as she slowly rotated her swivel chair to face Phillip Copeland, a man she had gone to extraordinary lengths to erase from her memory. It took all the strength she had to end the conference call with some semblance of authority and control. She schooled her features into one of mild surprise and irritation and hoped the shock that was wreaking havoc with her insides wasn't visible. His slight frame was draped in a tailored designer suit; glasses perched on his elegant nose, enhancing the arrogance he wore like a badge of honor. To her dismay, he hadn't aged a bit.

"Congratulations, Gorgeous," he said smoothly. "It's good to see you again."

"Lucifer," Nina said, her cool tone echoing her displeasure.

"That was mean," he said, frowning.

"No more than you deserve."

"I was hoping for a better reception. Maybe even a hug. It's been a long time, Nina."

"I can't imagine why you'd think that. I guess some things never change. You still believe the sun rises and sets on you."

"You thought so at one point in time," he said, inching closer.

"I wised up."

Nina stood up to her full five feet ten inches, towering over him with the additional three inches provided by her Louboutins. She suddenly felt claustrophobic and found refuge near a bookshelf at the far corner of the office.

"Why are you here?"

He pointed to the issue of *Executive Insider* on her desk. "Consider me impressed. I want to retain your services as a communications consultant."

"Why?"

He looked at her sheepishly. "I need help building my personal brand. I figure you'd be great for the messaging and media strategy, maybe even a little speech writing thrown in."

Nina couldn't believe what she was hearing. She hadn't seen the man in years and he just showed up out of the blue with a consulting offer, which frankly, sounded like a fun side project. A fun side project she had no business entertaining because it was coming from *him*.

"Why me, Phillip? Why now? There are a number of qualified people in the city who would do an outstanding job. In fact, I can tap my network and recommend someone."

Phillip knew this wasn't going to be easy but she wasn't giving him an inch. She glared at him with almond-shaped green eyes that shimmered like sunlight off the water during a sunset, an unusual color for a black woman. Her jet-black hair hung just past her shoulders, obviously professionally styled. Everything about her said chic, sophisticated, and confident, but he knew better. The air of confidence was a performance purely for his benefit. He was willing to play along for now.

"Your work is getting national attention. I want you to advise me."

"As I said, I'm happy to recommend someone."

"You get results," he said, refusing to back down.

She couldn't dispute that statement. As chief marketing officer, she had responsibilities for sales, media relations, customer experience, advertising and promotion, web services and corporate programs. Her ability to drive revenue and demonstrate return on investment for a function often criticized for its inability to do so was what had caught the attention of the editors at *Executive Insider*.

Nina's company-issued smartphone beeped and she was glad for the reprieve. She crossed the room in three brief strides and picked up the device. It was a text message from Gwen, her director of global marketing, explaining she would be late for their meeting.

"Unfortunately, I can't help you," she said, turning to Phillip. "My job is very demanding and at the end of the day, I just want to go home to my husband."

"I can appreciate that," he said with forced sympathy. "But I would try to make it as easy as possible for you. Maybe an hour or two a week for a few weeks?"

"The answer is still no," she said firmly.

Nina didn't know the real motive behind this sudden visit but she was willing to bet her Celtics courtside seat it had little to do with building his brand. Something big was brewing. It had to be to cause him to seek her out after all this time.

"Just think about it," she heard him say, his voice dragging her out of her thoughts.

"My answer won't change."

Phillip picked up a wedding photo from her desk. "Have you told your husband the truth?"

"Don't touch that!" She snatched the photo away from him.

"I guess I have my answer. Think about my offer."

"You don't hear very well, do you?"

"You'll come around."

"What if I don't?"

"I always achieve my objective, Nina."

"And what would that be?" she pressed, knowing full well his calculating nature wouldn't allow him to be honest.

"I want one of the top marketers in the country advising me. What else?"

Nina's mind raced after he exited her office. Maybe she was an idiot to think she could run forever, keep up the lies forever. If Phillip were to expose her, her marriage would be the first in a series of high value casualties. She had invested too much time and energy into living the perfect lie to allow that to happen.

CHAPTER TWO

Nina wasn't the type of woman who sat around waiting for things to happen but Phillip had her at a disadvantage. His sudden reappearance was a precursor to something much bigger and she shuddered to think what that might be. She'd told Marc enough white lies to ensure he didn't ask inconvenient questions but she also knew lies had a way of unraveling. When they did, lives usually changed forever. And Phillip knew all her secrets.

She busied herself preparing breakfast in the large eat-in kitchen of the modern four-bedroom colonial she shared with Marc. He protested initially when she wanted them to purchase it, arguing they didn't need a three thousand square foot house for the two of them, but Nina always looked at the big picture. For her, that included kids running around and breaking things. Their home was in an affluent suburb of eighteen thousand, thirty miles west of Boston— a town voted by *Money Magazine* as one of the best places to live in America. That was a major selling point for someone who had her entire future planned out. The local schools consistently scored high in the rankings of top public school systems in the state.

Nina turned around and caught Marc Kasai and his muscular six-foot-two frame leaning against the kitchen doorway with a lazy grin on his face. "It smells great in here. Do you need help?"

"I think I have it covered. I made all your favorites." Nina deposited a plate of scrambled eggs with bacon on the kitchen table and made a second trip to the stove to pick up the steaming hot Belgian Waffles. A quick trip to the refrigerator yielded a large carafe of freshly squeezed orange juice. Marc took care of the glasses, plates, and flatware and then sat down.

"Where did you go last night?" Marc asked, through a mouthful of eggs.

Nina was startled by the question but tried to sound casual. "What do you mean?"

"I reached for you in the middle of the night and you were gone."

"I couldn't sleep so I went downstairs to watch a little TV."

"We have a TV set in our bedroom."

Nina knew she was being defensive, but she wondered why Marc was making a big deal about this. It's not like he didn't know she suffered with bouts of insomnia. She just wasn't about to admit that this latest round was induced by a heartless bastard.

"I didn't want to disturb you. You were sleeping so peacefully."

He seemed satisfied with her answer.

The house telephone rang while Nina was clearing the dishes, shattering the serenity of their Sunday morning. An aggravated Nina answered.

"Yes?" she snapped.

"Why didn't you answer your cell phone?"

There was only one person she knew who exhibited this particular brand of arrogance.

"Why the heck are you calling my home?" She dropped her voice to a whisper so not to arouse her husband's suspicions. "How did you get this number?"

"You'd be amazed what you can find out if you know where to look."

"What do you want?"

"It's been five days since our last conversation. You only have two days left to accept my offer. I'm even willing to double your fee."

"That's two days to figure out how to get you off my back. Anything can happen."

"Don't get smart with me Nina. It's not a good idea."

"Really?" she asked sweetly, and then hung up.

"Who was that?" Marc asked, not missing a beat.

"A very pushy head hunter with no respect for boundaries. Nothing I can't handle."

"Strange you would get a call at home on a Sunday. Which firm does this headhunter work for?"

"It's not important. He won't be calling any more."

"How can you be so sure?" Marc insisted. "With the publicity you've been getting, Baseline's competitors are going to try and poach you."

"Well, they can't. I signed non-compete and non-disclosure agreements."

Marc looked like he wanted to discuss things further but Nina changed the subject.

"Don't you have a soccer match to get ready for?"

"I do. Thanks for breakfast," he said, dropping a quick kiss on her right cheek.

Nina reached for her purse on the counter after Marc headed upstairs. She took out her cell phone and went through the call log to see if Phillip's number had shown up. It was logged as an unknown number.

Nina punched speed dial number three. The call went to voicemail.

"Hey, it's me," she said. "Tell your playmate to go home. We have a category five storm on the horizon."

Charlene Hamilton was a force of nature, all ninety-eight pounds of her. The self-proclaimed chocolate fox and hair-styling maven had blown into Nina's life twenty-one years earlier when they were freshmen at Westwood High School. Charlene threatened to rearrange the intestines of a badly behaved boy who had been giving Nina a hard time. The discovery they shared a common Caribbean heritage sealed the friendship that had proved unbreakable over the years.

"How many people did you run off the road to get here so fast?" Nina teased as Charlene plopped down her favorite Coach bag on the kitchen counter.

"Child, please. You can't be throwing around words like 'category five' and not expect consequences."

"There's somewhere I need to be this weeken—"

Marc appeared around the doorway in full soccer garb. The conversation came to a halt.

"Looking luscious as always Marc," Charlene said shamelessly. "Don't hurt yourself on that soccer field now. We need you in peak condition."

"I won't break anything, Charlene," he said, humoring her. "I promise."

Nina shrugged her shoulders and gave Marc the you-know-how-she-is look. Marc bid both women goodbye and disappeared from view.

"Girl, if you ever get tired of him, I'll take him off your hands."

"Only if I'm in a box in the ground with worms for company."

"I can wait." Charlene grabbed the white porcelain jar marked cookies off the counter and headed for the kitchen table. She set the jar down and reached to the bottom and came up with an oatmeal raisin, her favorite.

Nina heard the engine of Marc's car roar to life in the garage. It was her cue to speak freely.

"I need to sleep over Friday night for a Saturday trip to Baltimore."

Charlene lived in Quincy, and from there, Nina could make it to Logan Airport in less than half an hour since Route 93 North weekend traffic was a cinch compared to weekdays. She would tell Marc she was spending the weekend with Charlene for some female bonding and retail therapy.

"Phillip came to see me at the office. It was not a happy reunion."

Charlene almost choked. "Stop lying."

Nina gave her best friend a recap of Phillip's visit.

"What are you going to do?"

"That's where Baltimore comes in."

"Who's in Baltimore?"

"A friend with special skills."

"Details, girl. Don't make me beat it out of you."

"Sonny Alvarez."

"The computer guy?"

"He's much more than a computer guy."

"Do I even want to know?"

"Probably not."

"Why don't you just tell your man the truth?"

"That's not an option," Nina said stiffly.

"How are you going to handle Phillip? Do you even have a plan besides Sonny?"

"I'm making it up as I go."

Charlene rolled her eyes at Nina. "You're asking for trouble, keeping this from Marc."

"How do you figure?"

"Tell him about Phillip before it's too late. Don't you think you've been hiding long enough?"

"You're my best friend. You're supposed to be helping me plot and scheme," Nina said half-jokingly. "I've kept the truth from Marc this long to protect us. Whatever Phillip has planned, I have to face it head on."

"Secrets have a way of coming back to bite you in the ass. I'm just saying."

"I can't worry about that right now. There's too much at stake. You have no idea."

"Such as?" Charlene asked sharply.

"Nothing you don't already know."

Nina hated lying to her best friend but there were certain truths she couldn't share with anyone, not even Charlene.

CHAPTER THREE

The Delta Airlines shuttle touched down at Baltimore-Washington International Airport a little past noon. A purposeful Nina made her way to ground transportation and jumped into the first available cab. She directed the driver to her destination and arrived twenty minutes later. She was greeted at the Havana Grill, a popular Cuban restaurant.

"Mr. Alvarez is expecting you," said the stout Latino man with the nose ring and a dragon tattoo on his left arm. "Follow me."

He led her through the restaurant filled with the chatter of lunchtime patrons. Strategically placed potted palm trees and ocean-themed artwork hugged the walls, giving the place a tropical flair. They arrived at a large booth in the far corner of the restaurant, where a beaming Sonny stood up and hugged her tightly. The maître'de said something to him in rapid Spanish then disappeared.

"What was that about?"

"He says I'm a lucky man."

"Oh," Nina said, blushing.

Sonny Alvarez looked like he'd just stepped off the cover of *GQ Magazine.* He possessed a sultry Latin charm that had women slipping him their phone numbers wherever he went. Born to a Mexican father and a Puerto Rican mother, the former Navy SEAL grew up in California and met Nina while she was a sophomore at Stanford and he was a Ph.D. candidate in Math and Computer Science. The National Security Agency came knocking and Sonny secured a position as one of their top analysts in the Cryptography Division. As far as Nina could tell, Sonny hadn't met a code he couldn't crack or a network he couldn't hack.

"So *mamacita*, how much trouble are you in?" he asked, as he pulled out a chair for Nina and took the one across from her.

"I came to see you, didn't I? That should be a clue."

Sonny leaned back in his chair and clasped both hands behind his head as he studied her.

"You're afraid. What are you running from?"

"My past. I was just minding my own business when it showed up uninvited."

"With baggage?"

"Enough to put Louis Vuitton out of business."

He laughed out loud as the waiter appeared to take their order. Nina ordered seafood with fried plantain chips; Sonny opted for red beans and rice with chicken.

"Sounds like unresolved personal issues. I don't see where I fit in."

Nina raked her fingers through her hair. "I wouldn't have come if I didn't think you could help me, Sonny."

Had she put all her faith in one place? What if Sonny balked at her request? He could get in serious trouble if he ever got caught helping her and frankly, she had no right to ask him to risk his freedom for her. But what choice did she have?

"Tell me then. What's got you so scared?"

"I made a decision years ago that probably saved my life. Not everyone was thrilled."

"Are you in physical danger?" He leaned forward, his face anxious.

"Worse."

"I see. What can I do?"

"What you do best. Get in and out without a trace." She felt vulnerable and exposed. Nina trusted Sonny but hated asking for favors.

"Wow. I suppose being a regular girl with regular problems is out of the question?"

"If I were, you wouldn't give me a second thought."

"You cut me deep, *mamacita*."

"It's true."

"You're not even supposed to know what I do for a living. If the agency finds out you came to me for help, I could be in serious trouble."

She hadn't thought her mere presence could put Sonny in jeopardy. She squeezed her eyes tightly, willing him to come to her rescue.

"But I owe you. You had my back when no one else did. I haven't forgotten. I'll help you on my personal time, away from work."

She didn't realize she was shaking. When she opened her eyes, Sonny's hands were covering hers.

"I'm sorry," she said. "I thought I saw my life being flushed down the toilet."

"Not as long as I'm around."

She punched him playfully in the arm. "That's for scaring me."

He pretended to be injured. "I would never say no to you, Nina."

"I couldn't take our friendship for granted."

"*Friendship*, huh? Whose fault was that?"

"It wouldn't have worked between us. It was better to spare you."

"You didn't invite me to your wedding."

"Would you have come?"

"No."

*   *   *

NINA READ THE NOTE FOR the third time and thought it was a trap. It had to be.

> *I've behaved abominably. Allow me to apologize.*

There was no signature at the bottom, but she didn't need one to know who'd sent it. She glanced at the stack of files on her neatly organized mahogany desk, and the two computers with dozens of emails and a loaded calendar all needing her attention. She was too tense to focus.

"I see you got my note."

The voice startled her. She turned around to find Phillip behind her.

"You have got to stop popping into my office unannounced," she said, exasperated. "Make an appointment like everybody else. Eric is in so much trouble."

"It's not your assistant's fault. Your boss and I are old friends. Plus the door was unlocked."

This news that Phillip and Jack were friends was disconcerting. How much had Phillip told Jack about their past together? She didn't dare ask Phillip, he would just use it as another opportunity to try and blackmail her. He was insinuating himself into her professional life and she didn't like it one bit. On the other hand, it might give her a chance to find out what he was up to. Plus, she'd spent so many years denying his existence, it shouldn't be too hard to deny a relationship ever existed in the first place if Jack started asking questions.

"What are you up to?" she asked suspiciously.

"I can admit when I'm wrong."

"To the best of my knowledge, hell has not yet frozen over."

Her screen saver caught his attention, a close-up of Nina and Marc on the beach in Mustique.

"Where are the kids?"

He knew damn well she didn't have any. Phillip Copeland was nothing if not thorough. She wouldn't be surprised if he had a dossier on her, dictionary-thick.

"Mind your business," she said brusquely. "You said you wanted to apologize. I'm listening. Then you can leave."

"Have dinner with me tonight."

The request caught her off guard. "Why?"

"Sometimes it helps to sort things out over a good meal. Maybe I came on a little too strong."

"I can't. I'll be leaving here late tonight."

"Jack's working you too hard. I think I'll have a word with him."

"And why would Jack Kendall listen to anything you have to say regarding his staff?"

"As I said, he and I go way back. We sit on the board together."

"What board?"

"The Board of Directors of Baseline Technologies," he said pointedly.

"I report directly to Jack. I would have known if there was a new addition to the board."

"I convinced them to delay the announcement. I wanted to be the one to tell you, after the board meeting this morning."

"Lucky me."

"Oh, come on, Nina. Let's sit down like two civilized people so I can properly apologize for my behavior. You have nothing to fear from me."

"I'm sure Jeffrey Dahmer said the same thing to his victims before he hacked them to pieces."

He chuckled. "A lesser man would be insulted, but I appreciate your sense of humor."

"It wasn't meant to be funny."

"I don't understand why you're being so stubborn. You're behaving as if I'm a criminal."

"Thanks for the invitation, but I have to decline."

"Don't be hasty. It's only dinner. I want you to see I'm not an ogre."

"Too late."

"You're wrong. Just give me a chance to prove it."

His insistence should have been a warning, but Nina's curiosity made the decision for her.

"Fine. Where?"

CHAPTER FOUR

N
ina pulled up to the Four Seasons Hotel on Boylston Street and handed the keys of her Porsche SUV to the valet attendant. The Bristol Lounge was on the second floor, a restaurant known for fantastic dining and conversation with Boston's movers and shakers. Tables offering a view of the Boston Public Gardens abutted floor-to-ceiling windows. The place was already packed for a week night and alive with the chatter and socializing of the after work crowd.

Phillip was nursing a drink at his table a few feet from the bar. He looked relieved when he saw her. "You made it. I wasn't sure you would come."

"I said I would."

He pulled out a chair so she could sit but she waved him off and pulled out her own chair opposite him.

"When a gentleman holds out a seat for you, it's polite to accept it," he admonished.

"You're not a gentleman so I'm off the hook." She could tell he was irritated, but for some reason, he needed to be on his best behavior tonight.

"Just relax. There's no reason we can't have an enjoyable evening."

"You're absolutely right. As soon as I order a drink, I will toast to that."

Nina figured she could catch more flies with honey, as the saying goes. If Phillip believed she was relaxed and ready to be an amiable companion, she might walk away having learned something.

"I saw you on *City Beat* a couple of weeks ago. You missed an opportunity to talk about how the foundation ties into what you're doing with the Developing World Economic Initiative."

"So you do pay attention." Phillip looked like he had just hit the Mega Millions jackpot— not that he needed the money.

"I was channel surfing. You happened to be on."

"Still, now you understand why I need your help."

"We're back on that subject again?"

"I was sincere in my offer, Nina. Jack gave me the inside story on how you helped Baseline regain lost market share, resurrected the brand, gained the respect of top business and technology analysts ... how your growth plans yielded a double digit percentage increase in revenue. It's virtually unheard of for a chief marketing officer to have that kind of impact on a company in such a short period of time. That kind of talent is rare. I want the best, and you're it."

He was actually flattering her. Now she really needed her guard up. Phillip's compliments usually came with strings attached. "Jack doesn't get in my way. He understands marketing in a way most CEOs don't. I proved to him marketing could be a revenue generator, not just a cost center."

"So that's the secret of your success—autonomy. I get it." He shook his head in admiration.

"Where's the waiter? I'm starving." Nina needed to stay focused, unaffected.

"Can we wait just a few more minutes?"

She hesitated. "Um ... sure, but why?"

"I have a surprise for you."

"I don't like surprises."

"Here she comes now."

He waived to a toothpick-thin woman with short red hair coiffed in the latest style. Her green linen dress was belted, emphasizing her tiny waist. As she got closer, Nina noticed striking blue eyes and flawless make-up. She greeted Phillip with a kiss on the cheek then turned her attention to Nina.

"Gosh darling, I thought you were exaggerating when you described her. She's a knock-out."

The woman had a strong British accent. Nina suddenly felt awkward and out of place. The stranger obviously knew of her.

"Nina, I'd like you to meet my wife, Geraldine. I asked her to join us ..."

Nina didn't hear anything past "wife." *He's married.* She tried to wrap her brain around that, tried to process how that made her feel, not that she should be feeling anything. It was just something she didn't anticipate. He wasn't wearing a wedding band, but if memory served her correctly, that's the way he liked it, no indication of attachments.

Nina regained her composure and exchanged pleasantries with Geraldine. Phillip signaled to the waiter and they finally ordered dinner.

"I told Geraldine all about you and the *Executive Insider* story. She insisted I invite you to dinner to get to know you better. She's a professor of Humanities at Tufts."

"That story on you was just brilliant," the Englishwoman gushed. "I told Phillip he absolutely had to procure your services, didn't I, darling?"

Nina eyed Phillip with malice for trying to manipulate her by dragging this poor woman into whatever scheme he had going. Her instincts told her Geraldine was a good soul who had no idea what she was in for.

"So this was your idea, Geraldine?" Nina asked.

"Well, of course. Phillip kept going on and on about you. You've made quite an impression on my husband. You had me worried for a while."

The glint in Geraldine's eyes told Nina the Brit was only kidding, but Nina couldn't help a snarky comeback. "Surely you jest. Have you met my husband? Any day now, I may fall off that pedestal he has me on."

Both women burst out laughing.

"I knew I'd like you," Geraldine said. "I could tell from your photograph."

Nina became alarmed. "What photograph?"

"The one on the magazine cover, of course. What other photograph would there be?"

"Sorry," Nina said, hedging on the fly. "I'm a little paranoid these days. You never know where your likeness might end up once it goes digital."

Phillip grinned inwardly. He had Nina exactly where he wanted her. He knew she and Geraldine would hit it off, and why not? They were both beautiful, intelligent, sophisticated women who were successful in their respective fields, and from what he could tell, they respected each other. This phase of his plan was working out perfectly.

"How long have you two been married?" Nina asked.

"It's been two years."

"You're practically newlyweds. How did you meet?"

"Don't bore Nina with mundane details of our life together," Phillip interjected.

"I'm not bored and neither is she."

Geraldine removed her napkin from the salad plate and placed it on her lap. "If I didn't know better, I'd say you two knew each other before tonight."

Nina went into a coughing fit and reached for a glass of ice water. She took a large sip. "I don't like to be interrupted when I'm about to hear a good story. That's all."

Nina shot Phillip a look of disdain, daring him to interrupt again. Geraldine looked baffled.

"We met at a café on Bond Street. Phillip was in the UK giving a series of lectures at Durham University. He practically spilled scalding hot tea all over my coat. He was so sweet I felt sorry for him. We ended up staying in that café until closing time. We couldn't stand being apart, so after a year of ridiculous long-distance phone bills and all-too-brief visits, we decided to get married. I moved to the States and the rest is history, as you Americans say."

"How charming. It must be difficult being away from your family."

"My parents are dead and my sister lives in South Africa."

Dinner was served, followed by dessert, during which time Geraldine excused herself to the ladies' room.

"What the hell was that?" Nina spat once she and Phillip were alone. "You brought your wife to get me to change my mind?"

"Are you upset you didn't have me all to yourself?" he asked mischievously.

"What? No, that's ridiculous. You asked—no, *begged*—me to come to dinner. So far, I don't hear any apologies. I walked into an ambush."

"Pipe down, Nina. I'm sorry I made you feel threatened. It wasn't my intention. I wasn't expecting you to be so hostile to the idea of helping me out. I thought a nice dinner with great food and conversation would be a do-over. Geraldine has been a great influence. I'm not the man you remember."

"She's not that gifted. No one is."

"When did you become so cynical?"

"My rose-colored glasses broke into tiny little pieces. My vision significantly improved after that."

Nina was getting tired of this conversation. She braced herself for whatever would come next.

"Look, I don't have the time to devote to your project. I work hours that would put a surgical resident to shame. Whatever time I have left I try to spend with Marc, who's no slouch in the workaholic department himself. I'm thirty-five and childless, which will become a permanent condition if I don't do something soon. I can barely balance it all. There's just no room for anything else."

Phillip cocked his head to one side, weighing her words carefully. It had never once occurred to him she might not be able to accept his offer for any other reason than she was being stubborn and wanted to hurt him. Other than the elephant-sized whopper she'd been telling that unsuspecting fool she married, he'd never known her to tell lies. In fact, she was just the opposite, which was why she was so dangerous to his ambition. He needed to dial up the pressure. And he knew just where to start.

"Are you having an affair with Sonny Alvarez?"

"What?" The question stunned Nina, but what was more disconcerting was the fact he brought up Sonny's name. How did he know Sonny and why did he think she was having an affair with him? Nina decided the best way to deal with this was to play it cool.

"I don't do affairs. That's more your department, isn't it?"

"You surprise me, Nina. Here you are talking about how wonderful your husband is, and you're cheating on him. Not that I blame this Sonny."

Nina was grateful Sonny had a cover job in case anyone came poking around. Phillip would have a coronary if he knew who Sonny worked for.

"Things aren't always as they appear. Sonny is a friend. And why are you having me followed?"

"It's clear you and Sonny Alvarez are lovers. To answer the second part of your question, I do background checks on all my employees, including who they associate with."

"It doesn't matter what you believe. The truth always wins out in the end. Secondly, I'm not your employee, and never will be, so you can call off your dogs. I wonder what Geraldine would make of all this?"

"Don't do anything stupid, Nina. I'll make you regret it."

Nina ignored the threat. "What do you want from her? How did you trap her into marrying you?"

"Geraldine and I were good friends before we started dating."

"You don't have friends," Nina countered. "You have targets. You and I both know she won't exit this marriage unscathed. You'll destroy her just like you did the others. And for once in your life, stop playing games and tell me the truth: why is there a bulls-eye on my back?"

CHAPTER FIVE

A married woman, still childless in her mid-thirties, is considered a failure in many non-western cultures. At least that's what Nina's mother-in-law, Claire Kasai, had told her one afternoon over drinks, soon after Nina and Marc were married. Claire went on to explain the expectations placed on women from such cultures, including their own Ivorian West African culture. It didn't matter what a woman accomplished professionally, Nina was told. If she failed to give her husband children, there was a certain stigma attached to her.

It sounded like outdated thinking to Nina at the time, an idea that had no place in a modern world where women had much more control over the choices that would impact their lives. Nina didn't believe such archaic rules applied to her marriage since Marc was American-born and didn't subscribe to that idea. They made the decision to put off starting a family so they could build their careers and extend the honeymoon phase through the first few years of their marriage.

For the past eight months, though, all efforts to conceive had been in vain. With their respective high-profile, high-stress jobs, Nina wasn't surprised they hadn't been successful. She made a promise to slow down and take more time to relax, but that hadn't happened. Instead, she was getting sucked in deeper and deeper into her responsibilities at work. On the home front, she was getting tired of the basal body temperature tracking, ovulation monitoring, and the post-coital legs-in-the-air routine. Marc was just as frustrated with what he affectionately referred to as his "monthly deposits."

Today they both ditched work and stayed home to do nothing in particular. Nina lounged on the sofa in the family room while Marc massaged her feet.

"This feels like heaven."

"You should let me do something about your hair, too," he said, grabbing a handful. "Right now it looks like a hurricane blew through the Amazon."

His quirky sense of humor was one of the things she loved most about him. "How long have you been sitting on that one?"

"A while. But I'm serious. You should let me practice on you. What if we have daughters? What if you're out of town and Charlene's not available? Don't you want peace of mind, knowing our girls won't go to school with hair like a troll's?"

Marc always looked at the big picture, thinking of every possibility from every angle. "Is that what you want, daughters?"

"Any child would be a blessing."

Nina suspected he was under mounting pressure from his family to produce a male heir. His younger brother, Thierry, loved the bachelor lifestyle and had no intentions of settling down and had told Nina as much. That left Marc to carry on the Kasai name. Claire Kasai erroneously believed her daughter-in-law cared more about her career than she did about having a family.

"I would prefer not to have girls," Nina announced.

"You don't mean that, *Cherie*?"

She sat up and looked at him. "I do mean it. I know it's not up to me, but the world isn't always kind to little girls. Or women, for that matter."

"Where is this coming from? I thought we wanted healthy children no matter the gender."

"As long as they're not girls."

Marc seemed unsure of what to say and gave her a forced smile. "You're going to miss out on a lot. Ballet lessons, first date, fashion crisis, boy crisis, senior prom, mother of the bride. I hear it's all about the dress."

"None of it's worth the potential horrors lurking around every corner."

Marc frowned in confusion but said nothing.

Nina knew it was selfish and irrational, but she didn't want a replay of her early years. She had mostly happy memories of her early childhood in Barbados, after her mother left her father when she was barely two years old and returned to the island to be near family. By the time she was eight, she was freakishly tall for a girl her age. To make matters worse, her small face emphasized her eyes, which looked like two enormous, green jack-o-lanterns. She was teased mercilessly by a group of kids who labeled her a witch—a damning moniker in Caribbean culture. She thought all the fuss over her features was left behind when she returned to the States at age ten, but it only got worse. None of the black kids would sit with her at lunch because they thought she was some kind of freak; her hair was too long, she had green eyes, and a funny accent. To add insult to injury, she was taller than everyone in her class, including the boys.

She rubbed Marc's shoulder reassuringly. "Sorry. I just had a flashback to my childhood. I meant to say it would be easier if we didn't have girls, especially if they looked like me. I just want to shield them from the misery I went through."

"They won't. I can see you storming the principal's office and demanding action if someone were to say boo to any child of ours. I can't imagine what it must have been like for you, feeling like there was something wrong with you. Looks like you got the last laugh."

"How so?"

"Look in the mirror. Why do you think I married you?"

"You said because I was smart and kind and I made you happy."

"True. But I didn't want to admit to you that one of the most elementary reasons I wanted to marry you. I was afraid you would accuse me of being sexist and turn down my proposal."

"What reason would that be?"

"I also married you because you're hot. I'm sorry, but I'm a man and that counts."

"Marc Kasai, you should be ashamed of yourself. You know how I feel about that."

"I know, which is why I compliment you sparingly when it comes to your looks."

Nina had almost missed out on marrying Marc. If she had moved one second too soon, they never would have met. He sought her out at a reception following a special lecture when she was winding down her MBA program at Harvard Business School. He stopped her just as she was headed out the door.

"I've been trying to get your attention all evening. I thought I might score some points if I did the manly thing and faced my rejection head-on."

"I didn't notice you." It was the best she could do not to come off like every other female in the room who looked at him like he was a lobster buffet at a seafood restaurant. He had intelligent eyes, a lean physique that moved like a panther, and sex appeal that would make Hollywood's leading men envious. Guys like him didn't fall for girls like her, Nina told herself. The smart thing to do was exit the situation as gracefully as possible.

Instead, they spent the rest of the reception glued to each other. She learned he was a managing director for global markets at Sullivan and Hewitt, a business management consulting firm; he spoke fluent French at the insistence of his parents, who had immigrated from the Ivory Coast, he had a younger brother and older sister, and his father was Chief of Neurosurgery at one of the state's leading hospitals.

Their year-long courtship brought Nina to life and made her believe anything was possible. Her newfound happiness had drowned out the history that told her she didn't deserve it. Her wedding day was everything she never dreamed of. There had been one conspicuously absent guest, a regrettable but necessary occurrence.

"I'm going to take a shower," she said to Marc, and jumped off the couch. Upon reaching their bedroom, she noticed the blinking light on the answering machine on the nightstand, and thought it was weird because she didn't hear the house phone ring. The message was from her gynecologist. Dr. Chaudhury wanted to see her right away.

CHAPTER SIX

———◆◇◆———

S
he would never be able to have children on her own. That was the bombshell diagnosis from Nina's doctor. Apparently, both her fallopian tubes were blocked because of massive scarring. IVF seemed to be the most viable option. Marc wasn't completely on board but Nina made the unilateral decision to move forward, and that led to a huge fight. They didn't speak to each other for three days. Once the smoke cleared and Nina had time to think things through calmly and rationally, she could see why Marc felt the way he did. They had been trying to get pregnant for almost a year, and that was stressing him out. He complained they never made love for fun anymore, everything was based on her ovulation cycle and she wouldn't let him touch her unless it was that time of the month. The pressure was causing him to be resentful and he suggested they consider adoption at some point if she couldn't get pregnant the old-fashioned way. That caused Nina to fly into a rage and she accused him of giving up without a fight. That led to an even longer, louder argument that ended with Marc moving to the guest bedroom.

This morning she was in a sour mood but the person knocking on the other side of the door was persistent.

"Come in," Nina said wearily.

"Surprise!"

Nina was astonished to see her younger sister barge into her office. Cassie was in her late-twenties, slightly chubby, yet sickeningly pretty. If a piece of clothing was short, tight or showed her cleavage, Cassie owned it. The Boston College dropout had a platinum credit card permanently attached to one hand, and a puppet string controlled by their father attached to the other.

Nina gave her a bright smile and a hug. "You didn't tell me you were coming over."

"I was at Downtown Crossing and thought I should come by and see what you're up to."

"Found anything good in the stores?"

"No, but my friend Kate says new inventory will be coming in at Neiman Marcus and she'll hold some items for us."

"I don't know, Cass. Marc is already complaining that I've taken up all the closet space. If I buy any more clothes or shoes, I think he's moving downstairs."

"Oh, please. Marc's not going anywhere."

"Maybe you're right. It's an empty threat. Name the date and the time and I'll be there."

Cassie seemed pleased. Nina had a guilt complex regarding her younger sibling. She didn't see her as much as she should. They were somewhat close, but Nina and the naïve and somewhat irresponsible Cassie were perpetually at different junctures in their lives. Cassie lacked direction and focus while Nina was single-minded in whatever she pursued. At the moment, it was motherhood. Cassie was the ultimate daddy's girl and he had no problem letting her wander through life aimlessly on his dime until the day when she figured out what she wanted to do with her life.

"Great, I can't wait. Dad says hello, by the way. He's still mad at you for skipping his birthday party."

"I always skip his birthday party, that's nothing new."

"He was hoping it might be different this year."

"He knows better."

"Come on, Nina," Cassie said impatiently. "How long do you intend to keep this up? Can't you give him another chance? This is getting ridiculous."

"I would expect that coming from you. The way you hero-worship him, though — that's what's ridiculous."

Cassie looked put out by the criticism. "What's that supposed to mean?"

"He's not who you think he is, Cassie. I've been trying to tell you this for a long time. Yet, you refuse to even consider my point of view."

"You're the one who's hard of hearing. Our father is getting old. Every time he reaches out to you, you reject him. Why can't you just be nice to him?" He's not going to be around forever and then you'll be sorry if you don't make up with him."

Nina was getting sick of Cassie's constant nagging about their father. Still, she was almost sympathetic to her sister's plight, since Nina had been the one who dashed her hopes of them ever being a happy family again.

I did it! It's graduation day and I made it through Stanford in three years and graduated summa cum laude. My honor's thesis was a walk through hell, but I went through worse to get here. I'm so happy Mom was able to see me graduate. She brought Uncle Archie, her favorite brother, who lives in New Mexico. Charlene came up from Boston, too, completing my little trio of cheerleaders. I'm officially independent now, thanks to hard work and the generosity of my step-dad, Trevor … wish he could've been here, too. We all miss him—another one gone too soon. But when he named me and Mom as beneficiaries on his insurance policy, he gave me what I needed to take care of incidentals and travel and whatever else struck my fancy while I was at school. Trevor will always be with me. And of course, Mr. Tibbs. I start a new job in New York in a few weeks. Charlene will only be an hour away, so we can see each other often. It means I can see Cassie more often, too, but I have to make sure he's not around.

Anyway, it's May in California and hot as heck. I wanted to ditch my cap and gown but Mom wanted to make sure we had enough pictures, you know, at least five hundred, to remember this moment by. The ceremony, which took place at Stanford Stadium, looked like the Astrodome during a Super Bowl game. Afterwards, Mom, Charlene, and I were going to head to the hotel, have a nice fancy lunch and fly to Los Angeles in the morning. We planned to play tourist for a week before I head to Dallas with my mother to spend the remaining time before I start my new job.

We were wrapping up some official pictures when I almost fainted. Not from the heat but because of the girl I saw running toward me— Cassie, now thirteen and quite lovely. Her presence meant only one thing, but I hoped I was wrong.

She almost tackled me to the ground. "I couldn't wait to see you, Nina," she said. "It took so long for the plane to get here last night, I thought we would miss your graduation, but luckily, Dad had the schedule all figured out."

"Dad?" I asked.

"Yes. Dad and my mom are here. He said we're gonna be a family again. Now that you graduated, you can come home. Dad said he could use his contacts to get you a job in Boston. Isn't that great news?"

I felt awful. The poor kid hadn't seen me in three years and I didn't say goodbye to her when I left. I was going to have to break her heart again, but it would have to wait. Theresa and Dad were approaching and everyone had to be on their best behavior for Cassie's sake. The introductions could have been less awkward, but under the circumstances, we all did okay. Theresa hugged me and congratulated me. She was polite enough to my mother and said it was nice to finally meet her. With Theresa, you never knew what she was thinking or feeling. Charlene was mostly taking it all in and keeping Cassie occupied while Archie stepped off to the side. Dad went to hug me and I wanted to hightail it out of there, but that would have drawn unwanted attention. When he hugged me, he whispered in my ear 'well done' and that he loved me. I don't think he was faking, but then again, it's my dad. He could make you believe anything.

The celebration didn't go exactly as planned. Me, Charlene and Mom didn't go back to the hotel right away. Instead we ended up at this Italian restaurant on the water…we seemed like any other family out having a Sunday afternoon brunch. Dad wanted to know my plans post-graduation and that's when things got a little hairy.

"I put in a call to a friend of mine who just started his own company. He could use somebody like you. You would run the marketing department with two other people. You would get to do things someone straight out of college wouldn't normally get to do at a more established company. The experience would be invaluable to your career in the long run. Say the word and the job is yours."

"Um ... that won't be possible," I said, chewing on my bottom lip.

"What's the problem? It's the chance of a lifetime. I'm sure some of your fellow graduates would kill for an opportunity like this."

Cassie chimed in, "Come on, Nina, say yes."

I looked at my mom and then at Charlene. They already knew the answer I was too afraid to give.

"Dad, I got an offer from a company in New York and I accepted. It's really great. It's with Winston and Shea."

He looked at me like he didn't know what I was talking about.

"They're a large marketing and PR firm with global offices—"

"I know who they are," he said curtly. "You'll just have to recant your acceptance. I'm sure they'll understand."

"I won't do that. I signed the offer letter. I have a start date."

"I went through a lot of trouble to get you this job with Ray. The least you can do is give it serious consideration."

By then the mood had soured and my mom had had just about enough. "Let it go, John. She already made a commitment. I'm sure there'll be other opportunities throughout her career where your influence will be helpful."

My dad didn't like being told what to do. "This is between Nina and me."

"Well, I'm making it my business," Mom replied, heatedly. "She's my child, too. I get a say."

The pair glared at each other, each willing the other to blink first. The stalemate was broken when Dad backed down, which was shocking.

He nodded at Theresa. "This is Nina's day and it should be about her."

Theresa opened her purse and handed me my graduation present from the both of them. It was a first-class trip for two to Italy, all expenses paid. And at the bottom of the envelope were car keys to a brand new Lexus sports car. At first I was touched by the gesture, and frankly blown away. But then this overwhelming sadness began to set in, strangling me. I had to get the hell out of there ... so I ran. I didn't know where I was going, but it didn't matter. I hated him for making me feel this way. I hated him for making me question his motives. I hated him for making me love him and loathe him at the same time. I would give anything to trade places with any one of my classmates, who could simply enjoy an indulgent graduation gift from her father.

Now I'm finally back at the hotel, but I don't feel like celebrating with Char and my mom...

"I don't want to fight, Nina."

"Good. Neither do I. It's not every day my little sister drops by to visit me. So what's new with you?"

Cassie was suddenly serious, the bubbly demeanor replaced by dread.

"What is it?" Nina asked. She instantly suspected Cassie's visit wasn't as spur-of-the-moment as she had made it out to be.

"Dad wants me to move in with him."

The news was surprising to Nina. "I wasn't expecting that. He pretty much let you run wild."

"He says it's time I get my act together and if I move in with him he can keep an eye on me and make sure I'm moving in the right direction."

"Why is he suddenly cracking the whip?"

Cassie shrugged. "I don't know."

Nina was intrigued. It's about time their father did something about Cassie. If he were occupied with her, then he wouldn't have time to fret about Nina's stubborn refusal to mend their relationship. "Yes, you do. Start talking."

Cassie started wringing her hands and paced the floor. Nina leaned up against her desk, arms folded. "This century, Cassie."

"You promise you won't get mad?"

Nina let out an exasperated sigh. "Yes, I promise not to yell too much, depending on what it is."

"Dad busted me and a friend smoking pot. At his house."

Nina could feel the laughter bubbling up in her throat but she did her best to control it. There was nothing funny about what her sister did, but it was the image, the look on their father's face when he discovered his princess engaged in illicit activities, that made her want to laugh out loud.

"I promised I wasn't going to yell, but what the hell were you thinking?"

"I didn't mean to, Nina. I was feeling kind of depressed and Spike said it would take the edge off and make me feel better."

"You should know better, Cassie. Marijuana can be a dangerous drug, not to mention, it's illegal. People get arrested for possession."

"I know," Cassie said, her embarrassment plain on her face. "It was just that one time, but dad freaked out, like I was a drug addict or something."

"One time is all it takes. It can lead to real trouble, Cassie, including other drugs. You shouldn't have touched it in the first place. And what do you have to be depressed about?"

"Just stuff."

"Cassie, you live in an expensive apartment in Back Bay, you blow more money on clothes and shoes than most people make in a year, and you don't have a job; it's all paid for by Dad. What "stuff" do you have going on that would cause you to turn to drugs?"

"I'm sorry. We can't all be perfect like you," Cassie said sarcastically.

Nina was taken aback by the biting tone of her comment. "I never claimed to be perfect. I just prefer to make my own way in the world. There's a certain freedom and pride that comes with it. And for the record, Dad is about to cut you off. Moving in with him is just the beginning. He'll make you give up your apartment and cut off the credit cards. You'll also have to give up the Z-4 sports car."

Cassie looked horrified. "Do you really think he will, Nina? I don't think I could survive living with him. He'd be breathing down my neck every second and constantly lecturing me. I'll just die if I have to go through that."

"There are worse things in this world than exercising a little discipline. Clearly you need it. You've been running around without a care in the world and now the party is over. It's time to start getting serious."

"You think I like being the screw-up? Do you know how it feels to be compared to you all the time and come up short? 'Nina went to Stanford and Harvard, Nina has a great husband, Nina has a great career, Nina is so accomplished.' I'm sick of hearing it."

"You don't know what you're talking about," Nina said angrily. "All of those things you just mentioned came at a price. That's the difference between you and me. I sacrifice for what I want. You're not willing to do the same."

"I'm not smart like you. I'm not strong like you."

"How would you know that? You never give yourself the chance to see what you're capable of. You accept the status quo because it's comfortable and rewards your behavior."

Cassie cracked her knuckles one after the other, an annoying childhood habit that drove Nina bonkers. "I never looked at it that way. But there's nothing I'm good at. I don't have everything all planned out. It's hard to figure out, okay?"

Nina felt sorry for her sister. She was handed everything and still couldn't get it together. The blame belonged squarely on the shoulders of their father.

"The way I see it, your best bet would be to return to BC and finish your degree. If you don't want to do that, then take some classes and see what you like. You may discover a passion for something you never thought of."

Cassie looked skeptical. "I don't know, sis. College isn't my thing. I don't want to spend years getting a degree just to end up doing nine to five in some office, trying to climb the corporate ladder."

Nina looked at her sister through narrowed eyes. "Is that a dig at me? I like my job. It's intellectually challenging and a great creative outlet."

"I didn't mean anything by it," Cassie said hurriedly. "Honest. I couldn't do what you do, it's just too hard."

"Let me know what you want to do. I'll help you any way I can. Moving in with Dad may not be the worst thing. It will give you some perspective while you figure things out."

* * *

NINA BACKED INTO A BARELY available parking spot on Mass Ave in Cambridge, a quarter mile from Christabelle's, the Caribbean restaurant she and Charlene dined at bi-monthly when they wanted to catch up on each other's lives or have a girl's night out. The owner, Christabelle Worthington, was originally from the island of Trinidad and was like a mother figure to the girls, a link to the island heritage they held dear. The restaurant interior combined red brick walls with a smooth, dark brown wooden floor. The tables were decked out in hot pink and pale blue tablecloths.

"What's wrong?" Charlene asked as soon as Nina pulled out a chair at their usual table.

"You already know I'm barren. Oh, my sister got busted smoking pot. By our father."

"You're shitting me," Charlene said, barely containing her giggles.

Nina gave Charlene the whole story, by which time their usual waiter, Crispin, arrived to take their order.

"Will you ladies have the usual?"

"No alcohol for me," Nina said. "I'll have the passion fruit juice."

"What about you, Charlene?"

"I'll have the usual," Charlene purred. "If you come with it."

An uncomfortable Crispin disappeared with their order.

"Why do you keep doing that?"

"Because I want him."

"He doesn't seem interested."

"He's interested. He just doesn't know it yet. I always get my man. He's no exception."

Crispin returned with their drinks and Nina asked for the night's specials. Everything sounded wonderful—and fattening. She settled on a crab dish that included Kallaloo, a popular Caribbean leaf vegetable, and Charlene ordered a jerk pork dish with chickpeas.

Crispin left the table and the two ladies relaxed, enjoying their drinks and each other's company.

"What is that old biatch doing here?" Charlene said distastefully, her face scrunched up, as if something foul was in the air.

"Who?" Nina followed Charlene's gaze.

Nina's heart sank. A dark-skinned woman with a moon face and large hoop earrings was making her way from the bar and heading straight for their table. As she got closer, Nina noticed the years had been kind to her. She was in her late forties by Nina's quick calculation, but her skin was just as smooth and wrinkle-free as the first day Nina laid eyes on her when she was a teenager. Constance Buckwell's smile was as fake as a Renoir in a trailer park.

"Is it really you, Nina?" she asked, unnecessarily.

"How are you, Constance?" Nina tried to keep the scorn out of her voice but it was futile. That woman was partially responsible for the misery in Nina's past and although she wished her no ill will, Nina couldn't stand to be around her for long.

"I'm doing good. I have a three-bedroom house in West Roxbury, a job and good health. I can't complain. The Lord has been good to me."

"Glad you're doing well."

Constance kept staring at Nina as if she was seeing her for the first time. It was awkward and unnerving; Nina just wanted her gone.

"Is there something else you wanted to say, Constance? Charlene and I are about to have dinner."

"I just can't believe my little Nina is grown, you're so … beautiful. More than those super models you see on TV and in the magazines. You must have men chasing you left and right."

Nina held up her left hand if it meant Constance would shut up and disappear. Constance's mouth opened and shut when she saw the near flawless three-carat princess cut diamond with a matching platinum band.

"Oh, looks like you married rich. Some people have all the luck," Constance said bitterly.

Nina felt her temper steadily rising. Luckily, Crispin arrived with their meal, offering a reprieve from the awkward encounter.

Charlene rudely banged her fork against her plate and Constance took the hint. She left their table, suggesting that Nina should come to her house and she would cook her all her favorites from when she was a teenager. Constance was barely out of earshot when Charlene let her tongue loose.

"That heifer is tripping. And what was that snide comment about some people having all the luck? Is it me or did she seem pissed that you were married? What the hell is wrong with some people?" Charlene concluded her tirade with an unladylike snort.

Nina had her suspicions as to why Constance was upset about her marital status, but she wasn't about to share them. "She was always a strange one. I wouldn't read too much into it."

"Didn't your father kick her to the curb for putting his business in the street?"

"Her services were no longer required."

Charlene gave Nina a look that said she was full of it.

"Okay, she got fired."

"Speaking of people from the past, what are you doing about the black cloud hanging over your head? I'm no expert, but aren't you supposed to reduce stress if you want to get pregnant?"

"It's been handled."

"In other words, you haven't heard from Sonny yet."

"You know I always have a plan B."

CHAPTER SEVEN

M arc paced back and forth on the living room floor, his face laced with anger. It didn't take long for Nina to discover the source of his wrath. He held up a photograph of Nina and Sonny Alvarez.

"Are you having an affair?" he asked, his jaw twitching.

Nina took two steps backwards, as if the damning photograph would cause her physical harm if she got close. She knew who had sent it and she berated herself for underestimating how low he could sink. By her way of thinking, Phillip figured if her marriage fell apart, she would come running to him and he could get her to do whatever he wanted. It's the way he manipulated people: get them in a vulnerable state and then swoop in for the kill or make some grand sweeping gesture that would get you all happy, and before you realized what was happening, it was too late.

"That's a strange question, Marc. When have I ever given you reason to think I was being unfaithful?"

"Never. Until now."

"Babe, you're getting worked up over nothing," Nina said calmly. "Sonny and I are old friends from Stanford. I met him for lunch to discuss business."

"On a Saturday? You said you were spending the weekend with Charlene. Look at the date on the bottom." He shoved the photo into her hands.

"It was a quick, unplanned trip. Sonny works for a research company and Jack came to me with the idea of hiring his firm. I told Jack I would take care of it because of my connection to Sonny. I wanted to get it out of the way—one less thing on my plate during the work week."

"Why haven't I heard about this Sonny until now? And if there's nothing going on, why lie to me about going to Charlene's?"

"I already explained that, Marc. I told Jack I would take care of it because I knew Sonny personally."

"So your boss called you on a Saturday, mentioned this research firm and you just decided to hop on a plane to Baltimore, just like that?"

Nina wiped her sweaty palms on her skirt and took deep calming breaths.

"Marc, I swear I'm not having an affair with Sonny or anyone else."

"Then can you please explain this? It came with the photographs." He pulled out a white sheet of paper from his back pocket and handed it to her.

Your wife is a liar. You deserve the truth.

The note was signed, "A concerned friend".

"Obviously someone is playing some kind of sick game."

"Why would someone follow you on a business trip, and why sign the note 'a concerned friend'?"

"Maybe one of your friends was in town and saw me with Sonny, thought I was cheating, and wanted to protect you."

Marc considered the possibility. "If one of my friends thought you were seeing another man, he would tell me, not send an anonymous note."

"Not Derek. You know he doesn't like me."

"That's not true."

"It is true. He wanted you to marry your ex-girlfriend and thought I got in the way of that."

"Come on, that happened ages ago."

"Yes, but it didn't stop her from reminding me on subsequent visits to the States that you married the wrong woman."

"Why am I just hearing about this?"

"Because I'm not going to come running to you every time someone says something insensitive about me. You asked me to marry you, not her."

Marc pulled out his cell phone and started dialing.

"What are you doing?" Nina asked, panicking.

"We're going to straighten this out right now. I'm calling Derek."

"Don't!" She grabbed at the phone.

Marc looked baffled. "What's the problem?"

"No problem. I don't want to get into a thing with Derek. Plus, I don't have any proof it's him, just a gut feeling."

"What do you suggest we do then?"

"Look, you can call Sonny yourself if it will make you feel better. I have his business card in my purse."

Marc shrugged. "That won't be necessary. I don't need to talk to Sonny. I'm trying to get the truth from my wife, not a stranger."

"I already told you the truth," Nina said, her voice rising. "I don't want to talk about this anymore. Why are you being so stubborn, anyway?"

"Because I'm not sure I believe you. Something's going on that you don't want me to know about. I'm not a fool, Nina. Don't treat me like one."

*　　*　　*

NINA TOOK THE LADDER UP to the attic, a place she rarely visited, and for good reason. The space was filled with reminders of her past she should have disposed of, but hadn't. She cleared a series of boxes and dragged an old exercise bike to a different corner. She reached behind a super-large box that had once contained their flat screen TV but was now home to used clothing she never got around to donating. She pulled out an old hat box labeled "Letters from Mom." She cleared a small space and sat down on the attic floor. She opened the box and removed all the letters on top. At the bottom was the only diary Nina had kept. The brown leather was slightly tarnished. She gingerly opened the cover and thumbed through the yellowing pages. What they contained had the power to destroy many lives, including hers and Phillip's. All it would take were the right pages falling into the wrong hands and *boom*—it would be all over. Phillip didn't know the diary existed, but what if finding out about it could get him to back off? Should she play his game? Did she have a choice?

Nina found Mr. Tibbs sitting precariously on an old rocking chair against the wall of the attic. He'd been her constant companion for most of her childhood and beyond. He was a dark brown, plush bear weighing about four pounds and measuring twelve inches tall. When she went off to college, he came with her too, and occupied a spot on her bed. Her roommate had teased her, saying she was too old to have a teddy bear, but Jess didn't understand that Mr. Tibbs was no ordinary bear. Nina couldn't part with him; they'd been through too much. She hadn't spoken to him in months, but her confrontation with Cassie in her office spooked Nina a bit.

"Cassie came by my office today, which was a nice surprise until she started talking about Dad. I wish she hadn't. I know he's getting older, but I'm not the one who needs to make peace with him … am I?

"I know it's my decision, Mr. Tibbs, but am I supposed to forget everything just because he's thinking about his mortality? How is that my problem? Cassie was going on and on about how I'm so mean to him and why can't I just take that step towards mending our relationship.

"You sound like Cassie, Mr. Tibbs. She said the same thing to me; will I be able to live with myself if something happened to him and I never got a chance to make things right. It's a gamble I'm willing to take, I guess. He has to be the one to fix this. For now, I'll leave Cassie to live in her fantasy world, but you and I know the truth, don't we?"

*   *   *

TRAFFIC WAS BACKED UP FOR miles on the Tobin Bridge heading toward Somerville, further ruffling Nina's already fraught nerves. Phillip's latest move sent the signal loud and clear that his intentions were serious. He would not take no for an answer. He knew her home address, where she worked, her comings and goings, and who her husband was. It was time she did some digging of her own.

Sean Merriman Investigative Services was housed on the second floor of a four-story brick building at thirty-two Highland Avenue. After being greeted by the receptionist and declining coffee, Nina was led into a private office by Sean Merriman himself. He wasn't what she expected for a PI.

With his blond good looks and pale blue eyes, he resembled a young Paul Newman. Merriman explained he had put in twenty years with the Boston PD before he struck out on his own. His office was decorated simply: a few file drawers, a desk, two chairs, a desktop computer, a phone and maps of the city on the wall.

"How can I help you? You said over the phone you were being blackmailed?"

"More like bullied, harassed."

"I see."

"I don't think you do, Mr. Merriman. If I don't find a way to stop him, he'll blow my life apart. There are things I haven't told my husband about this guy, important things, and he's threatening to expose me."

"So you want to put the brakes on, stop him in his tracks with something you can hold over his head?"

Nina removed a small envelope from her purse and produced the pictures and note Marc had received. "He sent these to my husband."

"You're sure these came from him?"

"Positive."

"Sounds like he has unfinished business with you and wants your attention. I have to tell you though, in my experience, secrets have a way of coming back to bite people in painful places. Sometimes, it's better to tell the truth and save the heartache. But then I would probably be out of business."

Merriman cocked a boyish grin. Nina knew he was right but that's not why she was hiring him. His job was to make sure her secret never came out and that meant neutralizing Phillip.

"Some secrets should stay buried. It's just better that way."

"Okay, if that's the way you want to play it. So, tell me about your blackmailer."

Nina wasn't sure where to begin. Her relationship with Phillip was complicated and there was a lot she didn't know about him in the years they were separated, or more accurately, there was a lot she didn't want to know, so she shut her eyes and closed her ears as much as she could. "He's well-respected in the Boston community, he did very well for himself as a corporate executive with Wellington Investments, and now he's in academia, a Professor at MIT Sloan School of Management."

"That's not what I was expecting to hear. I thought you were going to tell me about some sleazebag you had a relationship with, who was trying to shake you down."

"Who says he isn't? He's a rich sleazebag who wants something from me other than money. But he's a sleazebag, nevertheless."

"I see," Merriman said, stroking his non-existent beard. "Where would he hang out?"

"That's a good question I don't have an answer for, but I might know someone who can help me. He wouldn't be on campus much since it's summertime. Oh, he also runs the Dare to Dream Foundation, so I bet he has an office there. And just for fun, he sits on the board of several companies, including the one I work for. So if you can't find him in any of the places I mentioned, he's most likely in my office, harassing me."

"He comes to your office and you tolerate it?"

"He's a board member. As much as I want to call security on him, I can't. Plus, he's a friend of my boss's, the company CEO. It's better than showing up at my house, don't you think?"

"I suppose so."

"He's planning something big and I want to know what it is. People like him don't become concerned about their image and hire consultants for nothing. I want to know who he sees, where he goes— that might give me a clue as to what he's planning."

"What else?" There was an authority in Merriman's voice that told Nina he was a man who knew for certain there was more to this story.

She stared at him blankly. "What do you mean?"

"I've been doing this a long time, Nina. Something bad went down between the two of you, didn't it?"

She didn't bother denying it.

"You never told me his name. I kinda need that."

"Phillip Copeland."

Merriman's draw dropped. "You mean—"

"Yes."

"I don't know what to say. He's a big deal in this town, especially in the black community."

"Don't be impressed. It will only lead to disappointment."

"It looks like we're in business then. I'll take the case."

"Good. You should know that I need results fast."

"Understood."

"My cell phone is with me at all times. Use my private email account if it's something we can't discuss over the phone."

Merriman cracked a nervous smile. "About my fee ..."

She dug out a check from her purse and handed it to him. "This should cover all fees and expenses."

His eyes widened.

"Don't worry about it," she said, rising to leave. "You'll earn every penny."

"One last thing," Merriman said as Nina reached the door. "What's the real deal between you and Phillip Copeland? Who is he to you?"

"You ask too many questions," she said, a smile playing around the corners of her mouth. She left without another word.

CHAPTER EIGHT

B y the time July rolled around, Phillip was beginning to sweat and it had nothing to do with the summer heat. He walked into the lobby of Athena Biosciences located in what was commonly referred to as the "Innovation Cluster" near Kendall Square in Cambridge because of the number of biotech, pharmaceutical and high-tech startups that occupied the area. As he took the elevator to the executive floor, he reflected on his current circumstances. When he showed up at Nina's office a month ago, he thought his consulting offer and dinner invitation would have been enough to win her over, but he miscalculated her resolve, or maybe her hatred of him was more intense than he realized. Not even sending compromising photos of her with another man made a difference.

His backers were putting pressure on him to take care of any potential scandal lurking in the shadows that could derail the project. He had taken care of Tracey and he was confident she would keep quiet. He was shelling out enough cash every month to make sure she did. Theresa was a senior executive at a major cosmetics company in New York and was quite happy having as little contact with him as possible. Only Nina was left; his beautiful, infuriating, fiercely independent Nina. He thought getting sentimental was for fools but he had to admit it was great seeing her again. The strange thing was, he found he liked spending time with her. He was behaving like some lovesick teenager who kept finding reasons to see her. But make no mistake about it, he would break her if it became apparent she posed an imminent threat to his goals. He did it once and he could do it again. Only this time, it might get messier. He had to consider her husband. From what his investigator told him, Marc Kasai adored Nina and would battle to the death anyone who tried to hurt her. Plus, he had to tread carefully because Nina's father-in-law could become a valuable ally.

Ben Obasanjo had been a friend of Phillip's for almost thirty years. He was CEO of Athena, the first African-American to helm the company. He was responsible for turning the company around financially, and Athena now earned over $1 billion in profits annually, a record achievement for a firm its size.

"So you're really going to do this?" Ben asked, as he sat across from Phillip in his richly decorated office.

"I don't see why not. I have people crunching the data as we speak. I expect good news to come out of that."

"You know you can count on me."

"Yes. I need you to mobilize your contacts, potential high net worth donors who might see things our way and actually have the influence to get us where we want to go."

"Consider it done. What about that problem we discussed last week? Any closer to a resolution?"

"Nina is a little bit more stubborn than I anticipated, but nothing I can't fix. She won't be a problem."

"You better be sure, brethren, otherwise you could be finished even before we get this project off the ground."

Phillip knew Ben was right, he wasn't telling him anything he hadn't mulled around in his own mind a million times. He had confided in Ben about his recent challenges in getting Nina to see things through his lens.

"I introduced her to Geraldine."

Ben looked at Phillip curiously. "How did that go?"

"They like each other."

Ben slammed his palm against the desk with enthusiasm and a big grin. "There you go. It looks like things are working out, so what are you so worried about?"

"She has to be handled carefully and deliberately."

Ben nodded in agreement. "Makes sense. There's a lot of history there."

"Not just that. Her father-in-law might be very useful to us."

"Oh, yes. Doctor Paul Kasai. Good man. I've met him on a couple of occasions."

"Let's hope he's good enough to throw his support to the project."

Ben got suddenly serious. "We've known each other a long time, Phillip, and I believe you're a good man."

"Where are you going with this?"

Ben reached into his jacket pocket and pulled out a key. He opened the top desk drawer and removed a small manila envelope, the type with the bubble wrap inside.

"When you told me about your plans, I remembered something I had in my possession. I should have gotten rid of it years ago, but I didn't, and as time went by, I forgot about it."

"What is it?"

Phillip knew Ben well enough to know he didn't fool around. Whatever this was, it was major. He could see tiny beads of sweat forming on Ben's forehead.

Ben handed Phillip the envelope. "I think after you hear this, you'll know what to do."

"Hear?"

"It's not my place to pass judgment and I'll always be an ally. But you shouldn't have done it. Let's leave it at that."

*   *   *

THE FORTIETH WEDDING ANNIVERSARY OF Doctor and Mrs. Paul Kasai held two dramatic surprises for Nina. Waiters in black and white uniforms kept the champagne flowing and made sure the hot and cold hors d'oeuvre trays were never empty. The house was alive, filled with the animated chatter and laughter of Boston's elite. At every corner, the intellectually gifted, the cultured and refined, and masters of political and social ideals dispensed their opinions on everything from the war in Iraq and Afghanistan to Wall Street to the state of public education in Massachusetts and the nation. The eight thousand square foot mansion in Weston, an exclusive suburb favored by CEOs and doctors, was an eclectic mix of western opulence and African pride.

"There you are, *madame*. Doctor Kasai has been looking all over for you. He wants you to meet someone."

Nina excused herself from a conversation with a local bank vice president and turned her attention to the regal-looking woman with a salt and pepper bob. Claire Kasai had been a generally supportive mother-in-law, although Nina suspected she secretly would have preferred a daughter-in-law from their culture and background."

"Do you know who he wants me to meet?"

"He didn't say. You'll find him in the family room. I'm off to check on the caterers."

Doctor Paul Kasai was an imposing figure. In his mid-sixties, he had the agility of a man half his age, and a booming voice that could have you convulsing in laughter at one of his many impressions, or drowning in humiliation if you were privileged enough to work under him and human enough to have a bad day.

He sat across from a guest whose back was to Nina. His face lit up when he saw her.

"My dear, it's always a pleasure to see you. You have an admirer and I promised him an introduction. I'd like you to meet Doctor Phillip Copeland. He read the article in *Executive Insider* and hopes to persuade you to be a special guest lecturer for the marketing management course at MIT Sloan."

Phillip extended his hand in greeting. Nina forced a smile and shook his hand hastily. He did little to hide his amusement—or was it mockery? After mumbling something incomprehensible that she hoped sounded like a pleasantry, Nina took a seat next to her father-in-law.

"Doctor Copeland, how do you know Doctor Kasai?" Nina threw back her head, the challenge evident in her eyes.

"Phillip's foundation donates generously to the hospital, especially to breast cancer research," her father-in-law explained. "But I invited him here tonight to meet some potential donors to the campaign."

"Campaign?" Nina asked, puzzled.

"You may be looking at the next Governor of our state," her father-in-law announced proudly.

Nina felt like someone hit her in the head with a sledgehammer. She sat silent, willing her brain to function, hoping this was just her father-in-law teasing her. He was known to be a kidder and often had them in stitches. Yes, it had to be a joke.

"Are you teasing me again?" she asked him sweetly. "You got me pretty good the last time."

"Not at all dear. There are plenty of people in the room tonight, including myself, who like the idea. Phillip is well-respected in the community; he understands the issues and has a vision for moving the Commonwealth forward. Once we collect enough signatures to get him on the ballot, he'll have to give up his post at MIT. The primary could get rough, but we think he can win both the primary and the party nomination."

"I don't feel so good," Nina squeaked. "I'm going outside to get some fresh air."

*   *   *

NINA PARKED HERSELF IN HER father-in-law's library, comforted by the fact that Phillip was probably looking for her outside and wouldn't think to look for her indoors. She needed a few minutes to breathe and organize her thoughts. A lot of things were starting to make sense: the pseudo consulting offer and subsequent pressure and blackmail to get her to say yes, the apology dinner, the constant stalking, finding himself in the same place she was. It was all a ruse, designed to get into her good graces for his political gain. If she were firmly in his corner instead of fighting him, then he wouldn't have to worry about his dirty little secret coming out. In fact, if it did, he would be finished—politically, professionally, in every possible way for a person to be destroyed. He needed Nina to keep her mouth shut and she knew he would use any means necessary to that end.

"Why are you hiding from me, Nina? I don't bite."

His voice startled her. She was so engrossed in her own misery she didn't hear him come in. She stood up from the brown leather couch, folded her arms and leaned up against a large oak desk that contained Dr. Kasai's medical encyclopedia, a calendar, and an assortment of yellow stickies and writing utensils.

"You are a dirty, stinking rat, so yes, you do bite."

"Why are you so angry? You act as if I was asking you to give up your time for free. I was willing to pay you above market value for your services because I know how good you are. I take my responsibilities seriously."

"You might have everyone fooled with the good deeds routine, but not me. And God help the people of this state if you actually become a viable gubernatorial candidate."

"Don't be a bitch! No matter what you think of me, what I do matters. I have what it takes to make a difference in the lives of the citizens of this commonwealth. My private sector experience is a major asset, my foundation work says I'm in touch with the problems of everyday people and the less fortunate. My record in academia says I'm a scholar and can be pragmatic about the challenges facing the state."

"Save the stump speech, Phillip. I'm not the one you have to convince. I know what you're really like, so save your breath. But I will ask you to stop trying to trash my life. I wasn't amused by the photo you sent to my husband."

"He deserves the truth."

"There is no affair. And as someone who needs a favor from me, I suggest you start playing nice."

"You don't hold all the cards, Nina. You need to understand that."

"What is that supposed to mean?"

"It means you're not in control. I am."

"Oh really? Well control this." Nina reached for her purse on the couch and removed a piece of paper and handed it to Phillip. "I was going to give you this the next time you invited yourself to my office, but since you're here, why the heck not?"

He unfolded the paper and began to read. He no longer looked like a man calling the shots.

"What is this?"

"You know what it is. Writing things down can come in handy. You never know when you'll need that insurance policy. I'm willing to cash it in if you don't back the hell off."

Phillip ripped up the piece of paper into tiny little pieces, dumped it in the nearby trash receptacle and dusted off his palms as if that were the end of it.

Nina laughed. "You don't believe I'd give you the original, do you? Come on."

He moved closer to her, mere inches separating them. He cupped her face in his hands and held it firmly in place. "It looks like you want to play hard ball. But you should tread carefully because I'm way more experienced than you, a mere lamb I will sacrifice without hesitation if you cross me. You've established a good life for yourself, a great reputation both professionally and socially. What do you think would happen if this fabrication ever got out? What about your precious husband? What would it do to him and his family to be humiliated by your vicious lies? Have you thought about anybody but yourself in this ridiculous crusade you have against me? Grow the fuck up, Nina!"

Nina had a way of getting under his skin and now she had him by the proverbial balls. He needed to make her understand what was at stake and put aside her petty vendetta against him and look at the big picture. Why couldn't she see that this was good for both of them? If he became Governor, he would take her along for the ride, and it wouldn't be because of her association with him. She was brilliant, accomplished, and stunning, a lethal combination in politics. And who was to say Beacon Hill would be the end of it? Why not the White House?

Now he was struggling to suppress the terror rising up in his chest despite his display of nonchalance. His mouth went dry and he suddenly needed a stiff drink. The paper she handed him looked like the page from a diary and if it was, what else was written in it that could destroy him? He had to think fast. The ante had just been upped. He needed to rethink his strategy.

After Phillip left, Nina collapsed on the couch as she fought the hot bitter tears that threatened to spill out in a torrential downpour. Phillip's tirade left her feeling empty. Was the selfish brat accusation he leveled at her true? Had she been so single-minded in her hatred of him that she never gave a moment's thought to how trying to punish him might affect other people? But as miserable as she felt, there was hope. He had unwittingly given her the perfect weapon.

CHAPTER NINE

A fter she escaped the library, Nina's evening went from bad to worse. Trouble reappeared in the form of a very sexy and contentious Frenchwoman.

Merde!

Solange Dupond broke away from the small group socializing at the bottom of the grand staircase when she spotted Nina. Her sophisticated up-do and flawless café au lait complexion were the perfect compliment to the scarlet strapless dress that clung to her shapely figure like saran wrap. Solange radiated a sultriness that could strip the paint off an Aston Martin. The two had met once before and disliked each other on sight. Solange's contention that Marc was her one true love—and Nina was his backup plan, despite evidence to the contrary—only fueled their mutual loathing.

"*Bonne soirée,* Nina. You're looking well."

"*Merci.* So do you, but you already knew that."

"Of course. But I see you look the same as last time."

"Why wouldn't I?"

"You and Marc have been married for some time and one would expect things to change. *C'est une situation difficile, n'est ce pas?*"

"What situation are you referring to?"

"Five years and you still have not given your husband a baby. It must be hard knowing you're—how do you say in English?—inadequate, while for other women, it's … so easy."

The words hit Nina like a thousand needles boring into her skin all at once. The last thing she needed was her husband's bitchy ex-lover insulting her. Nina tried not to let her imagination run amuck, but that was an odd subject for Solange to bring up. And what did she mean that for other women it's so easy? Maybe she was being overly sensitive. Solange got her kicks from goading Nina, so she would just leave it at that.

"Your bitchiness is not charming, despite the accent. What are you doing here?"

"Boston is my new home."

"Since when?" Nina asked sharply.

"Our company is expanding into the U.S. market and we're looking to open our flagship store right here in Boston. Marc will be handling the expansion strategy personally."

Solange was head of merchandising for a French luxury retailer. She spoke four languages fluently and had spent a great deal of time in the U.S., so she was the natural choice for this assignment, Nina presumed. Despite her rationalizing, Nina felt the pang of insecurity tugging at her like a toddler at his mother's hem. Why had Marc kept that bit of information from her? Nina didn't care what kind of business Marc's firm had with Solange's company. The idea of her husband spending time with her in any capacity was unacceptable.

"How lucky for you they chose to open their first U.S. store in Boston."

"Luck had nothing to do with it, Nina. I'm very good at what I do. Very good."

"I could see why you would be. You've had plenty of practice lying on your back," Nina shot back."

Solange visibly flinched at the insult. "You're going to be very sorry you said that."

*   *   *

SHE HAD TO CHOOSE HER words carefully. If she showed the least bit of agitation, he would think she was being irrational and that would lead to another fight that would get her nowhere. The ride home was spent in silence but Nina wasn't about to let the matter drop. She sat at the edge of the bed brushing her hair before she separated it into four big plaits. Marc pulled back the covers and climbed in. He was ready to call it a night.

"Why didn't you tell me Solange Dupond was back in town and her company was one of your clients?"

Marc sat up slowly and let out a big yawn. "*Cherie*, it's two o'clock in the morning and I have an early meeting. Can we talk about this later? I just want to catch a few hours' sleep."

"I don't mean to be unreasonable, but I was humiliated tonight. It hurt having to hear from her that you'll be working together."

"I didn't tell you because I didn't get around to it yet. Solange just arrived yesterday. The conversations with her company are very preliminary, and nothing has been decided yet."

"I see. Solange certainly seems to think things have been decided."

"Why are you letting her rattle you?" he asked in frustration.

"Because I don't trust her," Nina snapped.

The truth was Solange made Nina nervous in a way no other woman did. Women like her caused men to forget their morals and values and a little thing like marriage vows wouldn't get in her way. Now that she was in close proximity to Marc for the foreseeable future, what would she do with that opportunity?

"You're reading too much into this. You have nothing to be nervous about. I, on the other hand, should be."

Nina was furious. "What the hell is that supposed to mean?"

"I'm going to sleep. See you in the morning."

Nina slid out of bed after she was sure Marc had fallen asleep, though it seemed to have happened the minute his head hit the pillow. She removed her smart phone from its charger and walked down the hall to the stairs leading to the first floor of the house. She hit speed dial number three.

"Are you sleeping?"

"The minute you start asking stupid questions, I know you're about to lose your damn mind," Charlene said, groggily. "Lay it on me."

"Solange is back."

"So?"

"What do you mean, so? She's circling like a vulture, making threats."

"Are you jealous of that skank?"

"No, don't be ridiculous. Maybe. Look, I don't know. She loathes me, Charlene."

"Stop worrying. He kicked her trifling ass to the curb, married himself a good woman and that's that."

"I don't trust her. And I can't afford another distraction right now. Things haven't been the best between Marc and I lately. I lied to his face about seeing Sonny and he's still suspicious."

Her insecurity was showing but she couldn't help it. She was genuinely afraid of the growing distance between herself and Marc. If she pushed him too far, it wouldn't be a stretch to imagine his ex could tempt him back into her arms. Then all the lying and cover up she'd been doing would be for nothing. The thought was unbearable.

"I told you secrets can come back to bite you in the ass," Charlene lectured. "Put yourself out of your misery and handle your business. Start by telling your husband that Phillip Copeland is really your father. The rest will take care of itself."

"I can't do that, Char," Nina said softly. "I've told too many lies already. The snowball is too big and I can't push it back up the hill."

"Well, it's about to bury you. I'll back you up if you tell Marc, though. You can't keep this up, girlfriend. If Marc hears it from someone else, you'll have one pissed off husband on your hands."

"Why do you have to make sense in the wee hours of the morning? I hate when you do that."

"Just keeping it real, girl. Just keeping it real."

After Charlene hung up, Nina could feel a deep-seated weariness seeping into her bones and winding its way into her spirit. Until Phillip showed up at her office more than two months ago, she and Marc had lived a relatively peaceful existence. He had accepted Nina's story that her father lived in another state and wanted nothing to do with her because they had a huge falling out over her decision to attend Stanford as an undergrad, a direct challenge to his wish that she attend Harvard, his alma mater. She had lived on edge the first year of their marriage, praying that they wouldn't run into Phillip on the street or at a supermarket or at the airport. She was finally able to relax when it seemed he had accepted the reality of their relationship.

Her reasons for keeping Phillip out of her life sounded selfish, but it was the only way she could stay sane and not end up an alcoholic, drug addict, or worse. It took a strength she didn't know she possessed to walk out and never look back, never considering how it would make him feel. He was the perfect chameleon, a really nice guy who cared about people and the issues that impacted the community— enough to start the Dare to Dream Foundation, dedicated to helping women and children combat poverty. He could be charming and kind when the mood struck him but Nina knew his other side: the controlling, manipulative, and viciously violent part of him.

By the time she left 48 Collinsworth Drive, that beautiful house with the perfectly manicured lawn and winding driveway that sat at the end of a cul de sac in an upper middle class suburb, she felt used, dirty, damaged, and ashamed. If she had allowed Phillip into her life after she got married, he would have destroyed her relationship simply out of spite. That was one of the reasons she didn't want Marc to know he'd been living less than an hour away from them for years. Her kind-hearted husband with his strong sense of family would have invited Phillip into their lives, setting the stage for another disaster. She wouldn't have the strength to survive a second time.

CHAPTER TEN

"It's almost over, babe," Nina said to Marc excitedly. "In a matter of hours, we could be pregnant. There's so much to look forward to: decorating the nursery, picking names, shopping for baby clothes, breasts the size of watermelons. And the best part will come when we hear our baby cry for the first time."

Marc was quiet, his eyes firmly on the road ahead, as they drove to the IVF facility in Boston.

"What's the matter?" Nina asked.

"I'm excited, too, *Cherie,* but I don't want you to be disappointed if it doesn't take on the first try. This could end up being a much longer journey than either one of us anticipated."

"I know that, Marc. But we agreed to give it a try."

"Is it worth sacrificing your health? We won't know what the side effects of these drugs are until years from now, and so much could happen in between."

Nina was getting irritated. "What's going on, Marc? Did you change your mind about starting a family?"

"Of course not."

"Then why the negative attitude?"

"Because I'm not willing to lose my wife to make it happen," he said fiercely. "Plenty of couples don't make it because of the strain the process puts on their marriage. How many fights have we had about this obsession of yours? You won't even consider alternative paths to parenthood."

"I'll consider alternative paths to parenthood if all else fails," she screeched. "This is our first shot at IVF. Let's see what happens before you jump to conclusions."

She hated the constant fighting between them and longed for the simpler days when they were absorbed in each other and she reveled in his adoration— when he made her feel like the most beautiful, amazing woman in the world who was a treasure to end all treasures. Lately, she felt like an insecure nag and could feel him withdrawing emotionally. On a couple of occasions, when he wasn't in bed when he should have been, she tracked him to the living room where she almost jumped out of her skin when she switched the light on and found that he was sitting in the dark. There was a kind of helpless look on his face she hadn't seen before and his eyes looked bleary. When she asked him what was wrong, he said it was just stress at work, kissed her on the forehead and told her to go back to bed.

Nina was lying on the gurney in a gown and surgical cap. Two enormous lights descended from the ceiling like aliens emerging from the mother ship. A vital signs monitor was off to her right and an instrument stand stood in the corner. She was awaiting the arrival of the anesthesiologist while the embryologist and other staff members busied themselves with preparation.

Doctor Bennett came by to say hello before Nina went under general anesthesia. She was a warm, likeable woman with soft brown eyes and an Afro.

"How are you feeling?"

"Excited and nervous."

"Don't be nervous. Your blood work, the follicles—everything looks fantastic. We expect to see several viable eggs."

"That's great." Nina turned to Marc, who hadn't said much since they entered the operating room.

"You see, babe? Doctor Bennett agrees with me. It's going to be just fine."

Marc nodded. Nina could see the wheels turning, as he tried to stay one step ahead, wondering what their next move would be if this first try didn't work. She squeezed his hand and mouthed the words "stop worrying."

"Good luck with everything, and I'll see you here again in a few days."

Doctor Bennett was about to leave, then thought better of it. "Nina, I know we ruled out surgery as an option to unblock the tubes because of the extent of the scarring, but I took another look at the x-rays a few days ago and it got me wondering about the cause of the damage. We've ruled out—"

As if on cue, the anesthesiologist entered brusquely and cut Doctor Bennett off with a greeting. Nina hoped no one could hear her heart slamming against her chest like a wrecking ball. Marc had accompanied her to every appointment since they undertook this journey, so Doctor Bennett obviously felt free to discuss her case with both of them present. But the question Nina knew Doctor Bennett was about to ask could never be asked in her husband's presence. She knew from the very beginning why she couldn't get pregnant and she had put on a good show of surprise for her husband's benefit when the doctor told her she couldn't conceive on her own. The truth only existed in her memory now.

Today I decided I couldn't take it any more. I tried to avoid going to him about it but now I'm really scared that if I don't see a doctor soon, I'll end up with some terrible disease whose name I can't pronounce. Mr. Tibbs thinks I should have said something three weeks ago when I started having abdominal pain. I had to be excused from Algebra last week to go to the nurse's office because the pain was so bad. And that wasn't the end of it. It hurt to pee, I mean really hurt, and the worst part? I have to go every five minutes. As embarrassing as it is, I have to tell my dad.

I found him in the living room watching World News Tonight with Peter Jennings. Peter is my favorite news anchor, but I'm never telling Dad that because I'm sure he'll find some way to turn it into something twisted he can use to manipulate me, like he did with the books. Theresa was working late and Constance was giving Cassie a bath, so it was the perfect time to talk to him. I was really nervous and Dad must have seen me wringing my hands out of the corner of his eyes.

"Stop hovering and have a seat."

My dad is wicked bossy. He's the boss at his job too, and I guess it's hard to be responsible for all those people, but I wish sometimes he would just chill out when he's home. I did as he said but didn't know where to begin.

"Well? What is it?"

"I ... I need to go to the doctor."

He looked at me like I was a three-headed monster. "Why do you need to see a doctor?"

"It hurts when I pee and my stomach hurts all the time."

"Really?

That's Dad's code word for "I think you're up to something."

"I didn't want to say anything before. I thought it would go away but it keeps getting worse."

He was quiet for a while, like he knew something I didn't, which he probably did. He shut the TV off, which surprised me.

"Who did you tell about this?" he asked, shaking my shoulders.

"Nobody. I haven't said anything. It's too embarrassing."

"Good," he said, relieved. "See that you don't."

"So can I go to the doctor?"

"Not yet," he said. He started to pace. "It's probably nothing serious. It could just be a yeast infection. It's no big deal. I'll talk to the pharmacist."

I don't know what a yeast infection is, so I looked it up in the encyclopedia. Maybe I need a medical dictionary, but I don't know how to get my hands on one. I mean, the only yeast I know of is the one Mom uses to make bread. I have no idea how you can get an infection from that. Maybe that's it, though, because I like bread a lot.

"But what if it gets worse?" I asked him.

"I said I'll take care of it. Just see that you don't tell anyone about this."

And then my dad acted like nothing happened. He went back to the sofa, flipped on the TV and continued watching the news. I didn't know what I was supposed to do, so I started to leave. Then he called me back to the living room.

"You know I love you, right? Very, very much."

I shook my head. Maybe he felt bad for yelling at me or because I had this yeast infection thing.

"How about a treat? That Madonna cassette you wanted? You won't have to spend your allowance money on it, and we could go to the mall to pick it up — if you don't mind being seen with dear old dad."

Well, Dad must have forgotten to call the pharmacist, because two days later I was doubled over in pain on my bedroom floor when Constance found me. I told her I didn't know what was wrong and asked her to call Dad. I read all about yeast infections, which was pretty yucky stuff, but nowhere did it say I was supposed to be on the floor crying.

Constance drove me to the doctor's office and Dad met us there. The doctor did an internal exam, which was way embarrassing — even worse than the time Melissa Matthews told Doug Johnson she liked him but he didn't like her back, and the whole school found out about it. The doctor was a man and I had to open my legs really wide while he put some cold, hard, metal thing in me. He took samples or whatever — I wasn't listening too much, since I was trying so hard not to cry.

Today the results came back. It turns out I don't have a yeast infection. What I have is much scarier. The doctor told Dad I had a sexually transmitted disease. Mr. Duggan talked about those in health class but you never think something like that is going to happen to you — at least, I never thought this would happen to me. Dad won't speak to me. He does that when he wants to punish me. I don't know what his problem is. I'm the one who should have an attitude.

A woozy Nina slowly opened her eyes to find a beaming Marc looking down at her.

"Welcome back, sleepy head."

"How did it go? How many eggs do we have?" She propped herself up on the pillow.

He leaned in closer and whispered, "The doctors were waiting for you to wake up so they could tell us, but I heard one of them say eleven."

Nina's eyes widened. "Eleven? Are you sure you heard right?"

"There's only one way to find out. Here comes Doctor Lee."

The embryologist, a burly Asian man with a baby face, approached them.

"Good news. We retrieved eleven healthy eggs, more than enough for a few rounds."

"We won't need a few rounds, Doctor Lee. The first one will take. You'll see."

"Keep that optimism going, but remember nothing is guaranteed. Doctor Bennett is going to prescribe some medications, so she'll see you before you leave."

"What kind of medication?"

"An antibiotic to prevent infection and a steroid to help reduce inflammation of the reproductive organs. The ovaries were working overtime to produce multiple eggs. Hormonal supplements will help support the endometrial lining so it's nice and thick and ready to support the embryos when we do the transfer. I'll see you in three days."

* * *

SIX WEEKS LATER, AFTER HER weekly staff meeting wrapped, Nina asked her assistant, Eric Zaslow, to remain behind. If she was serious about reducing her workload and stress levels, she had to take a closer look at her calendar. She was glad a couple of her direct reports were receptive to taking on additional responsibilities, grateful for the opportunity to beef up their resumes and boost their profiles.

"Killer flats, Nina. You giving up heels?"

Eric's knowledge of and penchant for high fashion were two of the things that enhanced their working relationship. He was always impeccably dressed from head to toe, in strong colors that offset his pale, almost translucent skin and jet-black hair. When Nina took over as CMO, Eric thought she was the second coming after having served under her predecessor, basically a despot in a designer suit. Nina's management style was laid back, but she demanded excellence. Eric thrived on the challenge. He was smart, efficient, and discreet. He also suffered from Obsessive Compulsive Disorder, an asset in his role.

"Not entirely. I'm a little tired of being the skyscraper around here."

Eric looked doubtful.

"Okay, I'm giving Marc a break from massaging my aching feet every night."

"Torture, I'm sure."

Her body was changing and she was afraid she would lose her balance and have an accident with heels. Flats were the safest choice, though she realized she had bigger priorities than fashion. She was beyond thrilled that her prediction had come to pass. She was in the first trimester of her pregnancy.

"What do we have on the calendar?"

"Your keynote presentation for the Marketing Executives International Conference."

"Shoot. I'll get that to you this week."

"You said that last week, and the week before. I can't make your powerpoint sparkle if I don't have content."

Nina snapped her fingers. "I'll take the Acela Train for the New York trip, work on the presentation on the way down, and refine it on the way back. Next item, please."

"Great light bulb moment. The rest should be a snap."

It was. Nina eliminated or cut short lunches, meetings, speeches and any work that could be delegated, freeing her to focus on her health and big picture challenges related to her role.

Later that day, Nina was powering down her computer when Eric came barging in after a single knock. He was grinning ear to ear.

"Somebody's been awfully good."

"What do you mean?"

He removed one hand from behind his back to reveal a Tiffany's shopping bag.

"This came by messenger a little earlier but I wanted to clear my desk before I gave it to you. So here it is," he said, handing her the bag. "Tomorrow, I want to hear what new fabulous jewelry Marc bought you this time."

After Eric left, a pumped-up Nina opened the bag. It was just like Marc to send her something sweet and special after they'd gone through a rough patch. Inside was a signature blue Tiffany gift box wrapped in white ribbon. Her hands nervously untied the ribbon and pulled aside the pristine white tissue paper. Inside was a beautiful sterling silver baby rattle. She felt her knees go weak as she removed the rattle from the box. The inscription read, *Baby Kasai.*

"Oh, Marc, you shouldn't have," she whispered. Nina could barely keep it together; her heart was overwhelmed with gratitude to the man who had changed her life, and who still never failed to show her how much he treasured her. She rubbed her stomach lovingly. "I can't wait for you to meet your dad. He'll be the most amazing man you ever meet."

She carefully deposited the rattle back into the box and noticed a white card sticking out from under the wrapping paper. *Congratulations, Gazella. I wish you every happiness.*

Nina recognized the handwriting as Phillip's and her joy instantly turned to anguish, then rage. If only he knew how much she despised that name and the reason behind it. She scanned her office for the heaviest thing she could find and settled on a marketing award she had won several years ago. She picked up the large, cube-like object made of heavy glass and pounded the rattle until all that remained was flattened, twisted metal.

CHAPTER ELEVEN

L unch patrons formed long lines at McDonald's, Pizzeria Regina, and Master Wok, and the clacking of the departure board updating every few minutes served as background noise for anxious travelers and commuters cruising the bookstores and newsstands for something that would make the wait bearable. South Station welcomed millions of people to Boston every year and was the perfect venue for an investigator to discuss a case with a client. It was also convenient, only a ten-minute walk from Nina's office.

"Please tell me you have good news." Nina didn't see the point in wasting time, since this was her first official face-to-face meeting with Sean Merriman since she hired him to investigate Phillip.

Merriman began cautiously. "No criminal record, perfect credit, no oddities in his finances. He goes to church at St. Patrick's every Sunday morning, the nine forty-five a.m. mass. He's married to a professor at Tufts who moved here from England," Merriman explained. "Second marriage for him, her first."

Actually it was Phillip's third marriage, but there was no way Merriman would have discovered that one. It went too far back and Nina was only interested in the here and now. She was a little disappointed Merriman hadn't turned up anything she didn't already know. His next words got her out of her funk.

"I think I may have found something you could use," he said, as he removed a brown manila envelope from his briefcase. "He's been taking trips to Worcester, mostly on the weekends. But on one week day in particular two weeks ago, he paid a visit to a St. Joseph's Catholic School, serving kids K-8."

"Worcester? Why would he visit a school that far away? Come on, Sean, don't keep me in suspense."

Merriman pushed the envelope across the table. Nina reached in and removed the contents. The first document caught her attention right away. It was a photograph of a little boy, around eight years old. The resemblance was uncanny. Nina felt her stomach churn. The boy had two front teeth missing, like most kids that age. He was a handsome little boy with copper brown skin, large round eyes and dimples. He wore a dress shirt and tie with a sweater that sported the school's emblem on the left breast pocket. She didn't need to be a detective to figure out who the boy's father was. The next document in the envelope was a birth certificate. The boy's name was listed as Alexander Phillip Forbes. His mother was twenty-five year-old Tracey Forbes. Nina did a quick math calculation and what she discovered made her sick to her stomach. Merriman must have sensed something was up because he kept asking her if she was okay.

"Do you want me to get you a drink? We could continue this later if you're not up for it."

"I'm fine. I just wasn't expecting this."

"You're upset that he has a son you didn't know about?"

"Yes and no. It's complicated."

"I could see that."

Nina picked up the photo again and traced her fingers across Alexander's face. She couldn't stop herself. She and Merriman agreed to be in touch soon and Merriman disappeared into the noisy crowd. Her emotions were all over the place. She didn't know what to do with what she just found out or why it was affecting her this way. Would she have been better off not knowing she had a brother? Obviously, Phillip hadn't bothered to mention the kid, not even to Cassie, which says he wanted to keep Alexander's existence hush-hush. Plus, now that Cassie was living with him, he couldn't tell her and risk Geraldine finding out. Nina was fairly certain Geraldine was uninformed about her husband's illegitimate son. She put the photo back into the envelope and tucked it under her arm. She asked Merriman to dig for dirt on Phillip but she wasn't sure she could handle any more surprises. She would have to consider calling off the investigator.

Nina decided she deserved a pick-me-up and indulging in the sweet, rich decadence of Aunt Clarice Cupcakes, just yards from where she was sitting, would make her feel better. They made the most delicious cupcakes she'd ever tasted. Even *Boston Magazine* agreed with her, three years in a row. She lightly tapped her fingers on the countertop while the server put together her order.

"My goodness, look at you. You grew into a breathtaking woman."

Nina turned around and stared at the stranger behind her, perplexed.

"You don't remember me, do you?" The woman had high cheekbones and wore her hair in tiny braids she pulled back in a bun.

"It's Jenny Obasanjo."

"Oh," Nina said, her memory coming into focus. "Your son used to pinch me and run away whenever I came to your house."

"That's right."

When Nina was growing up, Jenny and her husband Ben Obasanjo were close friends of her parents. Nina remembered Ben as an intense man who was in a perpetual state of seriousness. She had made a habit of ducking for cover whenever he was around, afraid that her mere presence would offend him. The irony was that his two sons, Kevin and Ben, Jr. were nuts in Nina's opinion, and would probably be treated for severe ADHD today.

"How is Doctor Obasanjo?"

"He's fine. We're divorced."

"I'm sorry."

"Don't be. It was for the best. How are your parents?"

"Divorced."

"A lot of that going around, I suppose." Jenny smiled warmly at Nina, and then looked down at her left hand.

"You're married. Good."

There was something about the way Jenny said it that made Nina curious. There was satisfaction and conviction in her tone. Nina picked up her order and paid the man behind the counter. Jenny said she had to pick up her brother, who was coming in on Amtrak from Philadelphia. When the women parted ways, Nina had an eerie feeling they would cross each other's path again.

CHAPTER TWELVE

Line three lit up on Nina's desk. She picked up the internal call.

"I have your mother on hold," Eric blurted. "She's not happy."

"Put her through."

Nina smiled to herself as the call came through. Daphne Lockwood's sole purpose in life was to keep her daughter's affairs running as smoothly as possible by dispensing her own fiery brand of mother-knows-best guidance. The distance that separated them made no difference. Daphne lived in Dallas, but acted as though she and Nina lived next door to each other. Her mother probably called Eric because Nina didn't pick up her cell phone, and she knew Eric was afraid of her.

Nina picked up the phone. Her mother didn't give her the chance to make polite inquiries about her health or well- being.

"Did your father buy you a baby gift? Why didn't you tell me he was causing trouble again? It wasn't enough he drove you away with his controlling, domineering ways?"

Nina would have to have a talk with Charlene about her loose tongue later. But she thanked God her mother never knew how awful things really were and never would.

"I didn't want to worry you, Mom."

"You know what this is, don't you? He wants to get in your good graces so he can control your life. Over my dead body that's going to happen."

"You're making too much of this, Mom. I'm not a kid anymore."

"But does your father know that?"

"Mom, I have no desire to figure out the inner workings of Phillip's brain."

"Have you told Marc?"

"I don't need Marc to fight my battles for me."

"In other words, no. When are you going to stop playing that man for a fool and tell him Phillip is your father, and he lives four towns away from you? Don't you think he deserves the truth? As patient as he is, no man wants to find out his wife has been deceiving him."

"Is that from personal experience?" Nina asked, flippantly.

"Don't you get fresh with me, young lady. Marc is a good man. I'd hate to see you lose him over some nonsense with your father."

Nina ended the conversation with her mother and promised to call her when she got home. Line three was lighting up again.

"What is it, Eric?"

"Um ... well ..."

The usually articulate and efficient Eric was at a loss for words. That was a sure sign of trouble. "Out with it."

"You know how you hate people showing up without an appointment?"

"You know the drill. Get rid of the person."

There was silence on the other end of the line.

"Was there something else, Eric?"

"She says if you don't see her, she'll cause a scene."

"That's crazy talk. Call security."

Nina had no idea who would be crazy enough to pull that stunt but—then it hit her. "Send her in."

Nina sat upright and assumed an authoritative posture while her fingers flew over the keyboard of her laptop. She barely looked up when Solange Dupond made her entrance.

"What's so important that you're interrupting my work day?"

"You are right," Solange said, taking a seat. "It is important."

"Let's hear it, then." Nina gave Solange her full attention out of simple courtesy.

Solange didn't speak right away. Her eyes wandered attentively around the office. Expensive leather chairs, mahogany bookshelves, and spotless glass front pieces were peppered throughout the ample space, along with paintings that had cost a small fortune. Nina's favorite thing about her office, however, were the large windows that gave the office a bright, cheery feeling.

"You have a very important job, *oui*?"

"I guess some people would say so. But I bet there's an insult in there somewhere."

"You have accomplished so much in your professional life. You have power, influence, and the respect of your co-workers—because you are so smart, hmm? But you are a failure as a wife."

"Your claws are showing. They make you look old."

Nina's play to Solange's vanity had the desired effect. Solange shot her a look that made Antarctica seem like a tropical destination. She straightened up in the chair and pasted a fake smile.

"I apologize. I did not come here to insult you, as you say."

"Really? Because I had a few more comebacks all ready to go."

"I wanted to apologize for my behavior at your in-laws anniversary party."

Nina eyed her uninvited guest with apprehension. "Did you get hit in the head on the way over here?"

"I know it may shock you, but I truly am sorry. I should not have made fun of you. I cannot imagine how difficult it must be to be childless after all this time. It was mean of me to be so inconsiderate. I hope you can forgive me."

Nina was bewildered. While the apology seemed heartfelt, she knew Solange couldn't be trusted. Either she wanted something from Nina or she was getting ready to drop a bombshell. Neither prospect sat well with Nina, who studied Solange for a long moment.

"You're trying too hard. What do you have up your sleeve?"

Solange feigned innocence. "Nothing. I just realized that was no way to behave to the wife of my ex-lover."

Nina didn't like the way Solange lingered on the word *lover*, as if she wanted to remind Nina that she and Marc had been intimate, something Nina preferred not to think about in the wake of his so-called business relationship with Solange and her company.

"We don't like each other. I know why I can't stand you but I never understood what your issue is with me. You and Marc had long broken up when I started dating him and I'm sure there were other women in between. Why aren't you mad at them?"

Solange shifted uncomfortably in her seat and wouldn't meet Nina's gaze. She was suddenly fascinated by her orange nail polish, as if the color had magically appeared on her fingers. Nina couldn't believe she had succeeded in stumping the woman who always knew how to push her buttons.

"Perhaps he was the one who got away from me. I did not think he would marry someone like you."

"Like me?"

"Someone so ordinary."

Who the hell did this woman think she was to barge into her office and tell her she's ordinary?

"I suppose you're extraordinary," Nina said with an amusement she didn't feel. "But the problem is, you're not. There are plenty of women like you who didn't make the final cut. He picked someone else. Pouting about it years later isn't going to change anything."

"You are so wrong. Don't keep Marc waiting to become a father. You know how African parents can be so intolerable of daughters-in-law who haven't produced a baby, especially a son. One day you could be in for a nasty surprise and discover that your husband may be a *Papa* and you are not the *Maman*."

Nina gripped the edge of her desk, closed her eyes and willed herself to calm down. The fact of the matter was, Solange was right about one thing. Marc was waiting to become a father because of her.

"I'm shocked that you would even say something like that, Solange. You claim to know Marc so well, yet you think he's capable of fathering a child outside our marriage?"

"The past has a funny way of changing the future. Marc could already be a father and not know it."

With that, Solange stood up and sashayed her way out of the office, leaving a stunned Nina in her wake.

CHAPTER THIRTEEN

S he did it again. Solange had successfully upset Nina's equilibrium and now she had her wound up so tight she could probably crack a hazelnut with her thoughts. When Nina had told Charlene that Solange implied that Marc might have a love child floating around somewhere, Charlene laughed it off and said Solange was a desperate skank who would do anything to come between Nina and Marc.

No matter how many times she told herself the Frenchwoman wanted to hurt her, Nina considered the possibility. Marc wouldn't be the first man to have an affair only to find out years later he'd fathered a child he never knew existed. That is until the mother decided it was time because the financial burden was too much or she was stricken with some terminal illness or for some other reason only the mother would be privy too.

Nina snapped out of her pity party when she noticed an incoming call from area code 410 on her smartphone. She didn't let it ring twice. She double-checked her office door to make sure it was locked against colleagues who might decide to just drop by.

"What did you find out?"

"Patience, *mamacita*. You have to buy me dinner first before I show you my goodies."

Nina giggled. "I can't. I'm ravenous. For information, that is."

Sonny provided a summary of what he'd discovered so far.

"I pulled his cell phone records. There are two numbers he calls regularly. One belongs to a Tracey Forbes from Worcester. He also makes regular monthly deposits in the amount of $8,000 to the same account."

The pieces of the puzzle were coming together. Eight grand a month for child support made sense since Alexander was attending a private school.

"What else did you find on Tracey?"

"She's twenty-five, a nurse at UMass Medical Center. I'll send you her address and contact details with the rest of the information."

"Who does the other number belong to?"

"Charlene Hamilton from Quincy, Mass."

Nina didn't move a muscle. Her heart plummeted from her chest into her stomach. She had to rationalize what she just heard. She was sure there was a perfectly reasonable explanation for this. Charlene just hasn't had a chance to tell her what it was yet. Plus, there was no reason to jump to conclusions.

"Nina, are you there? Are you all right, *mamacita*?"

"Yes. I'm fine."

"You know this woman?"

"She's my best friend."

"I'm sorry. Sounds complicated."

"You have no idea."

Sonny wasn't done with her yet, though. "I pulled some of his personal email communications. I'll send them to you but you'll need a password to open the file."

After Nina wrote down the password Sonny gave her, she hung up and tried to calm her rioting stomach. She was almost numb with fear about what the email contained. She was beginning to wonder if she'd stumbled upon a hornet's nest. Within minutes, she checked her phone and saw the email from Sonny in her inbox. She gingerly plugged in the password and waited for the document to launch.

She walked over to the window and perched herself on the edge. As her eyes skimmed over the words, she suppressed the overwhelming urge to vomit and it had nothing to do with morning sickness. Feelings of hurt and betrayal were invading her being with an intensity she couldn't control.

After a while she stopped reading. The smartphone fell from her hands to the floor and she made no effort to retrieve it. But the phone demanded to be acknowledged as it began ringing, the happy bouncy ringtone mocking her as if it knew how wretched she felt.

"I just emailed you some photographs," Sean Merriman said. "I don't know if they'll mean anything to you. Let me know if they do and what you want me to do about it."

A weak thank you was all Nina could muster. She was sure the photographs would send her over the edge and it was best to ignore it for now.

*   *   *

FORTY-EIGHT HOURS LATER, NINA MADE her way to the building at 50 Memorial Drive in Cambridge, which housed classrooms and offices for MIT's Sloan School of Management. The building was across the Charles River from Boston and adjacent to Kendall Square.

He was waiting for her at the podium inside one of the lecture halls with classroom style seating and computers on every desk. There was a vast projector at the front of the room. It looked like he had just wrapped up a lecture for one of his end of summer classes.

Nina sat in the very first row off to the left. He came down from the podium and sat two seats away from her, which was just as well. She didn't want to sit too close to him.

"Thank you for seeing me."

"You're being unnecessarily polite. I guess I should brace myself for the temper tantrum that's sure to follow. What evil deed am I being accused of now?"

"You need to stop it! Now. I mean it," Nina pleaded.

"What do you hope to gain by carrying on with my best friend behind my back?"

"Oh that," he said, not bothering to deny it.

"Yes, that."

He got up, adjusted his glasses, and stuck his hands in his pocket as he leaned against the podium. "I suppose it was only a matter of time. How did you find out?"

"It doesn't matter. Why are you so obsessed with hurting me?"

"Why does everything have to be about you? Believe it or not, you're not the center of my universe. And to be frank, Charlene is a grown woman and shouldn't have to report to you her every move."

"That's how you justify it?" Nina couldn't hide her disgust.

"I don't have to justify anything to you. Charlene and I have been friends for a long time. When you left for Stanford, she felt alone and abandoned. I helped her through a difficult time and she never forgot it. I don't expect you to understand that because in your narrow way of looking at the world, everything is either right or wrong, black or white."

Nina could feel her anger rising and fought to keep it under control. He had the nerve to stand there and explain it away as if it was totally normal for him to... she couldn't even bring herself to say the words. She would deal with Charlene and her betrayal later, but right now, she needed to pour Phillip a large dose of reality.

"You don't care about Charlene. She's like a sister to me and you had to taint that relationship, too. You don't care because you're incapable of understanding genuine human emotion and bonding, without conditions. And do you know why, Phillip?"

"Please, tell me. I've always wanted to be psychoanalyzed by someone with zero training to do so."

"Because you're a sociopath."

The pronouncement hung in the air. Phillip got deathly quiet and Nina needed a moment to catch her breath. She knew he was about to unleash his rage but she didn't care. Too many people let him get away with too much, including herself. It was time to stand up to the bully.

"Who the hell do you think you are?" he asked quietly. "What gives you the right to pass judgment on me? You forget that I'm your father and you need to show the proper respect, little girl."

His voiced inched up a notch. "I don't owe you an explanation for what I do and who I do it with. Your friend seemed perfectly content to spend time with me without a single complaint. The fact that she kept it from you is probably because she knows you're a self-righteous hypocrite."

Nina lost all control and began screaming at the top of her lungs, mostly as a release for the agony slicing through her heart. "You're my father! You're not supposed to be screwing my best friend. You've known her since she was fourteen. You are an unconscionable monster with an ugly contempt for women. You're not even sorry for what you did to me, your own daughter. I hate you. I really hate you."

Nina felt as if she was coming undone, but this was the very first time in her entire life she felt she could tell him exactly what she thought without repercussions, at least not the physical kind. Growing up, she was taught to fear him. She remembered the emotional blackmail he often subjected her to as if it were yesterday. If he was upset about something she did or said, he would shut down, ignore her. That was a feeling worse than death to a young girl who craved her father's love and approval.

Phillip was furious. She had no idea what she put him through and didn't seem to give a damn. Her continued assertion that he was a horrible person and a bad father made him want to throttle her until she took back every word of her ridiculous accusations. She hurt him in a way he'd never allowed another human being to hurt him, and he swore after she left, he never would again. She broke his heart into a million pieces, and yes, maybe he wanted payback.

"I'll be the bad guy if it saves you from having to examine your motives. You're so concerned with the feelings of others, but not once did you give me any consideration when you left home. Not once did you consider the fact that I might be worried about you.

"Years went by, not a single phone call to say dad I'm alive and okay. I had to hire someone to keep an eye on you when you were in college, to make sure you were safe. You got married and couldn't be bothered to invite me to your wedding. That was one of the most painful periods of my life. Whatever scraps of information I received after that was because I guilted your sister Cassie into telling me. You unfairly placed the burden of keeping your secret on her. You told your in-laws I had moved away and had no desire to be in contact you, while I lived in the same state, less than an hour away from you. And yes, your leaving really hurt your sister. She worshipped you and didn't understand why you wouldn't come home."

"You know why I had to …"

Nina didn't get to finish the sentence. She felt a sharp pain in her abdomen. She covered her mid-section protectively.

"What's wrong?" he asked sharply.

"Nothing. Just a little—oh, God …"

She grabbed the edge of the seat to balance herself and struggled to reach for her bag. Phillip walked over from the podium and picked it up.

"What are you doing?" she said weakly. "I have to call 9-1-1. Something's wrong with the baby."

"Sit tight. I'll call for help." He pulled his cell phone from his pocket.

The pain intensified, a sharp, wrenching pain that felt like her insides were being ripped apart. Nina screamed as she fell to the ground. She curled into the fetal position, holding on to her abdomen. Her screams escalated into primal, gut-wrenching sounds that could probably raise the dead. The last thing she remembered saying was, "Please help me. Please, help my baby." Then she passed out.

It looked like he got his wish for revenge. It wasn't the way he intended for it to happen. When she told him something was wrong with the baby, he wasn't sure what to think. He knew pregnant women often behaved as if the least little bit of discomfort they felt meant something horrible was about to befall their unborn child.

When her screams got louder, he realized it was serious. His anger at her over their argument and the ugly things she said to him kept playing in his mind as he watched her writhing in pain on the floor. It was the sight of blood on her skirt that brought his fury to an end. By the time he called for an ambulance, it was too late. His grandchild was gone.

CHAPTER FOURTEEN

Old man winter arrived in New England with a roar in early December, burying everything under a foot of snow. Nina wished it had buried her, too. She looked out of her living room window, taking in the picture-perfect image of untainted white powder covering the ground. It was mocking her. She had lost her baby because she was tainted—a tainted liar. Because she wasn't brave enough to tell the truth, her little boy was gone. Maybe she deserved it. What kind of mother would she have been if she couldn't teach her child to be courageous? She rubbed her cheeks against the blue customized baby blanket. She was going to bring him home from the hospital wrapped in its soft warmth. Now it was a reminder of the emptiness she felt.

The doctors told her women her age had a twenty-five to thirty-five percent chance of miscarrying. She was diagnosed with an inevitable miscarriage. The cramping she experienced had been followed by the opening of the cervix. Once that happened, there was no going back. The membranes ruptured and her baby was brutally ripped from her womb and expelled from her body in a flood of blood and tissue. Somehow, she had to find the strength to pick up the pieces and try again.

"I have something with your name on it. It's small and shiny."

Marc had been trying hard to make her feel better, putting aside his own grief to make sure she was all right. He did everything short of calling in the circus to cheer up his wife, but to no avail.

Nina slowly moved away from the window. She had an overwhelming urge to crawl back into bed and stay there indefinitely, but she opted for a seat on the sofa. Marc sat beside her.

"Don't you want to know what it is?"

"What?" she asked gloomily.

"The surprise I have for you," Marc answered, his enthusiasm waning.

"Oh. Maybe later," Nina responded weakly.

There was a long pause.

"I lost him too, Nina," Marc said softly.

She didn't know what to say. Her head told her that her husband was just as grief-stricken as she was, and that she should be comforting him as much as he did her. But she couldn't get past her loss and the humiliation of lying on the ground, bleeding out, and the only person who could help her was the man she despised most in this world. To make matters worse, he watched her suffering and delayed calling for help. It was too much to take. If God was trying to teach her a lesson, school was out as far as she was concerned.

"I'm sorry, babe. I know you're grieving, too. I don't know how to deal with this," she said, her voice fragile. "I don't know how to process what I'm feeling. I don't know how not to be angry. I'm barely holding it together."

"You don't have to hold it together, Nina," he said gently, pulling her into his arms. "That's what I'm here for. When you're better, I'm better."

His admission made her feel even more wretched than she already did. But it also reminded her what she was desperately fighting to preserve. She couldn't tell him about her father now. Maybe not ever.

She placed both hands on either side of his face and rubbed her forehead against his.

"I'm afraid that was our big chance to be a family," she whispered. "We may not get another one."

"I was looking forward to pediatrician visits and late night feedings," Marc said, his voice tinged with disappointment. "I even started working on assembling the crib. Maybe I acted too soon."

"Don't say that. We were well past the first trimester. We had every reason to be optimistic."

Nina leaned back into the comfort of the sofa. "How did you find out I was in trouble?"

"I got a call from a colleague of yours, named Phillip. He said he was expecting you for a scheduled meeting but when he got to his office, he found you passed out and bleeding on the floor. He called an ambulance right away."

Nina reminded herself that losing her temper was one of the reasons she lost her baby. If she hadn't confronted Phillip, he wouldn't have had the opportunity to make her vulnerable. He must have gone through her phone to find Marc's number. The idea of him rummaging through such a private part of her life made her want to spit.

"Was he at the hospital when you got there?"

"Yes. I thanked him on our behalf. He was very concerned about you. He was genuinely sorry when I told him you lost the baby."

Nina scoffed. "Yes, I'm sure he was all broken up about it."

Marc raised his eyebrow. "Why do you say that? He went out of his way to help a virtual stranger."

"I guess I should be thankful."

Nina couldn't keep the bitterness out of her voice. Marc wouldn't be so appreciative if he knew Phillip's lack of enthusiasm for helping her when she needed it most probably cost him his son. She would have to be careful of what she said from now on. She told Phillip he was a sociopath with no understanding of human bonding and emotion. He proved her right. So why did she feel so awful? What did she expect? That he would suddenly grow paternal feelings for her and forget every terrible thing she had accused him of? Why did she do this to herself? Why did she keep holding onto the hope that one day, he would see her as a real father would: a wonderful daughter who was deserving of his love and respect? Maybe she's the one who needed psychiatric help.

Marc's next question brought her back to reality. "Why were you in his office all the way in Cambridge?"

"The change of scenery seemed like a good idea. Jack asked me to follow up with him regarding the execution of our revamped corporate responsibility strategy. He's on the board of directors at Baseline and runs a foundation here in Boston."

Nina feigned boredom with the topic and flipped on the television. *Oprah* was on, featuring her Favorite Things. Nina wasn't much in the holiday mood, but she at least had the tree up. There was still some Christmas shopping left to do and not much time to do it. The one bright spot this holiday season would be her mother's visit in a few weeks. Oprah trotted out a purple cashmere sweater that piqued her interest.

"Remind me to pick up that sweater for my mother," she said to Marc. "I can't believe Christmas is around the corner. What a year we've had, huh?"

"Next year will be better."

"We get a do-over."

"How so?"

"We get to try again."

Marc walked over to the fireplace and picked up the poker. He stoked the almost dead embers, bringing them back to life.

"I don't know, Nina, it's too much pressure," he said, shaking his head. "We were happy before we started trying to conceive, before we found out there was a problem. Trying to get pregnant has taken over our lives. Maybe we need to make some decisions in the coming year."

She joined him at the fireplace and rubbed his shoulders. "You want us to quit, forget about having kids of our own?"

"We've been through a traumatic experience. I'm just saying we should give ourselves some time to heal and figure out our options."

"We were so close. A few more months and we would have had a healthy baby. Why is God punishing me? Haven't I been through enough?"

Marc frowned, took her by the hands and sat her down on the couch. "What are you talking about?"

The words were out of her mouth before she realized she had said them out loud. The last thing she wanted to do was give Marc another reason to doubt her. She said the most logical thing she could think of.

"Nothing. This has been a long process, one that took a toll on my body and our marriage. I feel like a rag doll that was mistakenly put in the washer on the spin cycle."

The doorbell ringing pierced their self-imposed silence. Nina nudged Marc to get it and he reluctantly untangled himself from her arms to answer it. He returned to the living room with Charlene in tow. It took enormous self-control for Nina not to roll her eyes in disgust.

"I'm in charge around here, at least for the weekend. Anybody got a problem with that?"

"No, ma'am," Marc said.

"Marc, I forgot the grocery list in my car, so go fetch it."

Marc kissed Nina on the forehead and headed out the door.

"Girl, you took a licking, but you have *got* to get out of this funk," she said, joining Nina on the sofa.

"He just stood there watching me, Char, like I was some stray dog that didn't matter. He took his sweet time calling for help."

Charlene looked away, unable to meet Nina's gaze.

"What is it, Char? Why can't you look me in the face? Don't you want to hear how your lover and I argued about you before he refused to call for help before it was too late?"

Charlene's mouth opened and closed like a fish out of water, gasping for air. "That's just nasty. Why would you say something like that to me?"

"Because it's the naked truth. And you're right. It's revolting to think of the two of you sleeping together."

"You better have some proof, Nina. You can't accuse me of some jacked up shit like this."

"Hand me your phone," Nina said.

Charlene looked dazed. "What for?"

"Are you refusing to hand it over?"

"Those drugs they gave you at the hospital must be messing with your head."

"Do you have so little respect for our friendship that you continue to lie, even after you've been found out?"

"You mean the way you've been lying to your husband?" Charlene answered brazenly.

"But I didn't lie to you, Charlene. And you don't even have the decency to be embarrassed when you know full well I wouldn't make an accusation like this without proof. What has he done to you?"

"You're grieving. It must be making you crazy, so I'll let this slide."

Before Nina knew what was happening, the palm of her hand connected with Charlene's face and made a loud crackling sound. Charlene was stunned, but not for long. Nina found herself on the receiving end of a retaliatory back hand that hurt worse than a bee sting. Nina got off the couch and headed to the kitchen where she took a bag of frozen vegetables from the freezer and applied it to her face. When she returned to the living room, Charlene looked madder than a rottweiler about to pounce on its victim. There was only one way this was going to end.

"You and Phillip deserve each other," Nina said with resignation. "You're a two-faced, backstabbing slut. Get out. This friendship is over."

Charlene picked up her purse and practically knocked over a visibly shaken Marc on her way out.

"Did you just curse out your best friend? I've never heard that kind of language come out of your mouth before. What's going on, Nina?"

"I'm tired, Marc. I'm just so tired."

*　　*　　*

"Sorry, Mr. Tibbs, I didn't mean to suffocate you. I'm a wreck. A selfish wreck who just threw away over twenty years of friendship. What did I do? I know you've always loved Char, but hear me out — she crossed a line she shouldn't have, and I don't know if I have it in me to forgive her.

"She had a *relationship* with Phillip. Phillip, of all people! Of course I have evidence, there are phone records and emails. I don't care what her reasons are. I know she doesn't know the whole story, but that's no excuse, Mr. Tibbs. It's just plain wrong.

"This hurts as badly as losing Noah. Noah Anthony. He was so real to me, Mr. Tibbs. I felt him kick. Marc and I would talk to him all the time.

"Marc. I haven't been the best wife lately. I know he's grieving too, but I've been sucking up all the air in the house with my incessant crying and foul mood. I should be looking after him, too, but he never complains. He's so worried about me, Mr. Tibbs. Maybe the truth is, I'm a little worried, too."

CHAPTER FIFTEEN

P hillip sat in his office at the Dare to Dream Foundation, wondering how everything could have gone so terribly wrong. For the first time in years, he was unsure what to do next, a feeling he despised because he was used to being in control. Every move he made up until now had been meticulously planned and he always had a plan B and C just in case. With Nina, all his careful planning had amounted to nil. They were at an impasse. She refused to cooperate from the beginning and now with the loss of her unborn child, and the end of her friendship with Charlene—and from Charlene's account, it was rather ugly— he failed to see any scenario under which she would become an ally or asset. For reasons he couldn't fathom, she had not revealed to her husband that he was her father, and from the looks of things, she had no intention of doing so. He chuckled to himself at the irony because that was the only thing working in his favor.

It didn't mean he was in the clear, however. There was the existence of that damned diary, which was pure fiction and obviously came from the mind of a very disturbed young girl. He had no idea she was so ill or had written down these crazy stories, which she actually believed. Maybe if he had been home more often this wouldn't have happened. She obviously needed his attention more than he realized. He traveled on business quite frequently and Theresa had her own career she was focused on. Constance did a decent job of taking care of both Nina and Cassie, but she was no substitute parent. When Nina left, he had one hell of a time explaining to

Theresa why his older daughter left without saying goodbye and refused to speak to him or accept his calls.

It wasn't long after Nina left that he and Theresa called it quits. The marriage was dying a slow death that neither one of them wanted to be the first to admit. Once Nina was removed from the equation, there was a gaping hole in the family dynamic. There was no way to salvage the marriage and the only logical thing to do was end it. They had an amicable divorce and Cassie went to live with her mother in New York, then returned to Boston for college, where she had been ever since. It wasn't lost on him that he had one daughter who worshipped him and another who despised him.

But maybe all was not lost. An idea began to formulate in his head. Marc Kasai had unwittingly given him an opening. He picked up the phone on his desk and dialed the number he swiped from Nina's smartphone when she had the miscarriage.

*   *   *

NINA WAS ADDING THE FINISHING touches to her appearance before she headed downstairs. Her dinner guests would arrive any minute and she needed to make sure she was present when they did. Marc wouldn't reveal too much about the surprise guests, except to say Nina would be thrilled to see them. It had been a while since they had company. The past month had been spent in isolation and mourning, so Nina was looking forward to this evening, a chance to socialize and have a little fun. Marc was concerned about the falling out between Nina and Charlene and wanted to know if their friendship was really over, which he couldn't grasp, because Charlene had always been part of their lives. Nina had alleviated his concern by informing him that the fight had been over a married man Charlene had been seeing. They'd sparred before in the past, and always made up. That explanation seemed to satisfy him and he hadn't broached the subject since.

Nina flung open the door, eager to welcome her dinner guests, and did a double take when she saw Geraldine.

"Ravishing as always, darling," Geraldine cooed.

Nina didn't know if she could take this. Why on earth would Marc invite her father to their home? Was this the night all her lies were going to come crashing down on her? Had Marc found out and planned to confront her tonight? Nah. Marc wasn't the type. Something more sinister was at play here. Nina looked past Geraldine, expecting Phillip to materialize any minute.

"He's finishing up a conversation in the car. I keep telling him he should get a mobile phone surgically implanted in his ear. And don't worry, Nina, your secret is safe with me." Geraldine winked at her

Nina was embarrassed. "He told you?"

"I've known for some time, dear. After we had dinner at the Bristol Lounge, I figured you were the daughter he never wanted to discuss with me."

Nina remembered her manners. "You can go right in," she said shakily. "I'll wait for Phillip."

Nina lay in wait in the foyer and watched Phillip approach the door. He raised his hand to push the doorbell when she opened it.

"You have some nerve showing up after what you did. Why are you here?"

"Your husband thinks I'm a hero. He wanted to thank me for getting you to the hospital and letting him know what was going on. It wouldn't be polite if I had turned him down."

"That's because he's a decent human being. Something you know nothing about."

"Don't be a hypocrite. You've been lying to the man for years. What are you going to do when he finds out I'm your father?"

"There's no way I'm telling him that my father killed his son."

"Must you be so dramatic? I was in shock. Confused. It took me a while to collect my bearings."

"How would you feel if someone killed your son?" Nina threw out nonchalantly.

Phillip averted his eyes and looked toward the staircase. "You have a very fertile imagination."

"Your denials are insulting. Tracy Forbes had your bastard child and you've kept it a secret. How much did you pay her to keep quiet about the fact she was underage when you got her pregnant? And you think you can become Governor with a long trail of despicable personal drama? This is a liberal state but voters will draw the line somewhere."

Marc interrupted before he got a chance to respond. "Get in here, you two. You're not allowed to discuss business tonight."

"This isn't over," Nina whispered to Phillip.

Both couples sat down to dinner in the elegant dining room. All the flatware, stemware and dishware had been carefully selected. Nina broke out a bottle of 1989 Chateau Haut Brion and poured for her guests first. She had to be the perfect hostess, even under duress.

"Thanks for accepting our invitation," Marc said. "My wife and I wanted to express our thanks for getting her the medical attention she needed. This dinner is the very least we could do."

"It's gratifying to see Nina has recovered," Phillip said. "I hope this dinner isn't uncomfortable for her."

"Nonsense," Nina said, smoothing her dress. "Why would I be uncomfortable in my own home?"

"You've been through a traumatic experience, dear," Geraldine said. "Having dinner guests so soon might be a bit much."

"I don't stay down for long, Geraldine. Soon I'll be back to my old self, ready to take on the world."

"That's the spirit." Geraldine raised her glass. "To taking on the world."

Everyone clinked their glasses in a toast then dug into appetizers: stuffed mushrooms infused with garlic, bread crumbs, two types of cheeses, mint leaves and a dash of cayenne pepper.

"How are your parents, Marc?" Phillip asked.

"You know my parents?" Marc was obviously surprised.

"Not very well, but I hope that will change in time. I donate to Breast cancer research at Mass General Hospital. Your father heads up Neurosurgery, right?"

"Yes, he does. I'm happy to make a formal introduction, if you'd like."

"I'm ahead of you on that score. Your father was kind enough to invite me to the anniversary celebration. As a matter of fact, I ran into your wife."

"Really? She didn't mention it."

Nina wanted to kick Phillip under the table until he howled in agony. He was blatantly baiting her, trying to get her to make a mistake or lose her temper. He had turned on the charm full throttle, obviously for Marc's benefit. It was nauseating. She didn't know what arm-twisting he did to get her husband to invite him to their home, but it made Nina leery. She didn't go through the trouble of keeping Phillip at a distance for over a decade only to have him invited into her private world.

"There were over a hundred people at that party. I can't be expected to remember every conversation I had that evening."

"You hurt my feelings, Nina. It's not every day I invite an executive from the private sector to lecture my class. Have you already forgotten our discussion?"

"You didn't mention that either, *Cherie*," Marc admonished.

"There's a lot your wife doesn't tell you," Phillip quipped.

"The time I spend with my husband is very precious. I don't bring up anything that doesn't benefit our relationship."

Nina turned to Geraldine for backup. "You understand. You're a busy professional as well."

Geraldine agreed.

By the time the main course was served, the atmosphere was much less tense, friendly even. Nina breathed a huge sigh of relief. It seemed they were through with minefields to navigate and traps she was afraid would spring — at least for the night. Marc discovered that Geraldine was conversational in French and she decided to practice her skills under the guidance of a fluent speaker. Phillip regaled them with tales of his travels and visions for the Dare to Dream Foundation.

"You, my dear, are an absolute genius in the kitchen," Geraldine gushed. "Marc, your wife can do it all. I'm bursting with envy."

"My Nina is a rare gem," Marc said.

"You see why I married him?" Nina said to her guests.

That remark got a chuckle out of everyone, including Phillip.

"Geraldine, if you help me clear the dishes, I'll tell you how to get that suit I wore on the cover of *Executive Insider* at a discount," Nina offered.

Geraldine didn't get a chance to respond. "I'll help you clear the dishes," Phillip offered.

Everyone looked at him like he had suddenly gone mad.

"That's not necessary," Nina said firmly. "Geraldine and I have it covered."

"I insist. You've worked very hard on this dinner."

To object further would raise questions she didn't want to answer. Nina acquiesced.

Once they were alone in the kitchen, all Phillip's niceties disappeared. "Now I understand why you've been fighting so hard," he said as he rested the dishes on the kitchen counter.

"Meaning?"

"Your husband loves you very much."

"Does that disappoint you?" Nina said, shoving dishes into the dishwasher.

"Why would it? I'm happy you've done well for yourself. You have a beautiful home, a great career, and a husband who adores you. Every father wants his children to be happy."

"Don't," Nina said, as she removed the chocolate flan from the refrigerator and placed it on the countertop. "Don't pretend you wanted what was best for me. You've only ever caused me pain and misery. That's why I left home and never looked back.

"I so wanted to have a normal father. I felt like some freak because of what you did to me. I couldn't tell Marc you lived close by. If he found out, he would have insisted on meeting you. I couldn't allow that to happen. You would have destroyed us like you do every relationship you have."

Phillip's brain went into overdrive. He recognized her deception for what it was: self-preservation, one of the most selfish human motives there was. Maybe his daughter was more like him than she was willing to admit. According to Cassie, Marc Kasai was a very patient man who lived by a strict moral code. To a man like that, finding out the wife he adores has been making a fool of him for years would not sit well. He could march right in there and tell Marc the truth, but Nina would retaliate in ways he couldn't afford. She might tell him that nonsense she'd been spewing about "what he did to her" and if she did, he could kiss a potential political ally goodbye. That was the kind of stuff he couldn't afford to get out because no one wanted to hear the truth. He needed to get his hands on that damn diary.

"How did it come to this, Nina?" he asked, his voice laced with something resembling regret.

"You want something I can't give you. Call it forgiveness, absolution, whatever. You want me to smile for the cameras and say what a great father you are and tell people in my demographic you would make a great Governor and they should vote for you. I can't do that.

"Even if you take me out of the equation, you have an illegitimate child with a young woman who was under age when you got her pregnant. You're on your third marriage, and to a foreigner at that. You had an affair with your daughter's best friend. And I don't even want to think about your business dealings when you were in the private sector. Looks like we have something in common other than DNA. We're both damaged goods."

CHAPTER SIXTEEN

Nina missed her best friend terribly, but what could she do? As long as Charlene was fooling around with Phillip, they couldn't be friends. She didn't even know if they were still seeing each other after their big blowout, but it didn't matter. Charlene's betrayal hurt Nina like someone had peeled her skin from her body.

It had been a hectic day at work, loaded with one marathon meeting after another. Nina just wanted to go home, curl up next to Marc and have him give her one of his achingly delicious foot rubs. She pulled into the garage and entered the kitchen through the side door. She flipped on the lights and stifled a scream. Marc was sitting at the table.

"Babe, you scared the heck out of me. Why were you sitting in the dark?"

"Just thinking. About us," he said, not looking at her.

Nina noticed a small suitcase, the one he used for short trips, next to his feet.

"You're traveling? Bummer. You won't believe the day I had. First of all—"

His response was curt and unexpected. "Don't bother. I won't be around to hear it. I'm going to New York. I'll be at my brother's place for a few days."

"You sound like you want to get away from me."

"I'm surprised you could figure that out. You've been so busy trying to keep your lies straight, I don't think you would have noticed I was gone."

Nina sat down across from him, her heart pounding in her ears. She'd told so many lies she didn't know which one he was referring to. It was best to proceed with caution.

"I don't know what you mean."

He shot her a look of disbelief. "You really don't know or are you pretending not to? You've become very good at pretending lately. Or maybe deceit has always been in your nature; maybe I just didn't pay close enough attention."

Crap! This was it. The category five storm she feared had now made landfall. No matter how angry Marc got, she had to keep herself in check. Charlene's warning about keeping secrets echoed in her head. She'd promised she would back Nina up when she decided to tell Marc about Phillip but since she tossed Charlene out of her life, her former BFF had no allegiance to her anymore. She felt naked without her sidekick.

"You obviously have something you need to discuss, so get to it."

"How can you be so casual about it?"

She struggled to keep the growing annoyance out of her voice. "Marc, please. Say what you have to say."

"You're a liar and a coward. The scary thing is, I don't know what else you're hiding. I don't know what else you're capable of. You had to have known the truth would come out eventually. The thing I don't get is why? Why would you concoct some story about a falling out with your father to explain his absence from your life?"

She kept her voice steady. She couldn't fall apart just yet. "How did you find out?"

"I had a hunch. I called Charlene. She had quite a lot to say."

"I bet she did."

He kept on going, as if she hadn't spoken. "I never made anything of the fact that you two shared the same last name, which I brushed off as coincidence. It doesn't make sense to me, Nina. Why would you hurt me this way? You sat at that dinner table and said nothing. There was plenty of opportunity over the years to say something and you didn't, which makes me think you never had any intention of telling me. Ever."

The look on his face broke her heart. He was utterly devastated, his eyes beseeching her for some truth or understanding that would rescue him from having to face the fact that he'd been betrayed.

Nina walked over to the kitchen sink and turned on the faucet. She splashed her face with cold water, as if the gesture would somehow give her the courage to be forthcoming. It had been relatively easy to sidestep Marc's curiosity with seemingly legitimate excuses. But now he was about to walk out of her life. There were others to consider, not just the two of them. If the truth came out, lives would be shattered. But maybe she didn't have to tell Marc the *whole* truth.

Her tongue felt heavy as she attempted to explain away the mess she had made. "You're right, Marc. I lied to you about Phillip because I didn't want him in our lives. I lied because sometimes the truth is better left unspoken."

He was flabbergasted. "That's it? That's your explanation? You don't think I deserve better?"

"You deserve to have a life free from the poison and influence of my father. That's the simplest way I can explain why I deceived you."

He stood up and slammed his palm on the table in a rare display of unbridled anger. "That's not good enough! You need to decide what's more important to you: The future of this marriage or keeping your secrets. And until you make that decision, I think it's best if we separate. This shouldn't be a shock to you, considering I've been begging you to confide in your husband for months and you blatantly disregarded those pleas."

His eyes were red, glistening from the tears he was struggling to hold back. He rubbed his nose on the sleeve of his shirt, picked up his bag and marched out of her life without a backward glance.

Nina headed to the attic without thinking, as if on autopilot. The habit of confiding in Mr. Tibbs was tough to break. The diary had to go. It was the only thing connecting her past to her present, apart from Phillip. She almost stumbled over Mr. Tibbs in her haste to retrieve it from its carefully concealed spot.

"What's the hurry, Mr. Tibbs? Marc just walked out because I couldn't bring myself to tell him our secret. I have no recourse but to destroy the diary. I know that was my only trump card, but Marc can't see what's written there. I *know* I can't go on this way forever. But if he sees what's in here… I don't know. I'm really confused right now. I just think people… well, they look at you differently once they find out, do you understand what I mean? We read *The Scarlet Letter* in high school, remember? We don't want to be branded by what happened. So I'm going to do the only thing that makes sense: burn it. All the awful things remembered in those pages will be gone forever."

Nina reached for the diary in its usual hiding place but it wasn't there. That was strange; she always kept it in the same spot. Maybe she was in a hurry last time and didn't put it back exactly in the usual spot—but that didn't make sense, either. She felt panic clawing at her but she did her best to shake it off. She dropped to her knees and went through the attic inch by inch, throwing aside boxes, books, and anything that could conceivably hide an eight by ten diary. She came up empty.

"Something's wrong, Mr. Tibbs." Nina raked her hair back with her fingers. "The diary isn't here. Do you know who took it?"

*   *   *

PHILLIP HADN'T FELT THIS GOOD in a long time. He sat in his den sipping chardonnay, enjoying the sound of paper going through the shredder. One by one, he fed the pages into the machine and the ripping sound was like a sweet symphony composed just for him. He congratulated himself on his cunning and how easy it had been. Marc, Nina, and even his wife bought the idea that he needed some privacy because he was expecting an important call the very night they all sat down to dinner. Marc gladly served up his home office. That gave Phillip the opportunity to do a little exploring, making his way up to the second floor. As he was walking down the hallway to the master bedroom, something made him look up. He saw the rope hanging from the ceiling. All he had to do was pressure Cassie into giving up her spare key Nina gave her in case of emergencies. The poor kid was so desperate for reconciliation between him and her older sister she was perfectly willing to accept his story that he was leaving Nina a surprise thank you gift for hosting him and Geraldine. Once in the attic, he just had to think like a woman who was hiding something. The diary wouldn't be in plain view. It would have to be hidden behind something or in something. The hat box behind the flat screen box seemed as good a place as any. His instincts had been dead on.

His solo celebration came to an abrupt and unwelcome end when a certain redhead poked her head in. "The movie is about to start, are you coming?"

"In a minute," he answered gruffly.

Geraldine's eyes fixated on the shredder and the book in Phillip's hand. "What are you doing?"

"Just shredding some business documents that contain sensitive information."

"Can't you do that later? The movie is about to start and the popcorn is getting cold."

Phillip was reluctant to leave but he didn't want to arouse suspicion. Geraldine knew his den was off limits when he wasn't around so he supposed there was no harm in returning to his task later.

CHAPTER SEVENTEEN

The mouthwatering aroma of cream of coconut in a luscious blend of spicy seasonings emanating from the kitchen took Nina back to her childhood. It was the most comforted and sane she'd felt since Marc left. The image of her mother in a red and white checkered apron, kneading the dough for the dumplings, brought a smile to her lips. This rich, hearty stew was the perfect culinary remedy for a cold and rainy January day. Her dejected spirit needed a lift and she was happy her mother had come to her rescue.

"I can't wait until the stew is done," Nina said. "How much longer?"

Daphne Lockwood, an attractive widow in her mid-fifties with flawless milk chocolate skin that mirrored her daughter's, looked up from her task.

"Not long. This dish used to cheer you right up when you were little."

Nina stood close to the stove, allowing the vapor from the bubbling stew to caress her face.

"Have you ever believed you were doing the right thing, only to end up with nothing?"

"You still have everything, if you want it," Daphne countered.

"How can you say that? I dumped my best friend, but not before calling her ugly names. My attempts at becoming a mother ended in failure. My marriage could be over, and Phillip stole my diary. I fail to see the upside of any of this."

Nina didn't want to feel sorry for herself, but it was difficult not to. Where had she gone wrong?

"Okay, one thing at a time. Charlene has always looked out for you. She listened to you. Told you what you needed to hear, not what you wanted to hear. Even though you're the same age, she was like a surrogate mother to you. Then you threw her out like an old pair of shoes. And why? Because she made a bad judgment call. Secondly, you can still have the family you deserve if you just have a little faith. Everything happens for a reason. Thirdly, you need to stop being stubborn and fix whatever problems you and Marc are having, and lastly, what the heck are you talking about, a stolen diary?"

Nina plopped herself down at the table and let out a frustrated sigh. "I just don't know how much more I can take, Mom. I know we all mess up and I should forgive Charlene, but I can't bring myself to do it. I may never be a mother and I need to accept that possiblility. And Marc, lying to him was wrong, but I felt I had no choice."

"What about the diary?" her mother asked, suspense locked on her face.

"I had a diary from when I was younger that had things in it that could cause a lot of trouble for Phillip. I made the mistake of tipping my hand and he stole it."

"What was in the diary that was so damaging Phillip would steal it? How do you know he took it?"

"I've had that diary for a lot of years and I always kept it in the same spot. Not even Marc knows I had it. You don't have to be Sherlock Holmes to put the pieces together. The diary disappeared after I blackmailed Phillip with one of the entries, and he came to our house for dinner. I'm positive it's him. Now, I have nothing left to fight him with."

Daphne sat next to her daughter and rubbed her arm comfortingly. "Nina, I had no idea that things had gotten so bad between the two of you, but stealing? It sounds like I don't know Phillip at all. What was in that diary that your father had to stoop so low to acquire it?"

Nina's stomach was in knots, her earlier hunger now replaced by a raw, piercing dread. She had hoped never to have this conversation with her mother, but her best laid plans had gone horribly awry. Her mother would never be the same. She was sure of it. But what choice did she have?

Nina watched as her mother removed the stew from the stove and placed it on the countertop. She reached into the cabinet for the soup bowls. She hummed an old gospel tune as she poured the stew in each bowl.

"I need to be sitting down for this?" she asked Nina.

"Yes, ma'm."

"Get the drink pitcher from the fridge and the glasses, will you?"

Nina obeyed. Her mother had a habit of making everything seem normal when she sensed she was in for some bad news. They sat at the table, poured drinks and placed spoons in their respective soup bowls.

"Start from the beginning."

"You already know about the hitting."

"Don't tell me it gets worse."

Nina gave in to the overwhelming urge to chicken out. She couldn't do it. "You know what, Mom? I don't want to talk about Phillip anymore. It's too depressing. Like you said, I have much more important matters that need my attention, like getting my husband back."

"You're not getting off that easy, Nina," her mother said. "Whatever you were going to say is important, so get to it."

Nina guzzled down a glass of the fruit cooler and poured another. She was halfway through emptying the second round when her mother practically ripped the glass from her hand, spilling most of the remaining contents on Nina's dress. With a hollow sense of calm, Nina reached for the napkin next to her bowl and soaked up whatever liquid she could from her dress. Her mother waited patiently for the next words to come out of her mouth.

"It's really hard to find the words. No matter which ones I come up with, I think it will hurt you more than me, mostly because I've had years to absorb it, question it, push it to the darkest recesses of my subconcious, and try to forget it."

"You're scaring me, Nina," her mother said, looking like she was about to be ill. "What did Phillip do to you? What did he do that has you all twisted up in knots, afraid to talk to your own mother?"

"Phillip is the reason you don't have grandchildren."

Daphne looked at Nina like she was descending into some unnamed mental state that was causing her to say strange things. "I already know about the miscarriage, remember?"

"I'm not talking about the miscarriage. It's a miracle I was pregnant in the first place. What I mean is… what I'm saying is the medical reason I can't get pregnant was, shall we say, induced by Phillip."

"I don't understand what you're saying," her mother said, dolefully.

"Phillip molested me for a number of years. I couldn't tell anyone: not you, not Charlene, not counselors at school, family, friends, and especially not my husband."

Nina wasn't sure her mother heard her at first. Daphne's expression was blank, as if all thought and emotion had been drained from her body. Nina was about to shake her out of her stupor when she came back to life.

"No, Nina. No. He couldn't have. It's not possible."

Nina watched her mother shake her head forcefully as she made a big fuss of digging her spoon into the still steaming hot stew.

"I wish it never happened, too. But he did. The worst part about it is he's not sorry. Not even a little bit."

"I don't understand Nina … you were ten years old when you came to live with him permanently. Why would he do something so heinous … especially after seeing you as an innocent, defenseless child?"

Nina took a deep breath. She was about to deliver another blow to her mother's already frayed emotions. "He didn't start when I was older. I didn't get the chance to figure out how to cope as an older kid, or find out how to be strong. I had to learn those skills as a ten-year old."

"Oh dear God," her mother said hoarsely. "Why didn't you tell me?"

Daphne looked like she was about to collapse. Nina stood up and moved next to her mother, holding her firmly in place. Nina knew better than to say anything at that moment. Whatever her mother was going through, she needed the stillness of the moment to come down from the blow she had been dealt.

"That bastard will pay for what he did, do you hear me? He'll pay even if it takes the last breath in my body to make it happen. Phillip. Copeland. Will. Pay."

"Revenge won't change what happened," Nina said acidly. "It won't give me my childhood back. It won't take away the feelings of worthlessness I struggled with. It won't take away the burden of keeping the secret all this time. I'll never get back what I lost. I don't want you to spend your energy thinking about him or how to get back at him."

"You amaze me, Nina. After everything your father has stolen from you, you think he doesn't deserve to be punished?"

"It's not about what he deserves. Don't you see? For so long it was all about him. I don't want it to be anymore."

Later that night as Nina was getting ready for bed, she made her way down the hall to say goodnight to her mother. She was about to knock when she thought she heard sobbing. She pressed her ear up against the door. She wasn't imagining things. She knocked gently then heard silence. She knocked again and waited. Her mother appeared at the door, with a tear-stained face and puffy eyes. "I'll stay with you if you want," Nina told her.

Her mother clutched her tightly all night, as if she were protecting Nina from some unseen evil that might befall her again.

*   *   *

BREAKFAST WAS A SOMBER OCCASION. Daphne insisted on helping Nina figure out how to pick up the pieces of her shattered life.

"You need to see somebody. A professional."

"I'm not going to see a shrink, Mom." Nina poured some orange juice for herself and her mother.

"Why not?"

"I've dealt with it all these years, there's no point in dredging it up again."

Nina could see the sadness creeping up in her mother's eyes. She reached across the kitchen table and stroked her mother's arms comfortingly.

"How did you manage to deal with something so horrific, so ..." Daphne's voice trailed off.

"Well, you know kids—they have very active imaginations. I would just pretend I was normal. I would do all the things kids my age did and when it happened, I would mentally check out until it was over and the next day I would pretend I was normal again. When I left for Stanford, I didn't feel alone at all. For the first time I was free and it was exhilarating. Eventually, it was almost as if it never happened because I cut him out of my life.

"I don't want to think about you going through that alone. It's too painful. Now I see I made a terrible mistake sending you here and I'm so sorry, Nina. I had no idea this is what was waiting for you. I thought I was being unselfish by letting you go because Phillip made a strong case.

"He said he wanted to get to know his daughter. He said it wasn't fair that I left with you after the divorce. He was in a position to send you to Harvard when the time came. You know I always had big dreams for you. I thought letting you go was the greatest gift I could give you, a future with endless possibility that your father could provide and I couldn't. I trusted him to take good care of you."

"Stop blaming yourself. Nobody has a crystal ball. You were married to the man once and had no reason to believe he was capable of this. Otherwise, you wouldn't have agreed."

"What about your younger sister?"

"What about Cassie?"

"Do you think ...?" Daphne couldn't complete the sentence.

"No way."

"How can you be so sure?"

"She had her mother to look out for her."

The minute the words left her mouth, Nina immediately regretted saying them. "Sorry. That came out wrong. You did something courageous. You put me first."

"And look what became of it. I left Phillip when you were less than two years old and returned to Barbados. I should have kept you until you were college age. If you were an adult, I'm sure this wouldn't have happened, Nina."

"No point in beating yourself up, Mom. It's not your fault and feeling guilty isn't going to do any good."

"I would have gotten you if you had given me even a hint anything was wrong. When we spoke, you always sounded so happy. I thought you were well taken care of and happy like you deserved to be."

"Abused children are really good actors. It's how they're trained—to be secretive and cover up the abuse."

"That's sick. That's why I want you to see a therapist. You need someone to help you come to terms with this."

"I have."

"Really? You can't bring yourself to tell your husband what happened to you. You couldn't even tell him Phillip was your father."

"I'll think about it. But no psychiatrist can give me what I want most. To have children of my own. How am I supposed to tell my husband I can't give him children because of my past? How am I going to justify that I knew why I couldn't get pregnant but neglected to tell him—"

Her mother went silent and looked past her shoulders. Nina turned around to follow her gaze.

Her eyes landed on Marc, who stood motionless at the kitchen entrance.

CHAPTER EIGHTEEN

Nina rose from the chair and took the longest steps she'd ever taken. She stood in front of her husband, stripped bare like the trees that lined their backyard in winter.

"You don't know what you just heard."

"Does it even matter anymore?"

"Of course it does, Marc," she insisted.

He laughed mirthlessly. "To think, I came back to work things out because I wanted to fight for us. Thank you for saving me the trouble."

She touched his shoulder. He brushed her hand away as if she were some toxic substance.

"It's not what you think. When I said I couldn't get pregnant because of my past, what I meant was …"

He cut her off rudely. "It doesn't matter. I don't want to hear any more of your lies."

Marc took the stairs two at a time, his long, powerful legs making quick work of the steps. Nina followed him into their bedroom. He opened the walk-in closet and grabbed a suitcase, which he proceeded to fill hurriedly and haphazardly.

"Where are you going?"

"Making our separation more permanent. I want a divorce."

Nina's head was spinning. "You don't mean that. I know you're angry and you should be. But you know me, Marc."

"Here I was thinking how unfair and cruel life could be. That we deserved to be a family but somehow, your body conspired to deny us that opportunity. All the while …"

Nina began to panic. The raw emotion in his voice brought home the gravity of the situation with stunning clarity. This was really happening. She couldn't get him to listen to her long enough to tell him what she never could before. The window of opportunity slammed shut with a resounding finality.

Marc zipped up the suitcase and left the bedroom. She followed him down the stairs like a stalking shadow. As if in slow motion he reached the bottom and turned to her.

"I know about Sonny Alvarez, another one of your lies. I heard you on the phone with Charlene, admitting that you lied to me about him." Marc then walked out for the final time.

*   *   *

HE DIDN'T SEE IT COMING. One minute he was on the phone with a potential donor and the next his ex-wife Daphne was standing mere inches from his desk with murder in her eyes. It had been fifteen years since he last saw her, at the disastrous family brunch following Nina's graduation ceremony, but he would recognize those eyes anywhere. They were the same blazing green eyes that stared back at him with defiance in the form of their daughter. For the first time ever, he was truly afraid of a woman's wrath. This one had hunted him down for a specific purpose. He bet it had something to do with her offspring and some crazy story said offspring may have relayed. Luckily, he had the diary, which was completely destroyed.

He came around from his desk to greet her and received a swift knee to the groin for his trouble. The excruciating pain brought him to his knees, with both hands covering his genitals in case she decided to take another shot. And if that wasn't enough, she spat on him to drive home her point.

"Even animals protect their young, Phillip. Since you couldn't do that, what does that make you?"

He slowly got off his knees and went back to his desk, limping. He sat down and assumed what he hoped was a bored expression.

"Don't ever do that again, Daphne. Next time, I won't be so civil."

"I don't give a flying fig about your civility. You don't deserve to live. And don't pull that smug crap with me either. I'm immune. I entrusted my daughter to you and this is how you repay my trust?"

"What are you babbling about, Daphne? I haven't seen you in 15 years and suddenly you barge in here and start accusing me of things I have no knowledge of."

"You're going sit there and deny it, you pompous son-of-a-bitch? You're going to deny that you raped your own daughter? My daughter?"

"I'm a very busy man. Either start making sense or get out."

"Stay away from my child, Phillip. Don't speak to her, don't write or email her, don't call her or visit her home or place of employment. Don't even breathe in her direction."

Daphne inched closer to him until he could see the whites of her eyeballs. "Do as I say. It would be the best thing for your health. Do you understand what I'm saying? I'm a grieving mother. I can't be responsible for my actions."

*   *   *

THE WEATHER OUTSIDE MATCHED NINA'S mood: a glum, rainy day with freezing temperatures. The Channel 5 meteorologist said the high would be a blustering twenty-five degrees. Nina wanted to be anywhere but the office, which she mistakenly believed would get her mind off her troubles. Emails remained unread and the red voicemail message button on her phone flashed like some ominous code she couldn't decipher. She cancelled most of her appointments, locked her door and decided to stay holed up all day, pretending to work on some important project she didn't have a name for.

"Nina, open up," he yelled.

He was the last person on earth she wanted to see. He obviously missed the "leave me the hell alone" memo. She reckoned she was moving slower than molasses as she dragged herself to the door. She unlocked the bolt and swung the door wide open in a wave of anger.

"What took you so long?"

"If you don't like it, then DON'T COME HERE, PHILLIP!"

Phillip could tell she'd been crying. Her body seemed tense, like a tree branch burdened by heavy snow right before it snapped under the pressure. "My goodness. What happened to you?"

"Did you come to gloat? Witness my ruin with your own eyes? Because I'm sure my mother told you to stay away from me."

Phillip flinched at the reminder of his rather unpleasant conversation with Daphne. "I don't take orders from your mother."

"Maybe you should. She can be fierce when crossed."

Nina went back to her swivel chair, propped her feet up on the desk, just the way she had them before she was rudely interrupted. She could tell he was uncomfortable. *Good*, she thought.

"Did you come to return my property? If not, then get the hell out. I have nothing to say to you."

"I don't have anything that belongs to you. Cassie told me your husband left. That's tough. As a veteran of two divorces, I thought I would offer my support."

If she wanted him to play the role of the concerned dad, that's what he would do. Obviously she wanted his attention and now she took it a step too far and told her mother that ridiculous story. With Daphne up in arms, he had to control that situation and Nina was the key. He had to get her mother to back off her ranting before she told some other idiot who would believe her. He'd come too far to turn back now. The primaries were less than a year away and he would announce his candidacy in a matter of weeks. This foolishness had to stop.

Nina couldn't take it anymore and she finally cracked. She knew full well he didn't give a damn about her marital state. Hysteria rose up in her throat and she started giggling like someone possessed. "You want to know something funny? I was going to burn the damn thing. I only found out you took it because I went to get it to start a bonfire.

"I couldn't stomach the idea of Marc finding out what happened to me. You marry someone and you think you know how they'll react to something, but there's always that tiny little part of you that's afraid of rejection, no matter how irrational it might seem. I don't think it would change how he feels about me, but that's a risk I wasn't willing to take.

"So don't you think for a second you got one over on me or you were so much more clever than me. All it says is that you're the same low-down coward you've always been, preying on the weak and not being man enough to face the consequences of your actions."

The violent streak that defined their history erupted like a raging storm that had been gathering strength near the horizon, waiting for the right moment to explode. She stopped his hand in mid-air before it could connect with her face, his favorite target.

"My reflexes are much faster now, don't you think?" Nina held his hand in a death-like grip, her fingernails drilling into his flesh.

He tried to wriggle his hand from her grip but she dropped it in a flash like the it was some filthy creature that made her skin crawl. He was visibly embarrassed but refused to give in. "You're lucky we're in a work environment. Otherwise, you wouldn't be standing."

"I disagree. But should you feel the urge to test me again, my kickboxing instructor is a three-time World Champion. He's taken a keen interest in making sure I have all the right moves."

"Don't get overconfident, Nina. I'm far more ruthless than you. That's why you'll never best me."

"I am my father's daughter. Who's to say I didn't inherit the ruthless gene? But I will confess to you right here, right now. I will make you pay. For everything."

Had he miscalculated everything? And if so, was there a chance to change course? The old saying, 'people never really change' was wrong. This girl was not the same girl who left home at eighteen. This woman was gutsy, determined, and had a combative streak a mile long. She had no respect for him and when people don't respect you, they don't fear you. He had to take a step back and regroup. He'd never conceded to anyone. Right now he was angry and disappointed, and felt backed into a corner. When he was backed into a corner, he tended to do bad things to get his way.

CHAPTER NINETEEN

T he corporate headquarters of Sullivan & Hewitt was housed in a large modern brick and glass building on Atlantic Avenue. Fortunately, the security guard on duty was familiar with Nina and didn't alert Marc to her presence. It had been several weeks since he moved out and all attempts at a face-to-face meeting failed. He kept giving her the same answer: they needed the time apart to reflect and do some soul searching before they could make any firm decisions about whether or not to end the marriage.

For Nina, there was nothing to think about. She had no intention of getting a divorce. It might take a lot of work, but she truly believed they could find their way back to each other and overcome the trust issues that ripped them apart. Since Marc wouldn't come to her, she decided to go to Marc.

She arrived in the large suite that supported Marc's office, as well as his assistant, Kendra Meeks, an impeccably styled, highly efficient brunette beauty in her early thirties.

"Hey, you," Nina said cheerfully as she tapped her fingers on the desk.

"Hello, Mrs. Kasai. How are you today?" Kendra wouldn't meet her eyes and kept filing and re-filing the same folder.

Nina wondered about the strange greeting. Kendra always called her by her first name. The stiff formality was unexpected. It made Nina uneasy.

"Why so formal all of a sudden, Kendra? Is Marc giving you grief? Just tell me and I'll straighten him out."

"It's nothing like that." Kendra offered a weak smile.

"Is he in a meeting?" Nina shifted her gaze to the closed door.

"Y-yes he is."

That's all the answer Nina needed. She sashayed her way to the door, but Kendra was closer and blocked her path.

"You can't go in there."

"Why not?"

"Because—"

"Don't worry about it. I already know." Nina winked at Kendra reassuringly.

She turned the doorknob slowly and willed it not to make a sound. It must have sensed the tension in her because she walked into the office and neither one of them heard her come in. Marc was leaning up against his desk, his view blocked by Solange, who was moving her hands seductively across his chest. They must have felt a presence in the room because Marc looked up and Solange followed his gaze.

She had startled them. Solange moved away from Marc reluctantly and Marc looked grumpy. Or maybe he was embarrassed, she couldn't quite tell.

Nina spoke first. "You two certainly didn't waste any time. I would expect that from Solange because she's a viper, but Marc, you surprise me."

Solange was defiant. "This is a business meeting. I was invited here, Nina. You're the one intruding."

"Is that what you call what you were doing? Business? Then this meeting's adjourned."

Solange looked at Marc, her eyes pleading with him to come to her rescue. Nina held her breath, praying she wouldn't be the one humiliated. When Marc gestured for Solange to go, Nina did a mental somersault.

Once they were alone, it took enormous self-control not to ask why Solange was in his office in the middle of the morning with her hands all over him. Nina studied Marc for a moment. His suit fit more loosely than the day he left their home. His eyes lacked clarity, a sure sign of sleep deprivation.

"When are you coming home?" she asked, putting her pride aside.

He returned to the chair behind his desk and picked up a stack of papers. "I have work to do."

Nina took the papers from him and threw them over her shoulder. They scattered like autumn leaves in the wind.

"Are you going to pick those up?" he demanded gruffly.

"Make me."

Marc thumped his fist against the gleaming cherry desk. "What do you want from me, woman?"

"I want you to talk to me. I want you to come home where you belong."

"That's not possible."

"Why? Have you already moved on with your ex?"

When he didn't answer, Nina became frantic. "Is it that easy for you to walk away, Marc?"

He looked her straight in the eye for the first time since she interrupted his interlude with the woman she'd always considered a threat. "As easy as it was for you to deceive me."

She guessed she deserved it. She tried not to make too much of the scene she walked in on even if every cell in her body was screaming that she might be losing him. She had to keep the conversation civil and focused, not emotional.

"There was nothing easy about it, Marc. You once told me that keeping my secrets was more important to me than keeping our marriage honest. That's not true."

"Why are you telling me this now?"

"I didn't get the chance to tell you the reasons I lied about Phillip. *All* the reasons."

Marc got up from his desk and walked over to the window, both hands stuck in his pockets. "I no longer trust you, Nina, and without trust, I don't see a way for us. I won't spend the rest of my life wondering if I can believe everything my wife tells me or waiting for the next bombshell to drop. I won't live that way."

The temperature in the room plummeted. Nina was in agony.

"You're so wrong," she managed to squeak out. "Things aren't always what they seem."

"I gave you ample opportunity to tell me the truth. You didn't. You left me with few options."

She walked over to the window and gently caressed his face. "I'm truly sorry, Marc. From the bottom of my heart, I'm sorry I lied to you."

She had done as much begging and groveling as her pride could take in one day. She picked up her purse and was about to leave, but she had to know.

"What did I walk in on, Marc?"

He looked in her direction briefly, then turned back to the window.

A concerned Kendra handed her a box of tissue. "I'm sorry, Nina. Whatever is going on between you and Marc is none of my business, but that Solange woman—"

Nina could see the disdain on Kendra's face. "Not a fan either, huh?"

Nina took a few steps toward the door when an idea occurred to her. After a few words with Kendra that played on the woman's sympathy, Nina walked out of the office armed with vital information and a new next move.

There was a spring in her step as she headed for the elevator. Her plan would work. But first, she had to get rid of the envelope with the Tufts University address that had been burning a hole in her purse.

Nina emerged from the elevator and was immediately accosted by an incensed Solange, who had been lying in wait.

"Marc doesn't want to be married to you anymore, Nina. It's time to move on. I'm sure you'll find another husband easily."

"Thanks for the vote of confidence, but I'll keep the one I have."

"It's hopeless to chase him. He won't come back. I warned you this would happen."

"Then your psychic powers should have told you that a husband and wife share a unique bond, especially when they love each other deeply, like Marc and I do."

"He doesn't share your opinion. We were making plans for tonight when you rudely interrupted."

Nina didn't flinch. "Just because you're an easy lay doesn't mean he's going to leave me for you. Married men lie, Solange. They're always planning to leave their wives for their lovers, but they never do. Why do you think you're still single?"

The last jab hit its target like a gun fired at close range. Solange was taken speechless. She gawked at Nina, the truth suddenly laid bare. Her embarrassment was cut short by the ringing of her cell phone. Solange dove into her purse to find the phone, which was apparently playing hide and seek. After a few frustrated seconds, success. Solange answered and began a conversation in rapid French.

Nina was about to walk away when something caught her attention. Just a few feet from Solange was a square piece of paper. Nina inched closer and picked it up. It was a photograph of a child, a boy between the ages of nine and ten, in Nina's best estimation. Something inside her began to ache. She was suddenly gripped by paralyzing fear. She looked up to see Solange staring at her.

"Who is this?" Nina asked, her hand trembling as she held out the photo.

"That's my son," Solange answered as if Nina had just asked her what time it was.

"Is he Marc's?"

Solange didn't answer. She simply took the photograph from Nina and left.

CHAPTER TWENTY

D aphne returned to Dallas, leaving a broken-hearted Nina behind. She had always relied on her mother's support but it was time to see what she was made of. It was time to pick up the broken pieces of her life, starting with getting her husband back. But what kind of relationship would they have when images of Marc and Solange with their son danced in her head at night? Did Marc know he had a son? Not that he would have told her, since they were separated. This was a game changer. If she wanted her husband back, that meant she'd have to accept his son, and his mother. Lately, Nina's brain cells were overloaded and she was afraid it would short circuit. But one particular situation continued to nag at her. Maybe it was time she put her stubborn pride on the back burner.

Finding a parking spot on Newbury Street in the middle of the day was an anomaly at best, so Nina enlisted the help of her assistant. Eric dropped his boss outside the Desert Rose Salon & Spa and promised to pick her up whenever she was finished. Nina felt guilty for asking the favor, but she had a schedule to keep, which did not include circling a two-block radius in the hopes that a parking spot would miraculously open up.

Nina walked into the salon and was warmly welcomed by Lynette, the receptionist, a soft-spoken twenty-something with five inch acrylic fingernails and too much make-up.

"Where have you been, girl? We miss you around here. The boss hasn't been the same since you stopped coming."

Nina's emotions were on tenterhooks and she responded to Lynnette with some mundane quip. She was glad to know Charlene was suffering from their breakup as much as she was. She focused her attention on the display behind the reception desk, rows and rows of beauty products in jars and bottles. The panorama of color had an oddly calming effect on her.

"I don't have an appointment, but do you think one of the girls could take me soon?"

"You know the boss will hook you up. What do you need?"

"A touch-up, deep conditioning, blow-dry, manicure, pedicure, herbal body wrap, thirty- minute massage and a facial."

"Work it, girl. Your man won't know what hit him."

"Who said anything about a man?" Nina asked, guiltily. "Can't a girl treat herself?"

"Who you fooling?" Lynette asked as she dialed an extension and got right to the point.

Within seconds, Charlene appeared in the waiting area.

"Your client needs you," Lynnette said.

*   *   *

CHARLENE'S OFFICE HADN'T CHANGED MUCH since Nina last visited. The basket of hair and beauty magazines sat next to a potted plant against the corner wall. Glamour shots of beautiful women in a multitude of hair-dos lined the wall and her appointment book sat at the center of a slightly disorganized desk. But the one constant that took on a different meaning for Nina were the personal photographs in ceramic picture frames next to the flat screen computer: High school graduation with both of them holding up their diplomas for the camera, Charlene on the arm of Marc's brother, Thierry, as they exited the church as Maid of Honor and Best Man at Marc and Nina's wedding, the grand opening of The Desert Rose and the two women toasting with champagne. Then it hit her. They were family, pure and simple.

Nina took a seat and tinkered with the bracelet on her left hand. "I'm sorry to impose. As you can see, I'm in need of the full treatment. I haven't had a chance to investigate alternative salons, so I shifted into auto pilot and ended up here."

"You're full of it," Charlene reprimanded. "It's not what's on the outside that needs fixing. Although you do look like you went a few rounds with an alley cat and lost."

"Thank you for the kind words. I see I've come to the right place."

"You're lucky I'm talking to you at all after the way you tossed me out. That was foul."

"What did you expect me to do?"

"I thought we were friends. You didn't have to do me like that. You could have listened."

"I was hurt and in no mood to be honest about why I was so pissed off."

"Really?" Charlene said in mock surprise. "I figured the miscarriage wasn't the only thing messing with your head."

"You were having an affair with Phillip when you knew he was causing problems for me," Nina said in frustration. "You don't think that was foul?"

"Look, I kept your secret. I helped you lie to your husband when you didn't want Phillip around. I never gave you grief about it. But me and Phillip, that had nothing to do with you."

Nina was bewildered by Charlene's nonchalant attitude, but she started to look at it from Charlene's point of view. It was time to do a little bit more listening and less talking.

"Okay. Tell Me. What was it about?"

"He was always in my corner. When you left for Stanford and I was feeling lost and alone, he would listen to me. Give me advice. It's because of him I have my own business today. He gave me seed money to open the first shop."

"What about recently?"

"We didn't see each other that often. It was a once in a while thing, but I called it off after you found out."

Hearing Charlene's version of the story was not what Nina expected. She made Phillip sound like a normal human being who wanted to extend a helping hand to his daughter's friend, a nice gesture. So her father could be nice to everybody except her. What a tragedy. But she wouldn't wallow in self-pity.

Nina told Charlene what Phillip had been doing to her when they were teenagers growing up and how Nina would cover up the abuse with lies, excuses, and perfection: She had perfect grades, was perfectly behaved, she was perfectly nice, and was perfectly dressed at all times. It was all a desperate cry for acceptance because she didn't feel she was good enough. If she were, her father wouldn't do bad things to her. That's how she rationalized it in her teenage brain, anyway. Maybe if her father saw that other people thought she was wonderful, then maybe he would too, and stop hurting her.

After Nina finished speaking, Charlene slowly backed away from her like a traumatized child who had just witnessed a heinous crime. She kept moving until she slammed into the closed door, numb to the impact on her body.

"If I knew... I didn't know...that's really messed up...I'm going to kill him, then I'll cut off his balls and feed them to pack of wild dogs."

Nina stood less than a foot away from her best friend, who looked even tinier than she already was. Charlene gnawed at her fingernails, a habit Nina hadn't seen in years, a quirk that only raised its head when Charlene was in crisis or under extreme duress.

"Wow. I didn't know you were so creative, Char," Nina joked, trying to diffuse the tension. "That's a really interesting visual."

"Why didn't you say something? I wouldn't have told anybody if that's what you wanted. I wouldn't have accepted his money. I wouldn't have..."

Nina knew what Charlene was struggling to say but couldn't bring herself to say the words in light of this new information. "I know you wouldn't have."

"You're my sister in every way it counts and you didn't say anything. Damn it, Nina, why?"

Nina joined Charlene on the floor, their backs up against the door. "People just don't talk about this kind of thing. From the beginning, I was trained to keep quiet. As I got older, it got easier and then I decided for my own reasons I would never tell."

Charlene was losing her battle to keep from tearing up. In all their years of friendship, Nina had never seen Charlene cry, not even when her parents died. But now, her friend wept silently.

"How did Marc react when you told him?" Charlene managed to ask through bouts of hiccups.

"I haven't told him. He left."

Charlene's head snapped to attention. "I can't afford high blood pressure. What do you mean he left?"

"He wants a divorce."

"Hell no. I turn my back for five minutes and y'all can't keep it together? Please tell me that heifer Solange isn't part of the problem?"

Nina gave Charlene a recap of events that unfolded while their friendship was on hiatus.

"Do you want him back?"

"Of course. The separation was not my idea."

"Don't you think he deserves the whole truth?"

"It might be too late."

"Did he serve you with divorce papers?"

"No. But if I get him back, he'll be coming with baggage."

"What do you mean?"

"He may have fathered a child with Solange."

Charlene's hand flew to her mouth in stunned disbelief. "What? Are you sure?"

"She didn't deny it."

"So what? You're his wife. You're not going to roll over and allow her take over your life, your man. You're just going to have to find a way to get along."

Afterwards Nina was preened, scrubbed, stretched and poked within an inch of her life. Four hours after her initial arrival, she emerged from the salon seemingly her old self, at least outwardly. Her insides were quivering like Jell-O as she got ready to execute phase two of her plan.

CHAPTER TWENTY-ONE

Nina presented her identification to the concierge at the Sherwood Plaza Hotel. She had convinced Kendra to call the hotel in advance to let them know she'd be joining her husband, and they should have a set of keys for suite 708 waiting for her.

"Is there anything else we can do for you this evening, Mrs. Kasai?" he asked.

"Have the flowers been delivered?"

"Yes, ma'm. Less than fifteen minutes ago."

Nina thanked him and took the elevator to the seventh floor. The one-bedroom suite her husband currently called home boasted thick, rich carpeting, an elegant living room decorated in classic designs and custom made furnishings of dark cherry and mahogany wood. She glanced at her watch. It was already seven p.m. and dinner would be arriving in fifteen minutes. Marc should make an appearance by seven-thirty. She had worked with Kendra to time this perfectly, accounting for traffic between Atlantic Avenue and Copley Square.

Nina sank into the pale green floral couch and clutched one of the throw pillows. She switched on the television and settled on one of the entertainment news shows. Taking in the latest celerity gossip, rumors, and tell-all books helped to take the nervous edge off. She was in the middle of learning who ruled the box office that weekend when the food arrived.

She directed the wait staff to the desk at the edge of the living room, near the windows. She picked up one of the bouquets of roses from the top of the fireplace and placed it in the center of the table. The unusual combination of red, yellow and white roses had been deliberately chosen for their meaning: red signifying love, yellow a reminder of their friendship, and white for humility.

Nina almost missed the sound of the key card being inserted into the door. She made it just in time to turn the handle and greet him.

"Good evening," she said pleasantly, careful not to sound desperate.

He was surprised to see her. Nina watched a plethora of emotions play across his face. He was trying hard to be annoyed but couldn't quite pull it off. The white, off the shoulder silk cocktail dress she'd chosen fit her body with precision. Her only jewelry was a pair of teardrop diamond earrings he bought her for their fifth wedding anniversary. Charlene decided to go in a different direction with her hair, opting for a headful of loose curls that hung freely around her shoulders. Her look had achieved its objective. He was hooked, and the hours she spent at Charlene's salon getting ready had been worth every torturous minute.

"How did you find out where I was staying?"

Nina didn't answer. She watched as his fingers fumbled nervously over the knot in the tie he was trying to loosen. She took a step closer and noticed his face was flushed and glistening with tiny beads of sweat. She could hear his heart beating wildly and figured he must have taken the stairs. It was precisely the kind of thing he would do if he missed his morning workout.

She slowly removed the tie from his neck and opened the top button on his dress shirt. "I don't want you to suffocate."

She took his briefcase as she had countless times before but he was hesitant to follow her lead. "I promise it's safe to come inside."

She was rewarded with an electrifying smile that made her heart turn over in her chest. She cleared her throat noisily. "I need a drink."

Dinner went better than she expected. They slipped back into easy companionship with their usual teasing, and anecdotes about family and work. Nina instinctively reached across the table and gently caressed Marc's hand. The aching she had suppressed since he left was like a rubber band about to snap.

"Don't do that," he said, withdrawing his hand from hers.

"Do I repulse you, Marc or do you prefer the touch of another?"

He looked perplexed. "I don't want to go down this road. It's better to make a clean break."

"I won't accept that. If you want to leave me, it can't be for Solange."

"How dare you question me after you betrayed me with another man?"

"You don't really believe I was sleeping with Sonny, Marc."

"I know what I heard. I've been in hell ever since."

"Is that why you took up with Solange again, especially now that she gave you what I couldn't?"

"You've lost me. What are you talking about?"

Is it possible that he really didn't know? That was exactly the sort of thing Solange would be quick to tell him. "I'm talking about your son, the one you had with her."

"Did you drink too much wine? You're not making any sense."

"Solange has a son."

"Yes, I know. I met his father."

"You did?" Nina asked dumfounded. "So he's not yours?"

It was Marc's turn to look dumfounded. "Where would you get a ridiculous idea like that?"

"I asked her if the boy was yours and she didn't answer."

"So you just took that as a yes. Nina, you're some piece of work."

"Don't make fun of me. I thought I was losing you to her."

He picked up a glass of ice water and got up from the table. He took small sips as he paced the floor. "You've been deceiving me for a long time. That's what drove me away. I honored my marriage vows. I don't know about you."

Her voice cracked with emotion. "I'm still the same girl you married, Marc. I haven't changed."

"Yes, you have. I watched it happen with my own eyes."

"I wasn't cheating on you with Sonny. I asked him to do me a personal favor. That's what I meant when I said I lied to you about him. I told you Jack wanted to hire his research firm but I was the one who needed his services."

"Why?"

"I'll tell you soon. I promise. That's why I came tonight. I don't want any more lies between us."

"Okay. Let's start with why we can't have children and the discussion I walked in on between you and your mother. I watched you go through grueling IVF treatments. Still, you hid the truth."

"Something happened when I was younger."

"You didn't think I had the right to know why my wife couldn't get pregnant?"

Nina had to concede that the time had come to stop running, stop hiding and lying. If she wanted to pull her marriage back from the brink, this would be her final opportunity to do so.

"I don't even know where to begin."

"The beginning is usually a good place. We were happy. But everything changed last summer."

"I was a coward then," she said simply. "I allowed fear to drive out common sense."

"You didn't just lie about some trivial thing. It was a series of calculated deceptions on your part starting with the nature of your relationship with Sonny Alvarez, then I come to find out your father lived only a few towns over from us and the list just kept growing from there. I couldn't take it any more."

"I had good reason."

"So you lied to me for my own good?" He stormed off in frustration towards the bedroom.

Nina followed, determined to have it out.

He removed his jacket and tossed it on the back of the chair. "You can go now. This evening was a mistake."

"If you want me gone, you'll have to carry me out."

She watched him strip down to his underwear. She averted her eyes when he caught her staring. He disappeared into the bathroom. Nina sat at the edge of the bed, her perfectly manicured fingernails digging into the mattress. She could hear the shower running. She closed her eyes tightly, trying not to think about his naked body.

He returned minutes later in a white terry robe, more collected, and stood mere inches from her.

"I asked you to leave."

"This is important."

"You didn't think so before."

"I made mistakes. We all do at one point or another. I was trying to hold on to us, maybe a little too tightly, and ... and we shattered like glass."

"How do you expect me to trust anything that comes out of your mouth?" he asked.

"Honestly, Marc, all of this was set in motion years ago, long before we met. I had no way of predicting that years later, it would come back to haunt me in so many ways, even impacting my ability to have babies."

He looked at her, his expression worried. He sat next to her on the bed. "What are you saying, Nina? Why can't we have children?"

"I said I would tell you everything and I will. But first I need to understand where you're coming from. Why you felt divorce was the only option for us."

He got up and started pacing around the room, as if to collect his thoughts.

"After the IVF took the first time, I couldn't believe our luck. As your pregnancy progressed and it looked like we were going to be a family of three, I couldn't have been more proud of you. When you miscarried, and I know it wasn't your fault ... I don't know. I felt like part of me died with our son. I wasn't sure we would get that lucky again. I felt cheated, twice. You wouldn't let me in. You excluded me from understanding why this was happening to us. From there, the other lies just compounded the loss and frustration I was feeling."

"I get it. I came here tonight to stop the lies."

Nina was nervous. There was so much to tell. She didn't know where to begin. She decided to work backwards. She signaled for him to sit. He pulled up a chair directly in front of her.

"I fooled myself into believing I could escape my past. And for a while, I did. But it found me again—the darkness, the shame. If I didn't tell you, the nightmare would lose its power and I would be normal. But I'm not normal, Marc."

His posture was defensive, as if he were preparing himself for an inevitable blow. His eyes were transfixed on hers.

"Say it. You're safe. Tell me what you haven't been able to since the day we met."

She hesitated. What if he ran out of the room in disgust and vowed never to have anything to do with her again? Would he refuse to believe it actually happened? She knew the kind of man she had married, yet she was riddled with doubt.

"I was molested when I was a little girl, Marc. It started when I was ten and went on for almost eight years. It was frequent and relentless. Somehow, I found a way to separate myself from my body ... it was the only way I could survive. College was the first real chance I had to end it, so I went to school in California. It was the furthest I could get from him without leaving the country. That's the reason I can't get pregnant. He gave me chlamydia when I was in my early teens. I didn't see a doctor right away because he wouldn't take me — there would have been too many questions and he didn't want that. By the time I finally got medical attention, an antibiotic cleared up the infection but I paid for it with damage to my tubes."

Her husband didn't react. His stone cold expression sent Nina into panic mode, afraid her confession had so repulsed him he couldn't bear to speak to her.

"Marc?" she whispered. "Please, say something."

When no response was forthcoming, she resigned herself to the inevitable. She would end up alone. But maybe he just needed some time to process what she had said. She would leave, and come back another time. She got up from the bed and dragged her feet slowly. They felt like lead. She headed for the door. Before she could turn the knob, she felt his hand on her shoulders. He spun her around to face him. The pain etched on his face was raw, his eyes clouded with deep sorrow. He guided her back to the bed and sat beside her.

His voice quivered with emotion. "Who did this to you, Nina?"

She almost forgot. She hadn't yet told him the worst part. "I'm ... well ... you're not going to believe this."

"It couldn't be worse that what I've already heard."

"I was abused by my own father."

There was a long pause, during which Nina watched horror, compassion, and disbelief wash over Marc's face.

"It's just not ... it's inhumane. It's vicious ... it's heinous." His hand trembled as he struggled to express his pain. "When you said you were abused, I thought it was by some deranged neighbor or a family friend. I could never have imagined that your own father did this."

He got up from the chair and started pacing again. "I'm going after him."

"You'll do no such thing," Nina said.

"What? How could you want to protect him, after what he—"

"He's not worth it. He has no power over me anymore."

As she said the words, she realized that all she needed to be free was to tell the truth. By lying, she had given Phillip the power to control her life.

"Why didn't you just tell me from the beginning and save us all this misery over something that wasn't your fault?"

"I was afraid if you knew I was an incest survivor, you'd find it revolting and wouldn't want me anymore."

Marc knelt before Nina and gently removed her three-inch stilettos. He massaged her left foot, then her right, as he had countless times before. A soft moan escaped her lips, his touch warm and comforting, yet undeniably exciting. He moved from her feet to her calves. His fingers fluttered across her bare skin in a dance that made her want to cry. She bit down on her lip. He stood up and leaned over her. His lips found hers and she opened her mouth eagerly, like a neglected plant suddenly awash in cool rain. Nina rolled onto the bed and pulled him on top of her. His fingers reached behind her and unzipped her dress. He peeled it off her body then went to work removing his robe.

"Are you sure?" he asked, his breathing ragged.

"Yes," she answered, her voice barely audible.

Nina could barely breathe as he made love to her slowly and delicately. She ran her fingers down the smoothness of his back and squeezed the tautness of his butt. He whimpered his approval, his hunger urging her to continue. His tongue flickered across her breasts and made its way down to her belly. She gasped when he parted her legs and plunged his tongue between her thighs. Her fingernails dug into his flesh, but he didn't care. Just when she thought she would faint, he slipped into her. She welcomed him with a sincere yearning that let him know he was home. He slipped his hand under her hips and she arched closer to him. As he went deeper inside her, her cries got louder and louder until they both climaxed.

Afterwards, Nina was caught in the grips of a hysteria she couldn't control. She buried her head in her husband's chest and wailed like a wounded creature. Marc hugged her tightly; somehow he understood this kind of emotional purging would help his wife escape the darkness she talked about.

Nina was still half asleep when she reached over for Marc and realized he was gone. She rubbed the sleep from her eyes and noticed the digital clock on the night stand read ten a.m. She had overslept but didn't mind. Maybe, just maybe, everything was going to be okay after all. She swung her legs over the edge of the bed and stood up. She immediately yelped in pain. Something had pricked the bottom of her foot and it hurt like hell. She looked down and found three roses held together by one of Marc's favorite ties. She picked them up and held them close to her heart. She plopped down on the bed, allowing herself a few more minutes to revel in the gesture. She was interrupted by the ringing telephone.

She picked up without thinking.

"I've been calling you all morning but you won't answer your mobile or your office line. Shall I come by your hotel?"

"No, you shall not," Nina answered coldly.

Solange was momentarily stunned. "Why are you in his room?"

"Because I'm his wife. What do you want Solange?"

"Marc and I have a very important business meeting this morning. I wanted to make sure he'll be there."

"Marc's a professional and very good at his job. If this meeting is as important as you claim, he'll be there. But I suspect your call has nothing to do with some so-called meeting."

"You are jealous, oui?"

"Goodbye Solange. I hope your son and his father gives you the family you want."

Why did she have to call and ruin a perfectly good morning? Nina griped.

CHAPTER TWENTY-TWO

Nina and Cassie were on their long-awaited shopping spree at Copley Place in historic Back Bay—four and a half acres of upscale shopping, high-end hotels, office buildings and a parking garage. An overpass connected the shopping area to the Prudential, Boston's second tallest building.

The girls had mapped out their shopping strategy in advance, which included stops at Jimmy Choo, Neiman Marcus and Burberry. They stood on the first floor, looking up at two massive white structures with stone carvings that connected each side of the mall. Their arms were already aching from the weight of their earlier purchases.

"Shall we go up?" Nina asked.

"Sure," Cassie said glumly.

"What's wrong, Cass? Aren't you excited about this anymore? Kate is waiting for us at Neimans."

They stepped on the escalator for the brief ride up.

"Be honest, Nina. Are you and Marc having problems?"

Nina almost lost her footing when the escalator got to the top of the floor and she didn't get off fast enough.

"Where is this coming from?"

"You haven't mentioned him all day. You usually can't go five minutes without saying his name."

"Today is our day, just us girls."

"There's more to it than that. Are you two even living together?"

Nina was flabbergasted. What was her sister getting at? "What's on your mind?"

"I saw Marc at a restaurant in Waltham. He didn't see me. He was having dinner with this woman."

"What did this woman looked like?" Nina asked calmly.

Her sister described Solange to the letter. This newsflash was not welcome, especially since Nina and Marc just reconciled. But perhaps a bit of probing would put things in perspective.

"What were you doing in Waltham?"

"Visiting Kate."

"When was this? When did you see Marc and Solange together?"

"Last month. They looked like they knew each other well. She kept flirting with him, touching him every chance she got. It was disgusting."

"Marc and I are good, Cassie. We hit a rough patch but we worked things out just a few days ago. Maybe Solange was taking advantage of the situation when you saw them together."

Before Cassie could formulate an appropriate comeback, they were at the entrance of Neimans. Cassie asked one of the ladies at the Clinique counter for Kate and was promptly directed to the women's apparel department, just beyond cosmetics.

Kate had a deep tan that made her clear grey eyes and freckles even more pronounced. Her dark brown hair was pulled back in an up-do held together by a banana clip. Cassie made the introductions.

"Cassie, I thought you said your sister was a size six," Kate said. "She looks like a four. I may need to replace some of the outfits I put aside."

"Don't worry about it," Nina said. "I'll start with what you have and see what fits. Thanks for helping us out."

"Not a problem. I'll be right back." Kate disappeared to retrieve the merchandise.

Cassie turned to Nina. "Are you sure you and Marc are okay?"

"Yes, Cassie, we are."

Kate returned with a rack full of outfits, and Nina and Cassie chose fitting rooms right next to each other. Nina hadn't had this much fun with her sister in a long time as they tried on multiple outfits, met each other at the floor length mirrors outside the fitting rooms, and gave a thumbs up or down on each other's choices.

The sisters emerged from the store with half a dozen outfits each and matching accessories.

"I'm starving," Cassie complained. "Let's find food."

As they walked and chatted, Nina let her mind drift as Cassie prattled about what so-and-so said to what's-her-name. When Nina collided with another shopper and dropped a bag, she came out of her daydreaming. She was in the midst of apologizing profusely when she looked up at the familiar redhead.

"Geraldine. I didn't see you," Nina said.

"That's quite all right, darling."

Geraldine's inquisitive eyes went from Cassie to Nina and back.

"It's okay, Geraldine. It's all out in the open. Marc knows Phillip is my father and poor Cassie doesn't have to lie for me anymore."

"Oh, thank God," Geraldine said, relief washing over her. "It's much better this way."

An idea occurred to Nina. In the spirit of being honest and doing away with lies, she had another confession to make to Geraldine and this seemed as good a time as any. They didn't see each other often and Nina didn't know if an opportunity would ever present itself again.

"Cassie, how about you go scope out the best place for us to have lunch? Text me when you find a place and they have a table ready for us."

Both Cassie and Geraldine looked at Nina with intense curiosity.

"I need to talk to Geraldine about something important," Nina explained.

Cassie obeyed, with curiosity written all over her face.

Geraldine parked herself on a nearby bench and Nina joined her, dropping her load of shopping bags on the ground.

"What's this about, dear?"

"I wanted to apologize for putting you in an awkward position when you and Phillip came to my house for dinner. It wasn't fair. I've learned my lesson about secrets."

"No need to apologize. Every girl has a secret or two. That's just the way it is."

"Secrets can be the death of a relationship. You should know that."

"Oh?"

"How did you feel when you found out your husband had a son he kept secret from you?"

Geraldine eyed Nina with comprehension. "You must be bloody joking. You?"

"Yes, I sent the picture and the information to your office at Tufts."

"Why?"

"I wanted to get back at Phillip, give him a dose of his own medicine."

"I see."

"Do you?"

"We got into a screaming match about it. He didn't seem to think it was important to tell me since it happened before we got together."

"You? Scream?"

"I can hold my own with the best of them."

Phillip's controlling behavior extended to his new marriage, Nina thought. His total lack of respect for the feelings of others was one of his worst traits. She could already see how this relationship would end, especially once Geraldine found out just how much she didn't know about her new husband.

"I'm afraid it doesn't end with a secret son," Nina warned.

Geraldine glanced at Nina sideways. "I don't know how much more my nerves can take. Finding out you were his daughter, and then about this son, well...maybe we married too soon. I feel like I'm living in the bloody twilight zone."

Nina wondered if this was the right time to tell her. But if not now, when? This impacted Geraldine too, and she deserved to know what she was dealing with. Phillip wasn't going to tell her and no matter what happened next, she would get hurt.

"This is hard for me, too, but Phillip is keeping something truly horrible from you. He'll deny it if you confront him about it, so be warned."

"What would that be?"

"He molested his own daughter."

Geraldine looked like she was about to explode. "What on earth would possess you to say something so obscene about your own father? Cassie adores her father, worships him, practically. Why would he do something so heinous?"

"I wasn't talking about Cassie."

Geraldine opened her mouth, closed it, then went into silent mode.

"I'm sorry I had to be the one tell you this," Nina said with sympathy. "The literature I've been reading says disclosure is part of the healing process. You had to know, you're part of his life."

Nina couldn't tell from her face if Geraldine believed her or not. She sat perfectly still. Her hands squeezing the edge of the bench was the only indication of movement.

"I can't believe it. It can't be true."

Her reaction was not surprising. "Ask him what happened the evening he gave me the *Famous Five* novels as a belated birthday gift. I was ten. I'm sure he remembers. The books were written by Enid Blyton. You may have read her work when you were a kid in England."

Geraldine turned pale, all color draining from her face. The reference to the books resonated with her. She knew Nina was telling the truth.

"That's absolutely ghastly," she said, as she continued to struggle between revulsion and compassion. "What have I gotten myself into?"

Geraldine reached for a cigarette and lighter from her purse as she nervously tapped her heels against the marble floor.

"You can't smoke in here," Nina said.

"I need something," she said, her hands trembling. "I married a pervert. Just brilliant."

"He doesn't come with a warning sign."

"He bloody well should," she said angrily. "I'm sorry, Nina. I had no idea. When Phillip talked about you, after I confronted him about not telling me you were his daughter, he made it sound like you were a rebellious child he couldn't control. He said you got into all kinds of trouble at school and he was worried sick about how you would end up."

"The only trouble I got into was when he slipped into my room at night, took what he wanted and didn't give a damn how it affected me. That's how he operated."

"Was there no one you could turn to?"

"He had me well-coached and plenty scared."

Geraldine reached for the cigarette again.

"Those things are bad for you," Nina joked.

"Death by cigarette is almost preferable to—" Geraldine was too distraught to finish the thought. She looked away from Nina, as if somehow her association with Phillip made her guilty, too.

"Don't beat yourself up. You couldn't have known. I told nobody until recently. But you should know things could get really bad before they get better."

"How could it possibly get worse?"

"Just protect yourself."

Geraldine looked at Nina woefully. "How could I have gotten it so wrong?"

"He can be very charming and generous. The dark side surfaces when he's challenged."

"Is that what happened with you?"

"I fought back when I was able to."

"Still, he's your father. Do you still love him?"

"Good luck, Geraldine."

CHAPTER TWENTY-THREE

———◆———

"Who else have you told?" Marc asked.

"Cassie and Geraldine." Nina placed the piping hot pasta dish in front of Marc. She joined him at their kitchen table for dinner, one of the most routine tasks of domestic life she now had a new appreciation for, after the near collapse of their marriage.

"How did it go?"

"Cassie was devastated but immediately went into her safe place: denial. Geraldine was in shock but she can hold her own against Phillip."

"I'm sure she will. She struck me as a fighter. Kind of like you. Maybe that's why the two of you get along."

"Perhaps. My mother wasn't so kind in her responses. She said he deserved to die and even kicked him in the groin for good measure."

"Wise woman, your mother."

"You agree with her?"

"Any man who would even think about his daughter that way should be shot."

"It's complicated, like I said."

"What's complicated about it?"

The little girl who saw Phillip Copeland as her daddy still existed somewhere deep inside Nina, and it was difficult to get rid of her. It was as if the adult Nina was split into two different people; one yearned for what could have been—a normal father-daughter relationship with goodnight kisses on the forehead, measured protectiveness against potential suitors, an understanding shoulder to cry on. The other was a woman who despised him and held her own over his particular brand of tyranny. She had to find a way to reconcile the two. Maybe it was time to take her mother's advice. At least, look into it.

"I don't know," she said, shrugging. "I guess some small part of me hopes he regrets what he did. That would humanize him."

Marc came around to her side of the table and wrapped his arms around her.

"You don't need him. You never did. You have to stop thinking of him as your father. It will only prolong your suffering."

"How do I do that, Marc?"

"Stop being afraid."

There was moisture splattering on his arm, one molecule at a time. She reached up and brushed away his tears with her fingertips. "Can you get me the Haagen Daz from the freezer? I don't feel like eating dinner. I'm going to have the whole tub and don't you dare try to stop me."

"Save some for me," he said.

Marc collected two spoons from the kitchen drawer and placed the ice-cream at the center of the table. They both dug in.

"Where were the adults, Nina?" he asked. "How come nobody stopped him? How come no one protected you?"

She shrugged nonchalantly. "Who would believe me even if I said something? Who would believe that a successful executive and community leader with a beautiful wife and the perfect family in a wealthy neighborhood was raping his daughter on a regular basis?"

"What about Theresa?"

"She was busy with her career. Probably didn't pay too much attention."

"She was responsible for you," he said wistfully. "She should be held accountable, too."

"I never faulted her for not coming to my rescue."

"Maybe you should."

"She wouldn't have turned him in even if she found out. He was the father of her only child."

"So you were the sacrificial lamb?"

"I never thought of it that way."

As the discussion continued, Nina had to gather up the courage to tell Marc that Phillip was partially responsible for the loss of their child. If they were going to have a fresh start, she needed to be one hundred percent honest about everything. Marc was devastated all over again. He threw a chair against the kitchen wall in a fit of rage. After she got him to calm down, he vowed for the second time that Phillip would pay for everything he took from them.

*   *   *

WHEN PHILLIP TURNED THE KEY into the door of his penthouse duplex, he wanted nothing more than to sit on the deck with several bottles of wine and enjoy the hilltop views of Brookline and Back Bay. He just wanted to forget this God-forsaken day ever happened. The primaries would be held in six months, followed by the Gubernatorial race two months later in November. And still, he had lingering issues that could derail his candidacy, which he was close to announcing.

Charlene barged into his office bright and early and broke into hysterics, calling him all sorts of vile names he didn't even think she had the vocabulary for. She threatened to tell anyone who would listen he was a rapist and it was only when he told her he wasn't above using violence to achieve his objectives did she back off. To make things worse, his wife had been been increasingly jumpy lately, avoiding him at every turn. When he confronted her about it, she claimed she was jittery because she recently quit smoking. Cassie was visiting her mother in New York, so he would have a little peace and quiet before Geraldine came home.

When he opened the door, all thoughts of a quiet evening suddenly grew legs and ran like hell. Sitting in his living room, as calm as could be, was Marc Kasai.

"You've let yourself in. This must be important." Phillip hoped he didn't sound as pissed as he felt at the intrusion.

"It is. Otherwise, I would have called first."

Phillip took the couch opposite Marc. "What can I do for you, Marc?"

"First, you're going to apologize to my wife and beg her to forgive you. Then you're going to tell family and friends what you did to her. And in your final act of contrition, you will seek psychiatric help for paedophilia. By then, I would have settled on an appropriate way to make you suffer."

It took everything he had to show restraint. Who the hell did this guy think he was? "Obviously you're mistaken," Phillip said with forced civility. "Everybody makes mistakes, so I'll chalk this up to confusion. I'm going to have to ask you to leave now."

"I see you don't like any of my suggestions," Marc observed. "Prison is a good option in cases like these. You know what they do to child molesters in prison, don't you?"

After Marc left, Phillip reached for a bottle of vodka in his liquor cabinet. He didn't bother using a glass. He drank straight from the bottle. His own child was out to get him, after everything he did for her. She wouldn't get away with it.

CHAPTER TWENTY-FOUR

The Framingham Worcester commuter rail came to a stop on platform three at South Station. Nina stepped off the train, one of the throngs of suburban dwellers who worked in the city. A panicked Eric was on the other line when she picked up her ringing cell phone.

"I don't know what you did, but one of our board members is looking for you. He's probably waiting for you at South Station with smoke coming out of his ears."

"Who is it?"

"Doctor Copeland."

"Did he say what he wanted?"

"No."

"How did he know I was taking the train in?"

"I'm sorry, Nina. He's really scary and I like my job. He could get me fired. I had to tell him."

Don't worry. I'll take care of it."

Nina hung up with much trepidation. She had no desire to go another round with Phillip. His reputation and credibility were unraveling fast. It began when Nina told her mother, then Charlene, then Marc, and then his wife.

A seething Phillip pounced on Nina the minute he spotted her walking towards the Dunkin Donuts inside the station. It was late spring and today was unseasonably warm, so Nina wanted to get her favorite iced coffee beverage.

"Where do you get off interfering in my marriage? How dare you?"

Nina ignored him and got in line to place her order.

He grabbed her arm. "I'm talking to you. I won't be dismissed, Nina."

"Get off me," Nina yelled loud enough so the other patrons in line could hear. They all stared at Phillip disapprovingly, which got him to back off, but then he starting hissing in her ears.

"Geraldine left me because you spewed some garbage to her and she was stupid enough to believe you. You're going fix this."

"Your wife left you because you're a lousy husband and she caught on. And I'm not a marriage counselor, so I can't fix anything."

It was Nina's turn to order. She observed Phillip out of the corner of her eyes, nervously appraising the crowd, as if plotting ways he could cause physical harm without being noticed. After she got her iced coffee, Nina continued walking towards the main exit. She would walk to her office by turning right on Summer Street. She figured as long as she was in a public space, he wouldn't try anything stupid.

She took a sip of her drink and adjusted the straps of her purse without saying a word, knowing full well her non-response would make him even angrier. It was a technique she learned from him and now she'd turned the tables.

"You need to stop this before somebody gets really hurt. You call Geraldine and tell her you made up the whole thing because you're angry with me."

"I can't do that. What I told her was true."

They came to an intersection and Nina stopped to let traffic go by. He got in her face, his eyes blazing with uncontained rage.

"Either you tell Geraldine you made a mistake or your precious Marc meets with an unfortunate accident."

Nina couldn't believe what she was hearing. She knew he had a violent streak, but murder? This was a whole other level of insanity.

"You're out of control. Get a grip on yourself. Take some pills. I don't care. But if you ever threaten anyone I care about again, I will ruin you."

*   *   *

ONE WEEK LATER, NINA WAS running six miles an hour on the treadmill at her local gym when a story on the flat screen TV in front of her caught her attention. She shut off her iPod and removed the ear buds so she could hear clearly. The story was about the Dare to Dream Foundation College Scholarship Awards. The reporter was interviewing the four recipients outside the foundation headquarters on High Street in Boston. Their glowing faces full of youthful promise, and talk of what the scholarship meant to them tugged at Nina. One of the students wanted to be a research scientist, while another had plans to study non-profit management so she could create her own foundation when she graduated from college. They talked about how the future they had planned wouldn't have been possible without the scholarships they just received. Nina didn't stick around to hear the rest of the story. She got off the treadmill and headed to the ladies' locker room.

Nina hopped in the shower, hoping somehow that the water would erase away the guilt and confusion she felt. There was no denying her father was making a positive impact in the community. He told her during that awful fight at her in-laws' anniversary celebration that what he does matters, and he was right. So who was she to interfere with his important work by insisting he be held accountable for what he did to her?

She was gearing up for the fight of her life and it was now clear the lives that would be impacted weren't confined to just family and friends. The news story she just heard proved that. But she also struggled with her own demons: how could she? What if she lost? What would that do to her? Worse than the answers to those questions was the idea of Phillip Copeland walking around, free to torment her another time, another place, or worse yet, turn his attention to some unsuspecting young girl. It had to end with her.

Her husband and mother ganged up on her and convinced her she needed to seek counseling. It was her own fault for having a meltdown when she came to the conclusion that her father never really loved her. All the hatred and resentment she'd built up inside over the years were simply protective gear. The most confusing part for her was wondering how she could want a monster to love her. That's when she realized she really needed her head examined.

*   *   *

A YEAR AGO HE WAS a man with endless possibilities. He had a bright political future ahead of him, he was unstoppable. Now he was holed up in his study, shattered, disbelieving, hope quickly fading. He was free falling and didn't know where or how he would land. The lies his daughter was spreading about him had taken on a life of their own. Ben had called him two days ago to tell him there was a rumor going around he was being accused of rape, and his supporters, the people who could make his dream of becoming Governor come true, were abandoning him in droves. There would be no big announcement of his candidacy before the Boston press. He had even hinted to his favorite reporters at the *Boston Sentinel* and Channel 5 that he would make a big announcement soon and left them to speculate.

His wife moved out of their home. She told him she'd be moving back to England because she couldn't take the shame and humiliation of being associated with a man accused of such a heinous crime. Wasn't it just like a woman to run out when she got whatever she could from a man? They all had a price: his daughters, his wives, his mistresses, all the same.

He was halfway through his second bottle of vodka when there was a knock at the door. It must be Cassie. She'd come back from visiting her mother the week before and had been tiptoeing around him ever since. He didn't feel like talking to anybody right now, but she already knew he was in, so it was pointless to pretend otherwise.

He must look worse than he thought; the expression on her face was shock. He took another swig of vodka.

"Yes?"

Cassie panicked. "I can come back later."

"You already disturbed me, so say what you have to say and stop wasting my time."

He knew it sounded mean but he couldn't help it. Cassie was sweet and always believed in him. He could use an ally right about now.

He softened his voice. "What's on your mind, Cassie?"

"What Nina said, it's not true, right? I mean, why would she say something so awful about you? Why, Dad?"

"You've been talking to Nina?"

"She called me and said we needed to talk. So we went out to dinner and she said you ... you ..."

"I know what she told you, and no, it's not true."

"Then why would she say such nasty things? She kept saying I was blind in my devotion to you and one day the awful truth would come out for everybody to hear. What's she talking about?"

"What did you say to her when she was telling you those lies?"

"I told her I didn't believe her and she needed to stop saying those things."

Phillip smiled, a real smile. "Good girl. I knew I could count on you. You're the only person who hasn't abandoned me, Cassie, and I want you to know how important it is to me. There are people out there who don't want me to run for Governor, and it's possible one of them is using your sister to ruin my reputation with these ugly lies. Thanks for defending me."

*   *   *

DR. ISSLER'S OFFICE WAS LOCATED in an office building on a tree-lined street in Wellesley, a wealthy suburb west of Boston. She was younger than Nina expected, early forties with hazel eyes and a bad case of adult acne. Her body language exuded a compassionate yet no-nonsense attitude Nina immediately liked.

Her office had just the right touches: not too cluttered, but enough knick knacks to make it welcoming. Her desk was neat, not a file out of place.

"What brings you to therapy, Nina?"

The direct approach was just fine with her. "I need to stop choking on my past, and accept certain realities."

"It sounds like you've given this a lot of thought."

"Over twenty years' worth."

Dr. Issler put on her glasses and she glanced through her notes. "What's your relationship with your father like now?"

"I don't know if there's a word or phrase to describe it. To say we're enemies would be an oversimplification of a complex relationship. For me, that is. I can't speak for him."

"I see. How does that translate into your feelings for him?"

Nina shifted uncomfortably. This should be a simple answer but it wasn't, to her chagrin.

"I still struggle with my feelings. Going back and forth between what is and what isn't; what I want that relationship to be and what it can never be."

"What do you want it to be?"

Nina hesitated. Mostly because she didn't want to sound ridiculous, like some orphaned kid who longed to have real parents again, no matter how remote the possibility. "I just want him to see me. I want him to care enough to be sorry."

"Why do you think he hasn't?"

"Because I fought back. He doesn't like to be challenged. When I left for Stanford, it was an open defiance to his authority. He had no say in the matter. By leaving when he wasn't expecting it, I stripped him of that power."

"Putting aside his attempts to regain control when he reappeared in your life a year ago, and everything that has happened since, do you think he would want the opportunity to start over if you gave him that chance?"

"I thought I caught a glimpse of what he could be as a father. What might have been possible. But now, I'm not so sure."

"Can you provide a bit more detail?"

"During the argument that led to my miscarriage, he said he was worried about me at school because I never called or wrote, and he had to send someone to keep an eye on me to make sure I was safe. He also said I was selfish, because my sister Cassie was devastated when I left, and I never gave any thought to how my leaving might have impacted her."

"Do you agree with his assessment that you were selfish for not considering your sister?"

"Coming from anyone else, perhaps. But not from him. His motives for doing or saying anything are never pure."

"Do you regret the way you left?"

"I regret the circumstances that caused me to leave my home and venture out into the world all alone. It was a survival tactic, but it worked. Sort of."

Dr. Issler looked through the notes again. "When Phillip first reappeared in your life, he threatened to disclose his identity to your husband if you didn't do what he asked. Why didn't you do what he asked?"

"Simple. He wanted control again. I refused to give it."

"What makes you say that?"

"He knows people who could do what he was asking. He didn't just show up in my office because he saw me on a magazine cover."

"Tell me about the magazine cover."

"It's a publication focused on corporate leadership. I made the cover of their annual 'Forty Under Forty' issue."

"That's impressive."

"That's what he said."

"He complimented you on your achievement?"

"He did."

"Do you think he was proud of you?"

Nobody knew how much time and energy she had dedicated to obsessing over whether or not he was proud of her, whether he knew how well she was doing on her own, all the while, still loathing him.

"At that point, his approval didn't matter. They were just empty words."

"Fair enough. You built a good life for yourself without his help and free of his influence. How did that change when he suddenly reappeared?"

"Outwardly I was strong, defiant, but inside, I was falling apart. He made me think about things I didn't want to, brought back memories I thought I had buried long ago. He basically disrupted the lie I was living."

Dr. Issler shook her head in the affirmative in solidarity with Nina. She took a sip of her vitamin water and cleared her throat.

"Why was it important to keep his identity a secret from your husband?"

"He's poison."

Doctor Issler thought about that for a minute. "Is that the only reason?"

"What other reason would there be?"

"You have to be fearless if this is going to work, Nina."

She knew coming to therapy meant she had to go to some gruesome places, but she deserved to maintain some level of dignity, didn't she? "He's into head games. He would try to diminish me in my husband's eyes out of spite."

"But you wouldn't allow him to do that, would you?"

"He doesn't think I have the guts to take him on. He told me I'm not ruthless enough."

"Is he right?"

It was a question that had occupied many of Nina's thoughts, and she still didn't have a concrete answer. "There is no easy answer. I have a conscience and he doesn't. I think about the impact any action I may take would have on others; he doesn't. He's a lot more selfish than I am."

There was silence in the room as Dr. Issler gave Nina a chance to collect her thoughts. Nina considered the ramifications of what was just discussed. She questioned for what seemed like the hundredth time if she had what it took to move forward with prosecuting her own father. Was there any legal precedence for this kind of situation?

Doctor Issler started up again. "This next series of questions may be especially uncomfortable to talk about, but I assure you, they need to be addressed in order to help facilitate your healing."

Nina was guarded in her response. "I'll do my best to answer the questions truthfully. But I reserve the right to put the brakes on."

Dr. Issler nodded. "How has the abuse affected your relationship with your husband?"

"In what context?"

"Victims of sexual abuse often have intimacy issues. Some find intercourse revolting because it's a reminder of the incest. Others engage in promiscuous behavior as a way to gain the affection they never got from the aggressor, sometimes as a means of self-degradation or punishment."

"If you're asking which category I fall into, the answer is none of them."

"How would you describe your sex life with your husband, or men in general before you got married?"

"Great and non-existent."

"I beg your pardon?"

"That's all you're getting from me."

Dr. Issler looked like an investigative reporter who had just stumbled on a story that could make a Pulitzer Prize-winning career. She leaned forward and lowered her glasses to the tip of her nose.

"Why?"

"I'm here. That should be at least one point in the fearless column."

"Are you embarrassed to talk about sex?"

"I don't have intimacy issues," Nina insisted."

Dr. Issler looked continued to push. "Did you date in college? Is that how you met your husband?"

"No, I didn't meet Marc in college. And since you won't let this go, I didn't date anyone in college."

"Why not?"

"You're the expert."

"You wanted control. For the first time, you were away from daddy, on your own, free to make your own decisions, including the decision of who to have sex with. It was your way of controlling your body, deciding who would have access to it and who wouldn't. You were punishing him by depriving the men who were interested in your affection."

Dr. Issler's observation couldn't be more accurate if she were sitting right next to Nina in one of her classes at Stanford. The scenario she just described was one Nina had almost forgotten. In her junior year, Jeff Wilson, a classmate in her global business management course was notorious for tormenting her for her lack of cooperation in the less is best wardrobe department.

"If you would lose the nun get-up, a tank top and miniskirt would do wonders for you," he said mischievously. "I'm just saying, you have to let your skin breathe."

Nina had given him the scathing, scornful look she had perfected, but he remained unfazed.

"I'm concerned for your health. And why are you wound tighter than a snare drum, anyway? Tell you what, because I'm such a caring guy, how about I come over to your dorm room later and help you relax and release, if you catch my drift?"

Jeff received a kick in the crotch for his trouble but it didn't dissuade him from his pursuit, which lasted right up until graduation. "I won't soon forget you Nina Copeland. You're one tough cookie."

"They were all pigs, only interested in one thing," Nina complained to her therapist. "I wouldn't allow them to use me the way he did."

"What made your husband different from all the other pigs?"

"We wanted the same things, and he was patient."

"Patient how?"

"He was attracted to me, but he wasn't aggressive. He put my feelings first."

"How did you know you were ready to be intimate with him?"

"Have you seen Marc?" Nina joked. "I couldn't hold out forever."

Dr. Issler chuckled. "So you still had a healthy view of sex?"

"I wasn't about to let what happened to me rob me of the capacity to enjoy one of the most basic human experiences. I've never connected with any man sexually the way I did with Marc. We're compatible in a lot of ways."

"And you didn't want your father to get in the way of your happiness?"

"Right. He used to tell me no man would want me because I was damaged."

"How did that make you feel?"

"I believed him. That's why I worked so hard to keep him away from Marc. I didn't want my husband's opinion of me to change."

"What about now? Do you still feel that way?"

Nina laughed nervously. "I'm in therapy. I think that pretty much says it all."

CHAPTER TWENTY-FIVE

Nina was running late for her session with Dr. Issler. She grabbed her car keys off the kitchen counter and was headed to the garage when the house phone rang. She ignored it but the ringing seemed to demand her attention. Against her better judgment, she picked up.

"Hello?"

"How could you do this to Dad?"

Nina was in a rush and had neither the time nor the desire to get into a shouting match over the phone.

"Cassie, I'm late for an appointment. Can we talk later?"

"Listen to me. You have to convince Geraldine to go back to Dad. He's freaking out and I'm scared for him, Nina."

"He created his own problems."

"Are you denying she left because of you?"

"No."

"What do you have to say for yourself?"

"I don't owe either one of you an explanation."

"Get over yourself, Nina."

"Tell that to your father."

"My father? So you're too good to be his daughter all of a sudden?"

"Yes."

"He was right about you. You don't care about anyone except yourself. After everything he did for you, this is the thanks he gets?"

"It's time to wake up, Cassie."

"I'm wide awake and I see how mean you really are."

"Open your eyes and see him for the selfish, manipulative sociopath that he is."

"Stop it!" Cassie screamed into the phone. "I don't believe you."

"Believe it. I already explained to you the best way I knew how what he did to me. I'm sorry you're struggling with the truth."

There was silence on the other line. Nina was afraid something had happened to Cassie. Could she have fainted?

"Cassie, are you there?"

"I-I-I d-don't ...you're wrong. Dad would never hurt us, Nina. Why are you doing this?"

"I have to, Cassie."

"Dad loves us."

"He loves you."

Nina felt resentment gnawing at her insides, threatening to rise up and strangle her. Therapy was going to be a long, painful ride.

*   *   *

AFTER APOLOGIZING PROFUSELY FOR BEING late, Nina took charge of the session.

"I just had a huge fight with my sister," she told Dr. Issler. "She's still in denial. I'm now the bad guy."

"What started the fight?"

"Phillip's life is falling apart. His wife left him and Cassie blames me."

"Is she right?"

"Sort of."

"Care to expand on that?"

"I told her about the abuse. I also provided information about an illegitimate child he fathered and never bothered to tell her about."

"Why did you do that?"

"I got tired. I didn't want to be pushed around anymore."

"Why won't your sister believe you?"

"Cassie is a daddy's girl through and through. She insisted that he loves us and wouldn't hurt his own daughter."

"What was your reponse?"

"I corrected her."

"How?"

"He loves Cassie, not me."

"How do you feel about that?"

"Resentful."

"A little jealous?"

"Perhaps."

"It's perfectly normal to crave parental love. Most children receive it freely, but yours came with conditions. Resentment is a natural reaction."

"I suppose so."

"Tell me about your relationship with Cassie."

"She's my sister and I love her, but we don't have much in common."

"What is she like?"

"She's young, impressionable, reckless."

"Why do you think that is?"

"He spoils her. She dropped out of college, makes excuses as to why she hasn't returned to complete her degree, has no ambition other than shopping for designer clothes and partying, all at his expense."

"She's your opposite."

"I don't want her to be my clone. She needs to be the best Cassie she can be. There's an eight-year age difference between us, so our perspectives on life are quite different."

"Are you afraid you'll lose her now that you've disclosed the abuse to her?"

"I don't care. She had both her parents to protect her from life. I had no one to protect me from him."

Dr. Issler shook her head, either in agreement or pride that her patient had a mini-breakthrough. Nina had come to the conclusion, with great difficulty that self-preservation had to be the cornerstone of her healing process. If she started thinking about how disclosing the abuse would impact others, the distraction would set her back years and slowly break down her resolve. She couldn't allow that to happen. The guilty party never thought about it, so why should she?

"Most victims have a difficult time getting to that point."

"I hate that word."

"You do?"

"It's dehumanizing."

Dr. Issler was intrigued. "Tell me why."

"It trivializes the human experience. Humans are complex creatures with complex relationships, beliefs, emotions and dreams. When someone is labeled a victim, the totality of their life experiences is overshadowed by their trauma. With that one label, it's as if everything else about that person is null and void."

A silence fell between them, each woman lost in her own thoughts. Dr. Issler cleared her throat and flipped through her notes, breaking the stillness.

"Last time our session ended before we could delve into this topic, but I'd like to bring it up again. You said you blamed your looks for the abuse?"

"I've had a complicated relationship with my looks, but we've come to accept each other."

"Why did you blame the abuse on your looks?"

"I got teased a lot growing up because I stuck out like a Go-Go dancer at a ballet recital. My mother kept telling me the other kids were jealous and I was going to turn into a great beauty one day."

"Do you think she was right?"

"I guess so. He certainly took notice."

"You mean your father?"

"I knew my looks had something to do with his behavior because he wouldn't shut up about it. I guess I latched on to that theory because I needed something that would explain why it was happening to me. There had to be a reason for the abuse. My looks were a natural scapegoat. It could also explain his insane bouts of jealousy."

"Jealous of whom?"

"Boys paid attention as I got older. "

"As an adult, how have your feelings about your appearance changed?"

"In college it didn't matter much. Once I entered the corporate world, I quickly learned that beautiful women could get by on their looks. But I made sure anybody who had a pulse knew I was highly capable. My performance had to be outstanding at all times."

"That's a lot of pressure to put on yourself."

"It was necessary."

CHAPTER TWENTY-SIX

On Thursday evening, Nina was home alone with pizza and a movie for company. When Marc was away, she took extra care to bolt every door and triple-checked to make sure the alarm was armed. They lived in a neighborhood where the crime statistics barely registered with the police department, but psychopaths didn't care what zip code you lived in.

She threw on her favorite cotton nightie, grabbed a plate of pizza, popped the disc in the DVD player and settled in for a quiet evening of entertainment. The opening credits were still rolling when the doorbell rang. She paused the movie and charged towards the front door like a raging bull.

"Who is it?" she shouted.

"Nina, open the door. It's me."

She froze for a split second, wondering what on earth he was doing at her home this late. She made it clear how she felt about him and couldn't imagine what was so important that he would show up unannounced. But then again, that seemed to be his favorite MO where she was concerned. She opened the door grudgingly. Phillip stood at the entrance with a silly grin on his face.

"You're crossing the line as always. This is my home. It's after nine o'clock at night."

"I have good news."

"There's this invention called the telephone. Use it."

"Are you going to let me in or would you prefer to have your neighbors call the cops because there's a suspicious looking black man standing at the door and no one's letting him in?"

"You weren't too concerned about the neighbors when you stole my diary," Nina griped, as she led him to the living room. "Or did you have someone else do your dirty work?"

"Goodness, Nina. Can't you let that go? I told you I don't have anything that belongs to you."

Nina offered a mirthless laugh. "What do you want?"

"Geraldine came back. I don't know what you said to her, but it worked."

"Is there a full moon out tonight?"

"She said the two of you met and you helped her see things in a new light."

"Did the light suck the grey matter from her brain?"

He sat down on the sofa and gestured for her to sit next to him. "I have something to give you."

"No thanks. You've given me plenty. I still carry the scars."

"Nina, please. I know I haven't always been the best father. I wasn't there for you as much as I should have. But I wanted to say thank you. You gave me my wife back and I wanted to express my gratitude," he said, removing a small black box from his jacket pocket.

It didn't make sense to Nina. After her conversation with Geraldine, she was positive there was no way she would stay with Phillip. Something must have happened to change her mind, something huge. Why would she go back to him? What was keeping her? Nina was sure she wouldn't like the answer. She of all people knew how Phillip operated and how persuasive he could be. Maybe he worked his particular brand of black magic on his wife. What a shame.

Nina took the box from him and moved to the far end of the sofa and opened it. Inside was a stunning cross, encrusted with dozens of small diamonds with a large birthstone, her birthstone in the center. Based on the brilliance of the stones, Nina estimated the gift to be worth tens of thousands of dollars. She was speechless.

"I know how important your faith is to you," he said.

"Then you should familiarize yourself with Leviticus Chapter 18. The gift is very generous, but I can't accept it." She returned the cross to the box and placed it in his hands.

He took her refusal as an affront. "You're my daughter. Why can't you accept a gift from your own father? I had this made especially for you. There's even an inscription."

He seemed genuinely baffled by her response. How odd. What did he expect? That she would jump into his arms, give him a big hug and tell him how much she loved it and he was the best dad ever? Well, that scenario already played out when she was a kid and it ended badly. She wasn't falling for that trick again.

"You know why I can't accept it."

"Don't do this, Nina. You said I was a sociopath who hated women, including you. That's the most painful thing anyone has ever said to me and it hurt even more because it came from my own daughter."

"Oh, sorry. I didn't know you had feelings. You should have told me sooner."

"This is funny to you?" he asked softly. "You think how I feel about you is funny?"

Her mood transformed from playful sarcasm to a dangerous place she had trained herself to avoid entirely. "That's the problem, Phillip. I don't know how you feel about me. I could only interpret your actions. Based on our history, I came to the painful realization that you weren't capable of giving me what I wanted: a father who wouldn't take advantage of a little girl's desire to be loved and accepted by her dad without conditions. I promise you, I'm fine with it. You don't have to pretend. Most kids take their parents' love for granted. I had to learn that I couldn't have what other kids had in that regard."

It was a jaded view she had spent years cultivating, another survival mechanism. It only hurt if she talked about it and she never had until now. She could feel the tightness rising in her chest and prayed to God she wouldn't start bawling right then and there.

"That's not how it is, Nina," he said, desperate for her to believe him. "I've always loved you. You have no idea how much. That will never change. You don't see it because you don't want to. You prefer to dwell on bitterness and negativity."

"It might be easy for you to dismiss what you obviously refuse to acknowledge and that way, you don't have to take responsibility. I never had that luxury. You took away who I was supposed to be, the woman I would have become, so I had to work like a dog to create a new me from scratch. Do you know how hard it is to create a new person from the damaged scraps that existed before?"

They both fell silent. When he reached over to hold her hand, she brushed it away.

"You were lost to me for eighteen years, Nina. A parent never stops being a parent."

"Don't talk to me about parenthood. Add that to the long list of things you took from me."

"I know you believe I was responsible for your miscarriage but you don't know the whole story."

"Enlighten me, then. You knew I was in trouble but delayed calling for help. Every second counted and the outcome could have been different if you weren't trying to be a control freak who wanted to teach me a lesson."

His expression was deeply melancholic, as if she had just twisted a sword in his chest. "That baby was my first grandchild. It took the ambulance at least fifteen minutes to get there. Everything happened quickly, from the time you said something was wrong to the time you passed out, it was a few short minutes. After the paramedics showed up, I stayed behind to clean up the blood on the floor the best way I could before I left for the hospital. The doctors said he was gone before the ambulance got there, all they could do was treat you."

Nina struggled to control the tears she could feel prickling at the corners of her eyes. The pain of losing her son came back with a rawness she hadn't experienced since the miscarriage. It didn't matter whether or not Phillip was telling the truth. She wouldn't have been in a situation that required her to put her body through grueling and highly invasive medical procedures in an effort to conceive, if he hadn't destroyed her ability to have children naturally.

She was about to fall apart. She wouldn't do it in front of him so she asked him to leave. He must have sensed she was on the edge because he didn't argue. He simply did what she asked.

After Phillip left, Nina wandered from room to room, pondering what it would have been like had her little boy lived. She could see his bouncer in the middle of the family room, his bottles lined up in the sterilizer on the kitchen counter. He would hold on to furniture as he cruised before he could walk. At feeding time, his high chair would be a mess and he would have food all over his face and head. She felt an intense longing inside. She would never get over the loss of her child. But maybe now that Phillip told her the whole story of that terrible day, she could put it in perspective. She stubbornly refused to believe Phillip might not be all bad, but she was appreciative of the fact that he told her the whole story. She had so few good memories of her childhood with him.

I couldn't believe it. After this morning's disaster of a driving lesson, Dad and I didn't kill each other. I just got my learner's permit last week, which was majorly cool, but Dad insisted that I learn how to drive stick. That's so ancient. Everyone at school is learning to drive on an automatic. Tara Gibson's dad got her an automatic Ford Mustang convertible the minute she got her permit but Dad said he's not Tara's dad. I have no idea why he wants me to drive a stick shift. You think he would have changed his mind since I rolled down the hill earlier this morning and almost smashed into a tree. I thought for sure he was going to start yelling at me or call me stupid or something, but he didn't. He was calm and understanding. Someone must have put a chill pill in his coffee this morning.

After the driving lesson, I was all shaken up about it but Dad put his arms around me and told me it was okay, we all make mistakes and I was doing great for someone who only had three driving lessons.

He said we should have some fun because it was such a nice day out. I thought he had to work but he said he'd rather spend the day with me, so he called the office and said he wouldn't be in. Maybe I'm wrong about Dad. Maybe he's not such a bad guy after all. If I don't think about the trouble he brings to my room at night, he's not so terrible.

Anyway, we ended up going to an amusement park and I've never seen Dad so relaxed or have so much fun. He wasn't scared to go on the rollercoasters with me, not even the Death Monster, the scariest rollercoaster ever. I felt really special, like I had the coolest dad in the world. We ate tons of ice cream, cotton candy and hotdogs, stuff Theresa wouldn't let me eat because she's a health nut. Dad even won me a stuffed giraffe. I like this dad better, the one who smiles, goes on scary rollercoasters and lets me eat treats. On the ride home, we made up stories about drivers on the road, based on the kinds of cars they were driving. It was a good day.

*   *   *

SHE DIDN'T RECALL EXACTLY WHEN it was decided or how. It had always been a possibility, swimming around in her head. It was discussed with Marc and her mother who said from the very beginning that this had to be done but the final decision would be hers. Something inside her said it was time. She felt terror like she'd never experienced before when she, the lone decider, moved forward.

Nina gripped the steering wheel tightly and sat perfectly still, hoping the bile forming in her mouth would dissipate and prevent her from having to sit in a cesspool of her own vomit. The two-hour police interrogation shook her to the core. It took her back to the mass grave of her childhood, and the ghosts lurking there. Every time she had to recall her father touching her, she died over and over again. Each time he hit her, there was another body to add to the count.

She opened the car door and spat. By sheer force of will, she calmed her insides long enough to call Marc. He picked up on the first ring.

"Are you all right?"

"I'll live."

"It was that bad?"

"Brutal."

"Did they believe you?"

"They said I make a 'credible' witness."

"That's good news."

"No, it isn't."

"Why not?"

"We haven't seen the worst of it. I have to relive everything I just told them on the witness stand. Only this time, his lawyer will be relentless in an attempt to break me and get him exonerated. It's a huge risk we're taking."

"Don't doubt yourself now. You'll do great."

"You have no idea the things they were asking me. Obscene things."

"You should have let me come with you."

"I endured it alone. I have to end it alone."

"We should plan a long trip after it's all over. For a couple of months or so."

"Can we leave now? I can pack quickly," she joked weakly.

"Soon, *Cherie*. Soon."

*   *   *

"OH MY GOD, NINA, YOU have to *do* something."

A hysterical Cassie was on the other end of the line. "Westwood Police questioned Dad about you. They showed up at his office and asked to speak to him. All the office staff saw it and they're gossiping about it. It was a bad scene, Nina. It was really bad. You have to tell them he didn't do anything. It was all a misunderstanding."

"He hasn't been arrested or charged with anything. Yet."

"This is all on you, Nina. Are you prepared to send our father to prison?"

"The Commonwealth will file charges based on their findings in the investigation. It's out of my hands."

"How could you be so *evil*?" she said hoarsely. "Don't you care about him at all?"

"As much as he cares about me."

"You'll go to hell for this."

"He took me there almost every day for eight years."

"You're not my sister. We're done, Nina."

"As you wish."

*   *   *

THURSDAY MORNING DAWNED WITH A bitter chill for Phillip Copeland, even though it was late August. He sat in his study downing a stiff drink. He didn't give a damn that it was too early in the day to be drinking. He needed it. He needed to take the edge off. He couldn't believe she was going through with it. He couldn't believe what was happening to him. When the Police hauled him in for questioning, it was surreal, like a bad B movie with no end in sight. He told them he wouldn't speak without an attorney. Luckily, Melinda Bosch, one of the city's toughest criminal defense lawyers with a reputation for aggressive cross-examination of prosecution witnesses, and a zero loss record to boot was available and agreed to represent him. She assured him this would never go to trial.

Their plan was simple. Deny that sexual abuse of any kind had ever taken place. No, he didn't know why his daughter would make such accusations. Melinda Bosch reprimanded the two detectives for hauling her client down to the station based on an outlandish story. It was obvious that these accusations were nothing more than the ramblings of a disturbed woman who wanted to get back at her father, for whatever reason. The cops reminded her it was their job to investigate any and all complaints. After an hour of denials, threats by his attorney, refusal to answer certain questions since they weren't in court and the tried and true invoking of the Fifth Amendment, Phillip left the station with his lawyer on his heels.

There was one thing Phillip hadn't counted on but he would soon remedy. One of the detectives mentioned that Nina told them Constance Buckwell was the only other person who could substantiate what she was saying. He hadn't spoken to Constance in years, not since he ran into her downtown a few years ago. She was still fawning all over him as she had when she was in his employ. He dismissed her behavior as he always had and hadn't thought much of the encounter. He had terminated her from her position as a caregiver for Cassie and to some extent Nina because she lacked discretion. What had she said and to whom? Why did Nina mention her specifically? He needed to squash that potential firebomb. He needed to see Constance immediately, before the cops got to her.

CHAPTER TWENTY-SEVEN

"It's always a pleasure to see you in my office, Nina," Jack Kendall beamed. Nina's boss, the CEO of Baseline, was a giant in the industry, though diminutive in stature. He was forever brushing an unruly mop of hair away from his eyes. She often teased him that the entire office should chip in to buy him a can of hairspray. There was a glint in his soft brown eyes, as if he had something mischievous up his sleeve.

"You might throw me out after you hear what I have to say."

"Never," he said jovially. "Did you share Baseline secrets with our competitors?"

"No."

"Then have a seat," he said, slapping the back of the chair around his mini conference table.

"A situation that could have major consequences for Baseline is taking shape. It involves one our board members, and I recommend he be removed before he can be linked to the company in any meaningful way."

"What's going on, Nina? This sounds serious."

"It is."

Nina didn't know how to tell Jack about her connection to Phillip. He had always been one of her biggest supporters, and she didn't want to compromise their relationship. She decided to go with a lie of omission.

"Dr. Copeland is being questioned by Westwood Police as the prime suspect in a sexual assault case."

"Impossible! I've known Phillip for years. I've never met a man with more integrity."

"We don't always know people as well as we think we do, Jack. Especially when it comes to their private lives."

"I can't believe it. Phillip wouldn't do something like this."

"I recommend we prepare ourselves in case he gets charged and there's a trial. A swift and quiet dismissal from the board would be best. I'll get our corporate communications and PR teams working on an appropriate response in the event it gets leaked to the media."

"Atta girl. I'll convene an emergency meeting of the board and apprise them of the situation."

Jack was still shaking his head in a state of shock when Nina left his office.

* * *

NINA ARRIVED A FEW MINUTES early for her session to break the news to Doctor Issler before they tackled this week's agenda.

"What's on your mind?" Dr. Issler asked.

"Something I never thought I'd do. I'm still grappling with it but it's been set in motion and I can't take it back."

"Wow, sounds serious. What is this *it* you're talking about?"

"I went to the police. An investigation is underway. There's no turning back now."

"You're forcing the perpetrator to face the consequences of his actions. That is huge, Nina. Kudos."

"I'm not doing back flips yet. This is huge, as you pointed out, but there's a lot at stake. Can I live with myself if he goes to prison? What about his young son who would never get a chance to know him until he's too old to be a father to him? I don't even know if he wants to be a father to Alexander, he doesn't even carry the Copeland name. What if he's found not guilty? How is he going to get his reputation back and what about me? I'll be seen as *that* girl."

Dr. Issler gave her a concerned look, like she was losing it. She knew she was on the verge of becoming hysterical so she had to take a deep breath and literally found herself lying on the clichéd therapist couch.

"Sorry. If it didn't come out of my mouth it would mess with my head."

"That's quite all right. You took a brave step. Most victims never go that far. You're speaking for all those who couldn't or wouldn't speak. That's quite courageous."

"I don't feel so brave. A lot of lives will be impacted, and not for the better, because of me."

"You sound worried about your father and the impact this action will have on him and others. What about you? How has disclosure affected your relationship with people around you?"

"I've been fortunate that my family has been supportive but you can't win everyone over. Cassie wants nothing to do with me, my mother and husband are already planning a conviction celebration and there are people in his corner who tell me this is a huge mistake I'll regret."

"People like who?"

"My aunt Elizabeth said I was a disgrace to the family and should be ashamed for putting my poor father through this. She said her brother had been an outstanding father I should be thankful I have. His friend Dr. Obasanjo told me I shouldn't allow bad advice to cloud my judgment and bring down a good man. He said whatever issues Phillip and I had could be resolved because that's what families do. They resolve their issues privately.

"I also told my boss. I let him know Philip is a liability the company can do without."

"Did you tell your boss who the victim was?"

"Of course not. I like my job. I also have a reputation to protect."

Doctor Issler removed her glasses. "That's—"

"Manipulative?"

"No. I was going to say that was a masterful move. You protected your job and destroyed his credibility in one brilliant stroke."

"Maybe I should take up chess. What do you think?"

Dr. Issler chuckled. "I want to revisit a question I've asked you before."

"Then why ask again?"

"Because circumstances have changed. Your answer could change."

Nina didn't get the point of this exercise but she would play along. "Okay. Ask away."

"If your father were to burst into the room at this moment, fall to his knees, admit what he did, tell you it wasn't your fault, and beg for your forgiveness, what would you do?"

"I already know it's not my fault."

"Really? Last session you talked about blaming yourself. Have you moved on that quickly?"

Nina gazed at a photo of Dr. Issler's Golden Retriever on her desk. *He has it easy,* Nina thought. No worries, no problems. Simple existence. He was loved and cherished, loyal and protective. Her human father could learn a lot from that dog.

"My head knows I'm not to blame and my heart will catch up soon. But he makes it difficult."

"How?"

"By pretending to care."

"What do you mean?"

"I was thinking of a rather expensive diamond cross he bought me. He claims it was a gesture of thanks for convincing his wife to give him another chance. I explained to him why I couldn't accept it. That was the last honest conversation I had with him. He also told me what happened the night I miscarried. For the first time in a long time, I saw him as human. He tried to comfort me when it was obvious talking about the miscarriage was still painful but I rejected him. I almost felt sorry about it."

"Is it possible the gift was a gesture of genuine thanks?"

"Anything is possible. But I have to keep reminding myself of who he is."

"As a way of protecting your emotions?"

"Yes. He can slit your throat and convince you it's your fault you fell on the knife."

"He has a powerful grip on your imagination."

"What are you going to do about it?"

CHAPTER TWENTY-EIGHT

T he stage was set for the *Commonwealth of Massachusetts versus Dr. John-Phillip Copeland*. There were ten counts of sexual abuse of a minor leveled at him, including aggravated child molestation, aggravated sexual battery, criminal solicitation of a minor, and lewd acts on a minor.

The case had all the makings of a TV crime drama: sex, betrayal, revenge, sibling rivalry, and marital discord. And that was before the opening statements were made. Nina dressed carefully that morning. It was late October and the temperatures were beginning to dip. She wanted to look chic yet sympathetic to a jury. She settled on a fitted sleeveless dress with a matching dress coat and belted waist. Her hair was pulled back in a sophisticated up-do. She went over and over again in her mind her rationale for doing this: *It made sense. It was sound. It was just. It was time.* Her mother came up from Dallas for the duration of the trial and Charlene had her second-in-command take over the salon so she could be available.

As they headed into the courtroom, Nina wondered if the District Attorney could secure a conviction against the defense. Melinda Bosch was one of the city's top trial lawyers, a partner at Atherton, McGrath & Jacobs, a law firm specializing in clients with deep pockets. She never lost a case. The DA also had a noteworthy record: the highest conviction rate of any DA over the past twenty years. Dan McCloud took over the job ten years ago and the cameras loved his youthful good looks, passion for crime fighting, and the not-so-subtle whispers of political appointment that seemed to follow in his wake.

Everyone stood as the bailiff announced Judge Michael Sokoff's entrance into the courtroom. Following the judge, the jury filed in and took their seats. It consisted of five men and seven women. Nina couldn't figure out if that was a good thing or not. Apart from a twenty-something female, the jury makeup gravitated to upper forties and higher. Would this group sympathize with the defense?

The judge addressed the courtroom.

"This case may be difficult for many of you in the courtroom today. You may find some of the testimony of a graphic and disturbing nature. I ask that you keep your emotions under control. I will not have my courtroom turned into a spectacle. We'll now hear Mr. McCloud's opening statement."

"Ladies and gentlemen, this case is about a man who had us all fooled while he perpetrated one of the most heinous crimes you could never imagine. And he got way with it for twenty-six long years. The victim? His own daughter."

McCloud slowly walked toward the defense table and pointed to her father. "This man, Doctor John-Phillip Copeland, distinguished professor at a world-class educational institution, philanthropist, corporate board member, and community leader, repeatedly and consistently raped his young daughter, beginning when she was just ten years old and he was a married man of thirty-two.

"He only stopped because she had the courage to end it by moving halfway around the country to attend college, instead of staying close to home."

The jurors' eyes were glued to McCloud. Nina fought to suppress the urge to look at the defense table but lost. He was furiously taking notes. *A bit early for that*, she thought, but that could be part of his strategy, nit pick every single word, challenge it, in an effort to wear her down and the state's case with her.

"You will hear from the plaintiff's former caregiver," McCloud continued. "A woman who has first-hand knowledge of the molestation the plaintiff suffered at the hands of her father. This caregiver lived under the same roof as the plaintiff and defendant. Doctor Maeve Issler, one of the world's leading experts on childhood sexual trauma and the plaintiff's therapist, will give expert testimony as it relates to this case. Multiple witnesses who knew the plaintiff as a child will testify to her crying out for help, but no one came to her rescue. We will expose the virtual conspiracy of silence surrounding the defendant, how the plaintiff was surrounded by adults who either knew or suspected the abuse was going on, but did nothing to stop it. Finally, you will hear from the plaintiff herself, a brave young woman who has come forward to seek justice by exposing a criminal and reclaiming her life. Thank you."

Phillip sat at the defense table as stiff as a board. He would show no emotion no matter what was said during the prosecution's case. He would turn on the charm when the jury looked in his direction, of course. He would appear confident, in control, a man who was one hundred percent innocent. A father who was devastated by what was going on. And depending on their reaction, he might even throw in a smile for good measure. Melinda warned him that things could get very ugly very fast. McCloud would be sure to bring out visuals to pull at the jury's heartstrings— pictures of a beautiful little girl who was being terrorized by her own father. Bosch had told him molestation was not a crime you wanted to be on trial for if you ever tangled with the legal system. Phillip remembered wanting to wring his attorney's neck. She had promised this case wouldn't go to trial. Apparently, Nina was a convincing, credible witness and the prosecution felt this case could be a slam dunk. Nina was smart, articulate and brave. That's the way the DA had described her in their meetings. She was all those things, Phillip thought to himself, but she would soon find out she shouldn't have crossed him.

McCloud took his seat and readjusted his glasses. The judge suppressed a cough and called on the defense to present its opening argument. Melinda Bosch was a pretty blond with a fierce attitude. Nina anticipated a battle of wills later on in the trial.

"You've just heard a very eloquent and heart-felt opening statement by Mr. McCloud," Bosch began. "You wouldn't be human if you didn't feel sorry for the plaintiff upon hearing that statement. Unfortunately for the prosecution, they forgot the one thing they need to build a case against my client: evidence, ladies and gentlemen. Why won't the state be able to prove its case? Because this trial is not about justice, it's about revenge."

The jurors leaned forward in their chairs. Bosch was putting on a show.

"The defense will present compelling evidence that the plaintiff manufactured this story of sexual abuse because she blames her father for an unfortunate miscarriage she suffered. Unable to have children, she told this ridiculous story to the police … and so here we are. You'll hear testimony that proves the plaintiff is a pathological liar, a manipulator. The state's entire case is based on portraying my client as a monster. It's their prerogative to do so, but when all the testimony is complete, my client will be exonerated."

McCloud called Daphne Lockwood to the stand and the bailiff swore her in. Nina's mother was feisty and fiercely protective, but this trial and everything that led up to it left her drowning in guilt and paralyzed by anger.

"Mrs. Lockwood, why was your daughter sent away from the love and security of the only family she'd ever known to live with virtual strangers?"

"I wanted Nina to know her father. When he said he wanted to raise her in America, I said yes. He had the resources to provide opportunities for her that I couldn't."

At the DA's prodding, her mother gave a description of the idyllic childhood Nina lived before she returned to the States, surrounded by a loving mother and stepfather and tons of cousins, aunts, and uncles.

"How did you meet the defendant?"

"I was a student at Fordham University in New York. I came to Boston with some girlfriends of mine and we met at the home of a mutual friend."

"How long were you and the defendant involved?"

"About six months. We were both busy with our studies and saw each other whenever we could."

"What was his reaction when you told him you were pregnant?"

"He wasn't happy. He said he wasn't ready to be a father. He had ambitions and a kid would just get in the way."

"How did you feel about his attitude?"

"I was disappointed, but I couldn't have an abortion. It's against my faith."

"Did you tell him this?"

"I did, and we got married, but parted ways almost two years later. I knew he only did it out of obligation. So I took my daughter and went back to my island home to be around family."

"Mrs. Lockwood, did you ever go back to college to finish your degree?"

"No," Daphne said sadly. "Once I had Nina, my life changed. I got married to my late husband and settled into raising a family."

"Did the defendant support you in any way?"

"He was good when it came to financial support. He sent a check regularly, but that was the extent of his parenting. He barely called and never visited."

Nina observed her father's reaction to this testimony. There was none. He looked straight ahead. It pissed Nina off. It was as if what her mother was saying didn't matter. He couldn't even give her the courtesy of paying attention.

"Mrs. Lockwood, was it difficult to let go of your daughter?"

"We were all saddened when she left. My husband had his doubts but I convinced him it would for the best. In the end, we were all wrong."

"Did Nina ever give you any indication that anything was wrong?"

"No. Nina was a very agreeable child. It took her a while to warm up to her new environment, but that was to be expected. She never complained."

"When did Nina tell you she was molested by her father?"

The defense objected. "Allegedly molested. My client hasn't been convicted of a crime."

"Sustained," said the judge.

"I'll rephrase the question. When did you learn there might have been an inappropriate relationship between Nina and her father?"

"In January of this year. I came to visit her after she lost her baby."

"How did you take the news?"

"I thought I didn't hear her correctly, but my daughter has never lied to me."

"So you believed her?"

"Yes. Nina wouldn't say something like that unless it happened. I wanted to die that day, because I did this to my daughter. I may as well have led her to his bed myself." Daphne sniffed loudly as she tried to compose herself.

"Can you tell the court exactly what your daughter said to you on that visit?" McCloud asked softly.

"It took several days to get the whole story, but she said all those letters she sent me, describing an ideal childhood, were only partially true. She said she didn't want me to worry so she omitted the bad stuff. She told me her father started in on her at age ten and didn't let up until she moved to California to attend Stanford."

Nina was uncomfortable. She wanted her mother off the stand. Conflicting emotions flittered across Daphne's face as she strained to hold herself together and complete her testimony. Nina sent up a silent prayer on her mother's behalf.

"Did she go into any detail? Did you ask questions?"

Her mother recounted the discussion she had with Nina in the kitchen that awful day when her mother made her favorite stew.

Daphne Lockwood broke down, sobbing uncontrollably. Between her meltdown and the nervous shuffling of papers, there was awkwardness in the air, as if no one knew what to say or do next. Nina looked at the jury. They wouldn't meet her gaze. Her father was unfazed, scribbling notes like a maniac.

McCloud handed her mother a box of tissue to wipe her tears and blow her nose.

"I'm sorry, am I done now?" she asked him.

The defense declined to cross-examine. McCloud had no more questions.

The judge dismissed her mother from the witness stand. Nina was thankful that her mother's ordeal was over. For now, anyway.

The next witness for the prosecution was Marc Kasai. He gave his wife a quick peck on the cheek, adjusted his tie and made his way to the stand. McCloud got the general questions out of the way first; how did Marc and Nina meet, how long they'd been married— the basics.

"How would you characterize your wife's interactions with her family?"

"Her mother is a strong, positive influence on her. With Cassie, things were a little bit different."

"Go on."

"There was always an underlying tension between them, even though they got along."

"What kind of tension?"

Marc looked at Nina nervously, as if in need of her approval. She nodded slightly, encouraging him.

"Whenever their father was mentioned, Nina would change the subject."

"Did you ever ask her about her dad?"

"She said they had a falling out about her choice of college and he lived in another state and didn't communicate with her."

"Did you ever try to get her to discuss her childhood?"

"Many times. Just before our wedding, I tried to get her to open up."

"What happened?"

"It was important to me that her dad attend our wedding, and my family wanted to meet him, too. She went berserk."

"Did she offer an explanation?"

"She said if I ever brought that viper into our lives, I'd regret it."

"Mr. Kasai, how did you find out your father-in-law was right here in Boston?"

Marc loosened his tie and glanced at his wife before he took a deep breath.

"I noticed suspicious phone calls and a change in my wife's behavior, so I asked her what was going on. She said it was just work-related stress. At the time we were trying to conceive, and she was under enormous pressure. I didn't think twice about that explanation. Later on, she and her best friend were no longer on speaking terms. I confronted Charlene and that's when she confirmed that Phillip Copeland was my wife's father."

"What was your wife's reaction when you revealed this to her?"

"She said she lied to me about the whereabouts of her father because he's a monster who would have destroyed us had she allowed him access to our lives."

"That's a pretty serious statement."

"I didn't know what it meant until she explained her father molested her for years."

"What was your reaction?"

"I was stunned. My heart broke for her. It took me a while to process what she was saying and what it meant."

"Did you believe her?"

"I never doubted her for a minute. A lot of things started to make sense."

"Such as?"

"She would change the channel whenever he was on TV."

"Mr. Kasai, you testified that this all seems to make sense to you, but how can you be sure that what your wife told you actually happened?"

"It's the reason we're having trouble conceiving," he said tersely, staring in Phillip's direction.

"Please clarify that statement."

"My wife is having trouble getting pregnant because her fallopian tubes are completely blocked by scar tissue. It's from when her father gave her chlamydia when he was molesting her."

The jurors looked at each other, confused, unsure if they heard right. Nina's mother squeezed her hand, reflecting a misery only a mother could feel. The defense objected. The judge called for a recess.

CHAPTER TWENTY-NINE

A fter a brief recess, the defense once again launched an objection.

"Your honor," Bosch said anxiously, "I object on the grounds that this is pure speculation. There is no proof that the plaintiff's condition has anything to do with my client, and therefore has no relevance in this case."

"If you would allow my witness to finish his testimony," McCloud said, "you'll see the relevance."

"Objection overruled," said the judge. "Don't make me regret it, Mr. McCloud."

"Thank you, Your Honor."

"Mr. Kasai, that's a rather inflammatory statement. Do you have any proof of this claim?"

"We went to see a reproductive specialist and found out about her condition, which was caused by an STD that went untreated when she was fourteen. It's in her medical records."

"How did she contract this STD?"

"From her father."

Bosch was furious. "Your Honor, there is nothing in my client's medical records to indicate he has ever been treated for chlamydia or any other STD."

"Your Honor, the defendant is a man of significant means and influence," McCloud said forcefully. "It's not inconceivable he could have been treated without it being noted in his file. Furthermore, the prosecution will be happy to produce a witness who can testify to the plaintiff's diagnosis and treatment for this particular disease."

"The defense is not aware of such a witness, Your Honor. We reserve the right to call our own expert."

Phillip remembered that incident. She was a freshman in high school when she came to him, complaining about a burning sensation. He thought it was some teenage girl ailment that would go away on its own. He had promised her he would go to the pharmacist, but he got busy and forgot. Next thing he knew, Constance had taken her to the doctor and he had to leave a business meeting to get to the doctor's office. When the doctor gave the diagnosis, he was shocked. What the heck was going on behind his back? he wondered at the time. Now she couldn't have children on her own because of it. Who the hell knew it would come to this?

The judge had had it with the dueling attorneys. He called them to the bench for a side bar. When it was over, a subdued McCloud had no further questions for Marc. It was time for Bosch to have her turn.

"Mr. Kasai, could you describe the kind of marriage you and your wife share?"

Marc relaxed his posture. "We are very happy. We share everything. She's my best friend."

"You share everything, yet she didn't tell you that her father was right here in Boston?"

"I already explained why."

"Yes, yes you did," Bosch said. "Mr. Kasai, isn't it true that your wife lied to you for months, and in fact, she went to great lengths to cover up the fact that her father was back in her life?"

"Can you blame her?"

"Isn't it true that your wife went behind your back and hired a private investigator to dig up dirt on my client and lied to you about it?"

""She was trying to—"

"Just answer the question, yes or no?"

"Yes."

"So your wife, who you adore and with whom you share everything, made a fool out of you by deliberately deceiving you repeatedly?"

McCloud would have none of it and objected vigorously. "Your Honor, defense council is badgering the witness, who already admitted his wife lied to him."

"Move it along, Ms. Bosch."

"No more questions for this witness."

Ronald Johnson, a friend of her father's for over twenty years, took the stand next. He was one of the few of her father's friends Nina truly liked. He was warm and caring and didn't tolerate bullshit. McCloud's questioning was brief, mostly focused on Johnson's observations of the relationship between Nina and her father, and his impression of Nina.

"You mentioned that the defendant took his daughter everywhere with him. Did you notice anything odd or strange about their interaction?"

He said nothing.

"Mr. Johnson, I asked you a question," McCloud pressed.

"No."

"May I remind you that you're under oath? I'll ask you again, did you notice anything out of the ordinary about the defendant's interaction with his daughter?"

Ronald took a deep breath and looked over at his friend at the defense table with a tinge of regret. Nina knew he wasn't testifying willingly. The prosecution had subpoenaed him.

"We were at a barbecue at a friend's house and I was teasing Nina about a crush she had on one of the boys at the party. She was about fifteen at the time. Her father overheard us and took her away. When I saw her about a half hour later, she looked like she had been crying."

"Then what happened?"

"She asked me if I she could come live with me and my family because her daddy was not a nice man. I'll never forget the look on her face," Ronald said, shaking his head. "Those big green eyes pleading with me. It's haunted me ever since."

"Why is that, Mr. Johnson?"

"I had this feeling that something wasn't right. It was the way she looked at me. I told myself I just felt sorry for her, but it wasn't until ..."

"Go on," the DA urged.

"It wasn't until a mutual acquaintance told me several months after the barbecue that there were rumors going around, that I started wondering if there was a connection."

"What rumors?"

Bosch objected. "We're here to deal in facts, not rumors and heresay."

"Your Honor, this establishes the don't ask, don't tell attitude surrounding this case. Mr. Johnson has had a personal relationship with both the defendant and the plaintiff and he should be allowed to tell the court what he knows."

"I'll allow it, but get to the point quickly."

"What rumors, Mr. Johnson?"

Ronald Johnson looked extremely uncomfortable. He began to sweat. He yanked a handkerchief from this jacket pocket and dabbed the sweat from his forehead. "She told me there was a rumor going around that Phillip was sleeping with his oldest daughter." He seemed relieved after getting that out.

"What was your reaction to such a shocking claim?"

"I was angry. I told the lady that it was a disgusting thing to say. Phillip had been my friend for many years and I knew how much he loved his children."

"Who is the woman who told you this disturbing story?"

"Charlotte Coleman."

"Is Mrs. Coleman in the courtroom today?"

He nodded.

"Please point her out for the jury."

Ronald did and McCloud concluded his questioning.

"Mr. Johnson, in all the time you've known Dr. Copeland, have you ever heard him speak ill of his daughter or say anything to indicate their relationship was rocky?" Bosch asked.

"No, not at all."

"In fact, my client had nothing but praise for his daughter, isn't that right?"

"Yes. Phillip bragged about both his girls, but he was always worried about Nina."

"Why is that?"

"He said he had to protect her from inappropriate boys because she was beautiful and naïve, a dangerous combination."

"You testified that Nina asked if she could live with you and your family, and it looked like she'd been crying. But couldn't it be argued that most teenage girls at some point pretend to hate their parents because they can't get their way?"

"Yes, I have three daughters, so I know."

Bosch smiled. "Did Nina ever ask you again if she could live with you?"

"No, she didn't."

"So this whole incident could be chalked up to a teenage girl angry with her father over a boy. You said he was a protective father. Isn't it possible that Dr. Copeland thought the boy she had a crush on was inappropriate or could bring harm to his 'naïve daughter,' to use your term?"

"Yes, it's possible."

After lunch, the prosecution called Charlotte Coleman to the stand. Charlotte was a short, round woman who looked like she was wearing every piece of jewelry she owned.

"Mrs. Coleman, were you and your family close to the defendant?"

"Yes, my husband and I have known Phillip for many years; he's godfather to our son, Nathan."

"In written testimony you stated that the defendant had a normal relationship with his daughter, but Mr. Johnson testified that you told him otherwise. Could you please explain the discrepancy?"

"At first they seemed normal, but then things got strange."

"What do you mean by that?"

"The way he controlled her—what she wore, who her friends were ... she couldn't have a sleepover, go to the mall, wear makeup."

"Where did you get this information?"

"My daughter, Zoe."

"Did anything else happen that made you think things had gotten *strange*?"

"I ran into Constance Buckwell."

"Constance Buckwell, the former caretaker of the defendant's children, including Nina?"

"Yes."

"What did Ms. Buckwell say to you?"

"She said it wasn't right what Phillip was doing to his daughter and he needed to stop."

"Did you ask her what she meant?"

"I did. She said he was sleeping with his own daughter and she caught him sneaking into her room at night many times."

"No further questions for this witness."

Bosch was anxious to start cross-examining Charlotte. "Is this the same Constance Buckwell who was dismissed by my client because she proved untrustworthy?"

"Yes."

"So it's fair to say that Ms. Buckwell has a history of being less than truthful?"

"I guess so."

"Thank you," a jubilant Bosch said as she walked back to the defense table.

*   *   *

IT WAS AN EXHAUSTING DAY of legal maneuvering and Nina was glad to see the inside of her bedroom. All she wanted to do was to sink into the Jacuzzi and let the bubbles take her troubles away, albeit temporarily. She hit the play button on the answering machine as she undressed and stopped cold.

"Nina, this is Constance. You need to stop this foolishness and leave that man alone. You can't prove nothing and you're just going to look silly in front of a bunch of strangers, you stupid girl. Anyway, don't say I didn't warn you."

Don't say I didn't warn you kept playing in Nina's head over and over again. Something was odd about that message. Why would Constance call her now that the trial had started? She must have been told she was to have no contact with either side of the case, since she was a key witness; frankly, she was *the* key to the prosecution's case.

Nina squashed the Jacuzzi idea and searched her purse for the piece of paper Constance had written her phone number on during their awkward encounter at Christabelle's last year. Constance picked up on the third ring.

"Thank God you picked up," Nina said anxiously. "What did you mean by that voice message you left me?"

"I can't talk right now, I'm at work."

"Don't hang up," Nina said sharply. She was already questioning the legality of calling Constance back, and she knew she'd lose her nerve if she had to call again. "Since the trial already started, you shouldn't have called me. You know that. I'm not going to tell the DA because I figure whatever you have to say must be important. So out with it."

"This trial won't end well for you. You're wasting your time."

"And I'm sure you're going to tell me why."

"I'm your star witness. That's what the prosecutor said."

"You have my attention."

"I don't know nothing. I didn't see nothing, didn't hear nothing. That's what I'm telling the court."

"I see."

"What happened was none of my business, anyway. You got what you deserved."

Nina could feel her rage simmering but she had to show restraint. "You're entitled to your feelings, even if they're disturbing."

"What did you expect? Always batting those big green eyes at him, Daddy can I have this, Daddy can I have that? You did whatever he asked. You were easy," she taunted Nina.

"I feel sorry for you."

"Life isn't fair, little girl. Was it fair that he was so obsessed with you that he couldn't see what was right under his nose? I wasn't asking for much. I could be discreet."

She wanted him for herself, Nina thought. *That's why she got pissed and wouldn't help me. Pathetic bitch!*

"Theresa hated you, too," Constance continued without pausing. "You were screwing her husband. They divorced because of you."

Nina wanted to cry at the sheer cruelty of the woman. She would have to tell McCloud that their key witness was planning to lie under oath. It would present a problem in that Constance was their key witness and Nina had no business communicating with her, but she would let McCloud earn his salary and figure out how to spin that to their advantage.

"You have to make this right. You've been a coward for far too long."

When Nina got downstairs, Marc had dinner ready. Her mother was in the family room, watching the evening news.

"We almost sent out a search party. What took you so long?"

"It was awful. She actually hates me."

"Who hates you?" her mother yelled from the family room.

Nina relayed a censored version of her conversation with Constance.

This upset her mother, who soon excused herself and said she was going to bed. Nina had learned that was her mother's code phrase for "I'll sit in my room and wallow in guilt and regret."

CHAPTER THIRTY

The telephone rang at three a.m. A drowsy Nina answered it.

"I have bad news."

She didn't need a psychic to tell her that. It was three in the morning.

"What is it?" she asked Dan McCloud.

"It's Constance Buckwell. She's dead, Nina."

Nina turned on the lamp on the nightstand and rubbed the sleep from her eyes.

"How could she be dead? I just spoke to her last night. She emphatically told me she was going to lie on the witness stand."

"It's a tough break, for her and for us." Dan McCloud couldn't hide his disappointment. Even at this ungodly hour, he was thinking like a lawyer.

"How did she die?" Nina asked.

"Heart attack. She was on her way home and collapsed on the bus. She made it to the hospital alive but died shortly afterwards."

"This isn't a good time to bring this up, but we just suffered a major setback and we need to rethink our strategy," McCloud said. "This case is going to come down to your testimony. I'm still optimistic about our chances, but you have to be the most compelling witness in this case. Your recollection of details is what's going to persuade a jury to vote for a conviction. Can you meet me at seven?"

Nina shook Marc awake. "We have big trouble."

"What?" he asked without moving.

"Constance is gone. No more star witness."

Marc popped up like a Jack-in-the-Box. "Where did she go?"

To hell is my best guess.

"She bought the farm."

"She ran away to buy a farm?"

"She's dead, Marc."

"Are you sure?"

Nina got out of bed and put on the main bedroom light. "Are you with me now? She had a heart attack."

"That's lousy news. Do you want to talk about it?"

"No."

"It's okay if you feel sad. You lived in the same house with her. I'm sure you have a lot of memories."

Nina had many memories, most of them confusing. One of the bright spots in her relationship with Constance came junior year in high school. Constance convinced her father to allow Nina to attend a two-week leadership camp. Only a handful of students were chosen from each school district, and Nina made the final cut. Her father had Nina on punishment for some stupid thing or another and said she couldn't go, no matter how Nina pleaded the benefits to her academic record. In the end, Constance won and Nina was allowed to attend. It changed Nina's life. Next to her grades, that camp was one of the most significant elements of her college application; it helped her get academic scholarships to top Ivy League schools. Nina would always be grateful to Constance for sticking up for her that one time.

"Dan wants us to meet with him at seven. Her loss will change our strategy for the trial."

* * *

NINA WOKE UP WITH A massive headache. The mood at the breakfast table was somber.

"How did she die?" her mother asked.

Marc relayed what little information they had to Daphne.

"Where does that leave us?" her mother asked. "She was supposed to be the centerpiece of the prosecution's case."

"We're meeting with the DA soon."

Nina started giggling without warning.

"What's so funny?" her husband asked.

"Her truth would have sent him to prison, her lies could have gotten him off."

Nina recalled her last conversation with Constance. Until the very end, she was loyal to her feelings for her former employer and was willing to perjure herself to protect him. It occurred to Nina that Constance was a disturbed woman whose sense of right and wrong was deeply flawed. It had to be. There was no way a normal person could allow abuse to continue because she was angry that the perpetrator was paying attention to the victim instead of her. Nina had read books on incest where in some cases, the mother of the victim would allow the abuse to happen and often participated in it. The experts said it was because such women were angry with their daughters and in most cases, wanted to preserve their financial security by keeping the father in the home. The only difference was that Constance wasn't her mother, but she was as much to blame as Phillip because she deliberately chose to remain quiet.

She survived her father and Constance. *And if it's the last thing I do,* Nina told herself, *I'll survive this trial, too.*

*　*　*

WHEN MELINDA BOSCH GAVE HIM the news of Constance's death, Phillip knew he was supposed to feel sorry but he didn't. She was the one loose end that could potentially send him to prison, no matter how much she claimed to be on his side. She could be easily duped and he didn't trust her not to crumble under the pressure of a criminal investigation. Some overzealous detective could get her to say what he wanted, and she wasn't smart enough to see through a tactic like that. If the prosecution's case rested on her testimony and she was no more, they had no case. They may as well dismiss all the charges against him. Another bright spot was that his loyal Cassie was in the courtroom this morning and would testify on his behalf.

When Team Nina arrived in the courtroom, the defense was already present. She looked in her father's direction and was rewarded with a smirk. Cassie, who was also present, ignored her. Nina welcomed a friendly face in the form of Charlene.

"How are you holding up?" her best friend inquired.

"I'm still in shock," Nina said.

"You're almost at the finish line."

"Someone keeps moving it. Are you ready for your smack down, Bosch-style?"

"I could take her, the way they do in the hood."

"Charlene, you grew up in Westwood," Nina admonished.

"That doesn't mean I don't know how they roll in the hood. Don't worry. I got your back."

The judge called the court to order.

"It's been brought to my attention that the prosecution's key witness has passed on. However, the State has decided to move forward with the case as scheduled. Your next witness, Mr. McCloud."

Charlene was sworn in.

"How long have you known the defendant, Ms. Hamilton?"

"Twenty-two years. He's the father of my best friend."

"Tell us about your relationship with the defendant's daughter."

"We met freshman year of high school and have been best friends ever since."

"In all the years you've been best friends, have you known Mrs. Kasai to be a liar?"

"No. We're brutally honest with each other, even when it hurts."

"Yet she never told you about her father?"

It was a brilliant strategy Nina acknowledged. Knock out the defense's argument before they had a chance to make it, thereby limiting any advantage they could derive from Charlene's testimony.

"I don't think she had any intention of telling anyone, including both me and her husband."

"Why not?"

"She told me it made her sick to her stomach and she was afraid people would judge her. She couldn't take it if we did, too."

"But you were her best friend," McCloud insisted.

"It didn't matter. She kept it private because she thought no one would understand."

"Why did she finally tell you?"

"She found out I was sleeping with him. She couldn't handle it so she ended our friendship. She told me later why she had been so angry with me—it was because he molested her."

"Please tell the court what Mrs. Kasai told you, in as much detail as possible."

"We were at my salon on Newbury Street. She explained that he got violent with her. She showed me a couple of fading scars, where he hit her. She then told me about the abuse. She said she had to be perfect at all times, as a way to get him to stop hurting her."

A couple of jurors were clearly uncomfortable with what they just heard and began fidgeting. Phillip, still defiant, looked straight at them.

"Ms. Hamilton, what happened when you and Mrs. Kasai were in the 10th grade?"

Charlene started chewing her fingernails.

"Answer the question," the judge ordered her.

"We were walking to school one day, chatting like we normally did. All of a sudden, she stopped talking. I looked over to find out why she stopped talking and she was standing in the middle of oncoming traffic."

"Then what happened?"

"I screamed out her name but she wouldn't move, like she was in a trance. There was a car coming at her full speed and the driver saw her almost too late. He braked hard and missed her by this much," Charlene said, holding up her thumb and index finger an inch apart.

"What else?"

"The driver was pissed. He got out of the car and started yelling at both of us."

"What did Nina say about this almost tragic event?"

"She said she just wanted it to stop."

"She wanted what to stop?"

"She wouldn't tell me. She said she wished the car had hit her, at least that way she'd be dead and wouldn't have to deal with it anymore."

"Was that normal behavior for Nina?"

"No. Nina doesn't do crazy."

"Did you call her parents?"

"She told me not to bother calling her father, it would just make things worse."

"Didn't you think that was odd?"

"I did."

"Why?"

"Her family was the black Brady Bunch, just with less kids. I thought they would want to know if she was in danger."

"So you never told her father about the incident?"

"No. Nina swore she would never do anything like that again. She made me promise to never speak of it. We never have ... until now."

"Is there anything else you recall during your teenage years that may have stood out, anything Nina might have said?"

"Nina seemed tense whenever she was around her father. He always wanted to know where she was, what time she was coming home. He would call my house to verify she was there."

"What did you make of that?"

"I thought he was a bit controlling but I understood ... at least, I thought I understood at the time."

"Can you explain what you mean by that statement?"

"Nina and I grew up in strict Caribbean households where you obeyed your parents. You never questioned them and they kept a tight rein over your life. I just thought Dr. Copeland was that way."

"Do you believe Nina was afraid of her father?"

"Objection," Bosch yelled.

"Withdrawn."

McCloud moved on to a different line of questioning after he took a sip of water.

"What can you tell the court about the role the defendant played in his daughter's wedding, if any?"

"What do you mean?"

"Well, was he the doting father of the bride? Did he give her away on her wedding day?"

"She didn't want him to know she was getting married. She said he didn't deserve the honor of walking her down the aisle, and she didn't want it mentioned again."

The DA thanked Charlene for her testimony and returned to his seat.

Bosch made a spectacle of sipping a glass of water, glancing at her notepad and clearing her throat before she approached Charlene.

"You testified that you and Mrs. Kasai are best friends, but she never mentioned this alleged abuse. That leads me to conclude either your friendship is not as close as you would have us believe, or," she paused for dramatic effect, "Mrs. Kasai is lying and this whole trial is a farce."

"Objection, Your Honor," a clearly annoyed McCloud shouted. "Ms. Hamilton is not on trial and defense counsel is out of line to call the plaintiff a liar before all the evidence is in."

"Ms. Bosch, stick to the facts, please," the judge admonished. "The jury may disregard the last statement. I will not tolerate grandstanding from either one of you."

Defense counsel apologized to the court, but her demeanor revealed a woman who wasn't in the least bit sorry.

"Ms. Hamilton, how well do you know my client?"

"Not very well."

"Really?" Bosch walked to the defense table and picked up a document.

"I'd like to enter this photograph as Exhibit A, Your Honor."

After the judge nodded his agreement, Bosch waved the photograph in front of Charlene. "Could you tell the court who the people are in this photo?"

The DA had gone over testimony regarding this particular piece of evidence with Charlene but she stalled anyway. Nina guessed she was embarrassed that her dalliance with her best friend's father was now out for all to see. Knowing Charlene, she didn't care what they thought. She was more worried about Nina.

Bosch was getting impatient and practically barked at Charlene to answer her question.

"It's a picture of me and Dr. Copeland."

"Where was it taken?"

"On vacation in St. Barts."

McCloud voiced his displeasure at the line of questioning. "I fail to see how this photo has any bearing on this trial. This is a criminal proceeding, not some tabloid TV show Your Honor."

Bosch eagerly responded. "This speaks directly to the credibility of this witness. She portrayed my client in a very damaging light, yet here she is, looking quite happy to be in his company on a luxury vacation."

Unfortunately for the prosecution, the judge allowed Bosch to continue her tirade against Charlene. Everything went downhill from there. Charlene was forced to admit that she deliberately kept Nina in the dark about the affair until Merriman found proof of her duplicity. Bosch trapped Charlene into admitting that an honest person would not consistently lie to her best friend. The defense all but discredited Charlene. But it wasn't enough for Bosch.

"Ms. Hamilton, did your best friend alert you to the fact that her husband never knew my client was her dad?"

"Yes."

"And you agreed to help her deceive her husband?"

"It wasn't like that."

"What was it like? We'd love to know."

Charlene stuck her chin out. Nina recognized the defiant glint in her eyes that said, *look bitch, you don't scare me.*

"Nina was always unhappy around her father and that went on for years. It wasn't hard to see she was better off without him in her life. If she had told me all those years ago what he did, his sorry ass would have been in jail because I would have gone to the cops myself."

The courtroom exploded in noisy chatter. The judge called for order and Bosch asked to have Charlene declared a hostile witness, which the judge refused to do.

"You testified that my client was controlling and overbearing. But isn't it fair to say that my client was doing what any caring parent would do, protecting his child from bad influences such as yourself?"

"I don't know what you mean."

"Have you ever tried marijuana, Ms. Hamilton?"

"A few times."

The prosecution objected.

"Your Honor, this line of questioning goes toward establishing the witness' history of questionable choices and the plaintiff's pattern of deceit."

"I'll allow this to go on but briefly. If you fail to prove relevance, you'll have to move on."

"Ever smoke in front of Mrs. Kasai?

"Once or twice."

"Did she ever try it?"

"Never."

"Tell the truth, Ms. Hamilton."

"She hated the way it smelled and it gave her a headache."

"So you and Nina Kasai have been keeping each other's secrets for years. My client knew you were a bad influence on his daughter and tried to shield her from you, is that right, Ms. Hamilton?"

"Nope."

The defense knew it was time to quit.

It was the prosecution's turn to clean up the debris from the bomb of Charlene's testimony. Dan McCloud would need a herculean effort on redirect to salvage her testimony.

"Of all the men in the world you could have dated, why were you having an affair with your best friend's father?"

"It didn't start out that way. He helped me a lot when I was going through some things. I didn't think anything of it because he was Nina's dad. He had known me since I was fourteen."

"What kind of help did he offer?"

"Advice about my future. Encouragement to pursue my career goals and later, he helped me set up my own business."

"When did the nature of your relationship change?"

"After I graduated from hair school. He would send me little gifts. We would have dinner sometimes."

"So he was pursuing you?"

"Yes."

"Did you feel indebted to him?"

"Yes."

"Pressure to accept his advances?"

"Yes."

"Why didn't you tell your best friend?

"I knew I would lose her."

"Your parents are deceased, is that right?"

"Yes."

"Do you have any other family?"

"A brother who lives in DC."

"Do you consider Mrs. Kasai family?"

"Yes. Doctor Copeland made it clear that if I told Nina we were seeing each other, I would lose her for good."

"Was he right?"

"Not quite. Our friendship was broken for a few weeks, but we managed to put it back together."

"Did the defendant use any other tricks to keep you at his side?"

"He said if I told Nina about our affair, he would call in the loan on my salon. He used his contacts at the bank to get me a loan to expand my business."

"Thank you, Ms. Hamilton."

CHAPTER THIRTY-ONE

Theresa's upcoming testimony was a source of great angst for Phillip. Their divorce was amicable and they pretty much kept out of each other's way, but their marriage was frayed with problems, mostly his inability to stay away from other women. He just knew the prosecution would make a big deal about it. There was nothing he hated more than his private life out there for others to see. That was one of the reasons this trial was tough on him. The press had mostly been low-key since this wasn't a regular rape trial. He wasn't sure if that worked in his favor or not. The last thing he wanted was a bunch of cameras in his face and to be the lead story on the six o'clock news. On the other hand, he was being accused of molesting his own daughter. The stigma of that would never go away, even when the jury came back with a not guilty verdict.

Nina watched as Theresa Jones, who had reverted back to her maiden name after she divorced Phillip, took the stand. She was average looking with large eyes and a mouth too wide for her face, but she had a killer body and a sharp wit that drew people to her. As a senior vice president for Bettencourt's, she had access to the best cosmetics and beauty products on the market and made the most of it. Nina imagined she wasn't pleased leaving New York to come to Boston for the trial. On the bright side, she would get to see Cassie. Theresa was a huge unknown in this equation. She could send the father of her only child to prison or portray Nina as a liar.

"Ms. Jones, how long were you and the defendant married?" McCloud inquired.

"Almost fifteen years."

"And how did Nina enter your lives?"

"When Phillip and I were dating, he told me he had a daughter with his ex-wife and maybe one day she would come to live with him, but he wanted her to be a little older."

"Why did he want her to be older?"

"He thought it might be an easier transition with an older child. She would be able to do things for herself while he was busy climbing the corporate ladder."

"How did you react?"

"I was okay with it. He was up front about it from the beginning, so when we got serious and started to discuss marriage, I knew I was coming into a ready-made family."

"According to earlier testimony by Mrs. Lockwood, the defendant virtually ignored his daughter after they divorced. How did he react to the prospect of actually having to raise a child?"

"He admitted he didn't want Nina at first, but once she was born and time went by, he came to terms with the situation and made plans to raise her."

Nina looked at her mother. This couldn't be easy for her.

"How did Nina adjust to having new parents practically overnight?"

"She missed her mother and her family back in the islands, which was to be expected, but she adjusted well to her new life. You know kids—they're resilient."

"How would you describe your relationship with Nina?"

"I tried to be a good substitute mother for her. I could never replace her biological mother."

"What was her relationship with her father like?"

"She was eager to get to know him. She asked a lot of questions. She wanted him to like her."

"Did he?"

"Yes."

"Would you say they grew close?"

"I would."

"What was the atmosphere in the household like?"

"Fine."

"Could you elaborate, Ms. Jones?"

"We were a typical American family in a lot of ways, a two-parent household. My own daughter, Cassie, was two years old when Nina came to live with us. Phillip worked a lot as an executive at Wellington Investments, but we had a comfortable life. Nina had everything she could ever want."

"Did that include being molested by her father?"

The defense objected. The DA withdrew the question.

"Ms. Jones, would you say the defendant and his daughter had a normal father-daughter relationship?"

"Yes. They sometimes clashed, but that's to be expected from a teenage girl."

"What did they clash about?"

"Rules, boys—that kind of thing. Phillip was very strict by some standards and insisted that Nina had chores and followed the rules. She wasn't allowed to have so much as a phone call from a boy."

"Why was that?"

"He thought she was too young, and that boys would distract her from her studies."

"How did Nina react?"

"She followed his rules, but like I said, there was conflict from time to time."

"How would the defendant react whenever his daughter voiced her displeasure regarding the rules?"

"He would give her the silent treatment. She hated that."

"In other words, he used psychological intimidation to get his daughter to cooperate."

"Objection."

"Keep the editorials to a minimum, Mr. McCloud," the judge admonished.

"Tell me, Ms. Jones, were you present when your ex-husband beat his teenage daughter senseless?"

Bosch objected on the grounds that the allegations had no basis in fact, and asked that the question be stricken from the record.

"Your Honor, these are not baseless allegations, not to the state, and certainly not to Nina Kasai, who will testify to the physical and sexual abuse she suffered at the hands of the defendant."

"Then save it for her testimony," a clearly annoyed Judge Sokoff said.

"Ms. Jones, were you aware that your ex-husband was molesting his older daughter?"

"No, I was not."

"You testified that you tried to be a good substitute mother for Nina. Wouldn't that mean looking out for her best interests and knowing if something was wrong?"

Theresa was visibly upset as her parenting skills were called into question. "I didn't see any signs to indicate any type of abuse was going on."

"Are you certain of that, Ms. Jones? There were no unexplained absences from your bed late at night? No weird noises or suspicious behavior on the part of the defendant?"

Theresa looked like she was about to bust out of the stand and head out of the building faster than a NASCAR driver.

"We're waiting, Ms. Jones." McCloud did little to hide his agitation.

"Phillip was a workaholic," Theresa said wearily. "He often worked late into the night."

"But you were suspicious at times?"

"The witness already answered the question," said defense counsel.

"Your Honor, Ms. Jones was married to the defendant for almost two decades. She would be well aware of his behaviors and habits."

The judge allowed the DA to continue the line of questioning.

"There were a few instances when I was waiting up for him and he came to bed late. When I asked him where he'd been, he said he was watching a late night program on TV."

"Didn't you find that odd? Especially if he knew you were waiting up for him?"

"I thought so but I didn't push the issue."

"Why not?"

"I don't know."

"Isn't it possible that you didn't want to know? You were afraid of what you might find out?"

"I didn't give it much thought."

"What was your sex life like with the defendant?"

The question was unexpected. Theresa was visibly embarrassed. The defense couldn't object fast enough.

"This is absurd, Your Honor."

"This line of questioning is highly relevant, Your Honor. I'm establishing whether or not the defendant had unique sexual proclivities that would substantiate the Commonwealth's case."

The judge directed Theresa to answer the question. Bosch was not happy.

"It was fine."

"Did you and your ex-husband have an active sex life?"

"Y-yes."

"How often?"

"What?"

"How often did you and the defendant engage in marital sex?"

"Phillip and I worked a lot," Theresa mumbled.

"Once a week, several times a week, once a month?" McCloud was not about to go easy on Theresa.

"It varied."

"At any time during your marriage, was there a decline in the frequency of sex?"

"All married couples go through dry spells."

"A simple yes or no will do."

"Yes."

"When?"

"I don't recall exactly."

McCloud wasn't getting the response he wanted, so he changed tactics.

"Did the defendant ever cheat on you during your marriage?"

Theresa looked like she was about to be sick. "We had our troubles like everyone else."

"So he *did* cheat, correct?"

"Yes."

"Was this a one-time thing or were there multiple instances of infidelity?"

"It happened more than once."

"Were you aware of who the women were?"

"Sometimes."

"Would you describe them as young?"

"What do mean by 'young'?"

"Significantly younger than the defendant, twenty years or more his junior."

"I guess so."

"Is it safe to say the defendant had an appetite for young girls?"

Bosch objected. "He's leading the witness, Your Honor."

Theresa looked in her ex-husband's direction. It couldn't be easy for her, given they shared a daughter and had to be in each other's lives.

"I guess so."

"Why did you and your ex-husband divorce?"

"Irreconcilable differences."

"Well, what was the final blow to the marriage?"

Theresa wouldn't answer right away. She kept folding and unfolding her hands.

"We're waiting, Ms. Jones. What finally ended your marriage?"

"Phillip wouldn't forgive me for cheating just to get back at him."

The defense's cross-examination zeroed in on the fact that Theresa had no way of knowing the exact age of the women her ex was involved with, and therefore couldn't say for sure they were at least twenty years Phillip's junior. Bosch also scored points by getting Theresa to share additional observations about Phillip's treatment of Nina in her presence, which painted Phillip as a stellar father.

Lieutenant John O'Reilly was sworn in. As lead investigator on the case, his testimony would carry a lot of weight. A twenty-five year veteran of the Westwood Police Department, O'Reilly was thorough, relentless and always nailed his man.

"Lieutenant, please tell us what Nina Kasai said to you on the day of July 15th of this year." McCloud was deliberate and confident.

"Mrs. Kasai came to the police precinct and said she wanted to report a crime. I took her into the interrogation room and questioned her about the crime and who the perpetrator was."

"What was the crime and who was the perpetrator?"

"Sexual assault. The perpetrator was her father."

"Did she indicate where this crime took place?"

"At the family residence, 48 Collinsworth Drive in Westwood."

"Who lived with her at that residence?"

"Her father, stepmother, baby sister, and Constance Buckwell, their caregiver."

"When did this crime take place?"

"Alleged crime," Bosch pointed out.

"Over an eight-year period, beginning when Mrs. Kasai was a ten-year-old child to when she was almost eighteen."

"Where in the house would these alleged assaults take place?"

"The acts were mostly confined to her bedroom."

"Did you find her story to be credible?"

"I found Mrs. Kasai to be a very credible witness."

"Why is that, Lieutenant?"

"Her recollection of certain incidents, the time frame, the consistency in her story."

"In our interview, you used the term 'conspiracy of silence' to indicate that many people knew of the plaintiff's plight but refused to help her. Is that your professional opinion of this case based on your investigation?"

"It is."

"What is that conclusion based on?"

"The majority of witnesses interviewed indicated they thought something was wrong, that was consistent throughout the interviews. The only variation was Constance Buckwell."

"Were they outraged, sad, indifferent?"

"Mostly indifferent. They treated the defendant as if he were a god and the allegations against him were just an annoyance."

"What do you mean, they treated him like a god?"

"They talked about all the good he did for the community or for them personally, what a great man he is."

"Lieutenant, is there any evidence to corroborate Mrs. Kasai's recollection of events?"

"Yes. We visited the property, her former residence. The layout was exactly as she described in her deposition."

"Was the property empty when you visited?"

"No, it's been occupied by the current owner."

"Did anything about that visit stand out?"

"Mrs. Kasai's room was directly across from Ms. Buckwell's room."

"In other words, she could see who went in and out of that room?"

"Correct."

"Were the rooms close enough so someone in one of the two rooms could hear what was going on in the other?"

"Yes, they were."

The DA presented photographs of the house as Exhibit A. Nina began to choke up as memories came flooding back. She could hear the stupid whistling sound he made whenever he came to her room. She remembered trying to climb out the window one night when it was ten degrees outside. She got stuck and had to come in hurriedly before he found her trying to escape. She knew a beating would have followed had he caught her.

The defense approached the witness.

"Lieutenant, did any of the witnesses you interviewed produce any evidence to prove that my client abused his daughter?"

"No."

"Did any of the witnesses you interviewed, at any time in the last several years, come forward to report abuse?"

"No."

"Did any of the witnesses ask the plaintiff if her father molested her?"

"No."

"Thank you, Lieutenant."

The trial broke for lunch. Nina was on her way from the ladies' room when she saw him. There was no alternative route to the courthouse entrance where Marc and her mother were waiting. He walked right up to her, taking a quick look to make sure nobody was watching.

"I'll get off free and clear. All of this will be for nothing. People pretend to be outraged, but the truth is, they secretly think you're a slut."

Nina thought of a dozen comebacks. She chose to walk away without uttering a single word.

Cassie ambushed Nina on the courthouse steps.

"Dad is going to get off. How will that make you look?"

"I didn't know you cared, Cassie. Don't worry about me, though. Unlike you, I don't need him to survive."

"That's not true," she said tersely.

"What will you do if he gets convicted? Who will pay your bills? Where will you live?"

Cassie's bravado disappeared as she was forced to confront the possibility of life without her father. Nina could tell she still believed he was innocent; everything would go back to the way it was after the trial.

"He promised to take care of me."

"Don't count on that. His defense is very costly. He may not have the luxury of being quite as generous as he used to be."

Dr. Maeve Issler was sworn in. While she had her hands on the bible, Nina ventured a glance at the defense table. He didn't look happy. Bosch had fought hard to strike Dr. Issler from the witness list, claiming that as Nina's psychiatrist, she would be biased against the defendant. The state won on the grounds that Dr. Issler's impeccable record and extensive expertise on the subject made her impartial.

"Dr. Issler, what is the nature of your relationship with Nina Kasai?" McCloud asked, as he retrieved a document from his briefcase.

"She's my patient."

"And what was she seeing you about?"

"Emotional healing stemming from an incestuous relationship she had with her father." Bosch objected, claiming the statement was prejudicial. The judge allowed it.

"What was your initial impression of Nina?"

"She struck me as highly intelligent and driven, very much in control, or so it seemed at the time. She resented having to seek therapy."

"Why did she feel resentful?"

"She said the idea of having to seek therapy made her feel like she would be living the abuse all over again. She went on to say that she had spent the better part of the last eighteen years carving out a life for herself, free from her father."

McCloud paced the floor, hands in his pocket. "Why would she feel ashamed? She wasn't the instigator or perpetrator."

"Victims of sexual molestation often feel shame and guilt over the abuse. They blame themselves because they believe something about them triggered the abuse."

"Could you explain to the court in layman's terms what your findings were after treating Nina Kasai?"

"Nina exhibited classic symptoms of someone who was molested and who has been forced to confront the situation."

"Please elaborate."

"Victims often exhibit traits such as high levels of secrecy, almost living a double life in some cases. They're prone to psychological conditioning by their aggressors, for example, 'you'll destroy this family if the truth ever comes out'. Sometimes it extends to comments about the victim's physical appearance. They're told they're special, beautiful, etcetera. If the perpetrator is married, the wife is painted as cold, unfeeling, and mean."

"What about relationships with the opposite sex?"

"Perpetrators often discourage victims from interest in the opposite sex. If the female victim has a boyfriend, the perpetrator will make it difficult for her to see him and in many cases, demand that she terminate the relationship."

"Dr. Issler, how many cases of sexual abuse have you treated or consulted on during your career?"

"Hundreds."

"How does Nina compare to what you consider a classic case of sexual abuse?"

"In many ways, Nina's case is typical, yet atypical."

The DA look puzzled and so did the jury. "What do you mean?"

"In many cases, incest survivors take on a sense of displaced anger, either at themselves or their partners. Nina directed her anger at the perpetrator. She didn't engage in some of the self-destructive behaviors victims of incest often exhibit, such as alcoholism or drug abuse, for example."

"Can you think of anything else that makes Nina different from most victims?"

"She has built a fortress around her emotions. Like many victims, she has spent most of her adult life atoning for what she considers a mortal sin."

"In what ways?"

"She had to be successful in all her endeavors whether it be career, marriage, or friendship. She's involved in many charities and does volunteer work despite a demanding career. It's her way of saying to the world, 'I'm worthy in spite of my damaged past'. She has internalized that characterization because she heard it repeatedly from her father."

"What is your professional opinion of the defendant based on your sessions with Nina?"

"Defense objects," Bosch said. "Dr. Issler's opinion of my client is not relevant to this case since she has never met him."

The judge overruled the objection.

"Based on my evaluation of Nina and my expertise on the subject, Dr. Copeland is what we shrinks call a textbook sociopath."

"For those of us unfamiliar with the term, can you please explain what you mean?"

"Sociopaths by definition are superficially charming, domineering individuals who feel no remorse or shame about what they do to their victims. They don't recognize the rights of others and they feel everything they do is justifiable. Their feelings of entitlement drive them to do whatever it takes to meet their objectives and nothing stands in their way. They typically surround themselves with people they enlist to help them do their dirty work. In many cases, those accomplices end up being victims, because most sociopaths are covertly hostile."

"That's a pretty grim picture. Could a sociopath be dangerous?"

"Absolutely. They allow nothing to stand in their way once they've identified an opportunity to get what they want."

"Dr. Issler, what is your professional analysis of this case?"

"There is no doubt in my mind that Nina Kasai was molested by her father."

The silence was deafening.

"Your witness," McCloud said to Bosch.

"Dr. Issler, is it possible for someone to fabricate a story of sexual molestation?"

"I suppose anything is possible."

"Yes or no?"

"Yes, it's possible."

"Thank you. No further questions for this witness."

CHAPTER THIRTY-TWO

The prosecution's case was winding down with only three witnesses left: Jenny Obasanjo, Sean Merriman, and Nina. She had survived relatively in tact so far, but now came the ultimate test. Would she be able to sustain an onslaught from the defense? Her mother organized a prayer meeting with Nina's pastor to ask God for strength and guidance. Her in-laws had called to wish her luck. Marc was making plans for their post-trial getaway. He would take a month's vacation and work remotely the rest of the time they were away.

Jenny was sworn in and took a seat. Nina was surprised the defense didn't strongly object to her as a witness since she was the ex-wife of one of their key character witnesses. They wouldn't have acquiesced so easily unless they felt confident they could negate her testimony. The DA approached.

"How do you know the defendant?"

"Phillip and my ex-husband have been friends for close to thirty years. We spent time together with the Copelands while we were married."

"What was your reaction when you heard the defendant was being charged with sexual assault against his own daughter?"

"It didn't surprise me."

Nervous murmurs came from the courtroom. There were murmurs coming from the gallery and Dan McCloud looked pleased with the response.

"Why weren't you surprised by these stunning allegations?"

"Because he's guilty. He defiled that precious little girl and acted like it was no big deal."

"You seem very sure of yourself."

"I am."

"What leads you to believe he's guilty?"

"The tape. It was all on the tape."

"Could you please tell the court what tape you're referring to?"

"Ben, my ex-husband, began recording incoming phone calls to our home."

"Why did he do that?" McCloud suppressed a smirk.

"Our nanny at the time was good friends with Constance Buckwell, who worked for the Copelands. The two of them would trade gossip about what was going on in the homes of their respective employers. Ben is a very private man and didn't want his household affairs discussed by the help, so he wanted proof before he fired Gloria."

"Gloria was your nanny?"

"Yes."

"What did your ex-husband discover on the tape?"

Jenny got emotional, tears pricking the corner of her eyes.

"I know this is difficult," McCloud said, "but you have to tell us exactly what was said on that tape."

"Constance told Gloria that Phillip was—"

Jenny began to hiccup uncontrollably. The DA poured a glass of water from the pitcher at the prosecution's table and handed it to her. After she gulped down the water, McCloud pressed on.

"What did Constance tell Gloria?"

"That Phillip was fucking his own daughter."

There was an eerie silence in the courtroom. The only noise was the clock ticking its second hand. Nina looked at her father. He lowered his gaze. When the DA was satisfied the dramatic impact had hit its mark, he continued.

"How did Dr. Obasanjo react to this devastating revelation?"

"He was as shocked as I was."

"Did you say anything, tell anyone?"

"No. Ben asked me not to."

"Why?"

"He said if the authorities got wind of the tape, they would remove Nina from the home and put her in foster care until her mother could come get her. He said he would talk to Phillip and tell him to cut it out."

"And did he?"

"I don't know. Ben never told me whether he did or not."

"What happened to the tape?"

"Ben destroyed it."

McCloud's eyes widened dramatically. He made sure the jury could see him. "Did you see him do this?"

"He told me he did."

"So it's your testimony here today that your ex-husband, Dr. Benjamin Obasanjo, was in possession of a recording that proves beyond the shadow of a doubt that the defendant molested his own daughter?"

"That is my testimony."

They all come tumbling down, Phillip thought. No Constance to get trapped by the prosecution, no tape that could be misconstrued, thanks to Ben. It would come down to his word against Nina's. He couldn't wait for Bosch to go at her. So far, he had no reason not to be optimistic. The burden of proof was on the prosecution. All the defense had to do was raise reasonable doubt and there was plenty to go around.

The defense pounced on Jenny.

"Did this tape really exist, or is this story a total fabrication by a bitter divorcée who saw an opportunity to get even with her ex?"

"No," Jenny said forcefully. "The tape existed. I heard it with my own ears."

"So you're saying your ex-husband destroyed evidence of a crime?"

"Yes. Phillip knew Ben would never turn him in. That's why he was comfortable all this time, until now."

"What do you do for a living?"

"I'm a physical therapist."

"What did you do before that?"

The prosecution objected. "I fail to see what Ms. Obasanjo's career has to do with this trial."

"I'm getting to that."

"Sometime this decade, Ms. Bosch," the judge said.

"I was a receptionist."

"And before that, you worked part-time as a security guard while living with your sister, is that right?"

"Yes," a mortified Jenny said.

"Ms. Obasanjo, did you fall on hard times after you and your ex-husband divorced?"

"I guess you could say that."

"In fact, you and your ex-husband had a rather acrimonious divorce in which you were left with nothing, including your children, whom you lost in a bitter custody fight."

"Ben can be mean."

"You don't get along with your ex-husband, do you?"

"Our relationship is strained."

"And you would love nothing more than payback?"

"What I said about the tape is the truth. None of that other stuff matters. He heard it and I heard it."

"Yet this mysterious tape seems to have disappeared without a trace, and we only have the word of an angry ex-wife who wants to stick it to her husband as proof that it ever existed. Thank you, Ms. Obasanjo."

The people called Sean Merriman, twenty-year veteran of the Boston Police Department and private investigator, to testify.

"Mr. Merriman, why did Nina Kasai hire you?"

"She was being blackmailed and she wanted information to protect herself."

"What did the blackmailer want?"

"He wanted her to work on a project for him and threatened to expose their connection to her unsuspecting husband if she didn't cooperate."

"Why was it important for her to keep their connection a secret?"

"She didn't go into details. She only acknowledged he had done something really horrific."

"Did she reveal to you what their connection was?"

"No."

"What did Nina want you to do?"

"Find any information she could use to make him back off and leave her alone."

"Did she identify the blackmailer?"

"Yes. She said it was Phillip Copeland."

"Were you surprised?"

"Very much so."

"Why?"

"Because he's an important man in this town. From my observation, Nina was a little afraid of him. I couldn't imagine what he did that was so bad, being who he is."

"Did you find anything that could have helped your client 'get him off her back' as you say?"

"Yes. I found out that Dr. Copeland had an illegitimate child, a little boy of eight."

"What else?"

"That the boy's mother was underage when she became pregnant."

"Your Honor, I'd like to enter into evidence Exhibit B, the birth certificate of Alexander Phillip Forbes. You will see that the defendant is listed as the child's father. Exhibit C is the birth certificate of Tracey M. Forbes."

The judge accepted the documents into evidence. Merriman was thanked for his testimony.

The defense had one point to make.

"In your line of work, have you ever come across someone lying about their age?"

"Yes."

"So isn't it possible that Ms. Forbes lied about her age when she was with my client, claiming to be older than she was?"

"I suppose it's possible."

"No further questions."

Now it was up to Nina to clinch the verdict. Before she got called to testify, The DA's paralegal appeared in the courtroom and slipped a note to McCloud. He read it and asked for permission to approach the bench. After talking to the judge for a few seconds, the defense was asked to join the side bar. Bosch was clearly unhappy. The judge announced that new evidence had come to light, evidence the attorneys needed time to examine.

"What's going on?" Nina asked McCloud.

"We just hit the jackpot, thanks to you and a wife who wants to see justice done."

"Huh?"

"We just got word that Geraldine Copeland is in possession of pages from a diary—your diary."

"I'm confused. He stole the diary from my house and I don't think he would have left it lying around. Besides, Geraldine went back to England."

"I know that's what you told me, but apparently there's more to it. I still want to put you on the stand while we sort this out."

The bombshell revelations kept coming. According to the DA, Geraldine, who would be called to testify, snuck into Phillip's den one evening, after she had discovered him shredding pages from what looked like a diary. Her curiosity was satisfied but not in the way she had hoped. She took the pages he hadn't yet shredded, scanned them and put the diary back the way she had found it. Phillip was none the wiser.

Nina would have to provide a sample of her handwriting for comparison and handwriting analysis by an expert. The discovery process for that piece of evidence had to be authenticated. In the meantime, the trial would move forward.

Phillip was blasting his attorney in an intense conversation at the defense table. "You have to suppress that piece of evidence and make sure my wife never takes the stand."

Bosch looked at him gravely. "What's in that diary, Phillip? I can't be blindsided a second time. Your wife contacting the DA is a disaster."

"Then it's your job to make sure she doesn't testify. That's what I'm paying you for."

"I need to know everything that's in that diary and how you got your hands on it. The answers could jeopardize this case and I need the details to prepare a proper defense."

"I told you my daughter is disturbed. I didn't even read most of the damn thing," he lied. "The only thing in that diary was the rambling of a girl who clearly needs professional help. That hack Issler who took the stand should lose her license because she couldn't see through Nina's lies and confusion."

His lawyer didn't push the issue any further and only promised to the do the best job she possibly could under the circumstances, which Phillip was grateful for. *That* bitch *Geraldine*, he thought. How could she betray him like that? Was there a single woman on the planet who was trustworthy?

CHAPTER THIRTY-THREE

One week later, Geraldine Copeland took the stand. Nina smiled to herself as McCloud made a show of praising Geraldine for her courage in coming forward to see justice done at great personal cost. He told her everyone in the courtroom understood how difficult it was for her to testify against her own husband, that she put justice ahead of her personal feelings and she was a hero for doing so.

"Could you tell the court, in your own words, why you're here today?" McCloud began.

Geraldine fidgeted nervously. "I found out something truly ghastly. I couldn't live with myself if I stayed quiet. Gosh, that would make me a monster. Like my ... like Phillip."

"And what did you find out that was so ... ghastly?"

"His daughter told me he molested her when she was a little girl. I could barely believe it. It was just too awful to comprehend, that the man I married ..." Geraldine couldn't say it. She turned as red as her hair.

"I know how difficult this is for you," McCloud said sympathetically. "When you say his daughter, are you referring to Nina Kasai?"

"Yes."

"Did you believe her?"

"I didn't want to at first, but Nina was very certain. She talked about the first time he attacked her with clarity and reference to a series of children's books he had given her as a birthday present when the first

211

incident took place. I read those same books when I was growing up in England. I knew she wasn't lying."

"For the record, could you tell the court the name of the books?"

"It was the *Famous Five* series written by Enid Blyton."

McCloud entered a couple of the books as exhibit B and held it up for everyone to see. "Was there something else that convinced you that your husband had committed these horrible acts?"

"I found her diary. Nina's diary."

"Could you explain how you came to find this diary and what it contained?"

"It was in Phillip's study. One evening, I poked my head in to remind him we were supposed to be watching a film. There was paper in the shredder. I asked what he was doing and he said shredding sensitive business information. The diary was next to him."

"What happened after that?"

"I got curious. I waited a few days, and went to the study when I knew he wouldn't be home for hours. I found the diary in a desk drawer. Most of the pages were already destroyed. I read what was left. It made me violently nauseous."

"I'm sorry to hear that, but please, go on."

"I knew it would only be a matter of time before it would be completely destroyed and gone forever, so I scanned whatever was left and kept them hidden."

"Why did you do that?"

Geraldine toyed with her pearl necklace and remained quiet, her face pensive as if trying to recollect what drove her actions. Nina felt sympathy for her. She knew what it was like to love someone who did awful things.

"I'm not quite sure. I knew Phillip and his daughter were not on the best of terms, and when I read the diary, I understood why. Phillip blatantly lied to me about why their relationship was so acrimonious. He said she was a rebellious girl and he had difficulty controlling her. I knew that diary was the only existing proof the abuse had taken place. It just seemed the right thing to do to hold on to something like that. I had no idea it would come to this."

Phillip sat fuming at the defense table. She set him up plain and simple. He knew he should have kept the den locked like he usually did, but for some reason he was exceptionally busy that week and kept forgetting to lock it. He was confident that no one, especially Geraldine, would dare to enter without his permission. While he was so worried about his daughter causing trouble for him, he couldn't have anticipated that his agreeable, proper British wife would be the one who would do him in. It didn't matter. The defense had yet to put on its case. Cold-blooded killers have gotten off on technicalities. There was no way he was going down for something he didn't do.

"One last question. I know this is very distressing to you but could you share with the court some of the things you discovered in the diary?"

Geraldine closed her eyes then opened them. She was expressionless. Everyone in the courtroom waited on pins and needles to hear what would come out of her mouth next.

"The few pages I was able to salvage had dates on them. The entries referenced the act, how she felt dirty afterwards and wanted to be somebody else."

"Thank you so much."

Before the words were out of McCloud's mouth, Bosch pounced on an obviously weary and uncomfortable Geraldine. "How do you know this diary belonged to Nina Kasai?"

"Because she told me about the abuse. The account in the diary matches what she told me."

"Did these pages reference my client by his first name?"

"No."

"What about his last name?"

"There was no mention of it."

"Did you ask my client about this diary?"

"No, I did not."

"So just to summarize, you found a diary in the home you shared with my client, assumed it documented his abuse of his daughter, but there is no reference to him or his daughter by name and you can't prove the diary belonged to her?"

"Well …

"Thank you, Mrs. Copeland."

McCloud asked for a redirect. "Why didn't you ask your husband who the diary belonged to or how he came to have it in his possession?"

"After I read what was in it, I couldn't. I knew I was dealing with someone not entirely sane, in my opinion."

*   *   *

IT WAS FINALLY HER TURN, the day she'd been dreading for weeks. But it also meant the trial would soon come to a close. Nina was elegantly dressed in a charcoal grey suit and white silk blouse. Her hair was pulled back in the usual chignon.

"I want the jury to clearly see your face when you testify, to show them you have nothing to hide," McCloud had said to her. Now he approached with gentle understanding, yet firm professionalism.

"Are you nervous?"

"No, but let me know when I should be."

Her response yielded nervous laughter from the courtroom.

"What are your feelings toward the defendant?"

Nina contemplated the question. There was still no easy answer. "It's complicated."

"Why is that?

"How much time do you have?"

Dan McCloud smiled. "Why don't you tell the court, in as straightforward a manner as possible, why your relationship with the defendant is complicated?"

"He's the only father I've known since I was ten. I loved him very much at one point in my life. But I also grew to both fear and loathe him."

She could feel herself getting emotional and bit down hard on her lips to shift the pain from emotional to physical.

"Describe for the court what it was like in the first few days after you met your father for the first time."

Nina cleared her throat. "He said he could see I was raised well and I was a well-mannered, polite young lady. He looked forward to us getting to know each other. He said he would provide me with everything and anything I needed and never had to worry."

"How did that make you feel?"

"I was ecstatic. Who wouldn't be?" I wasn't sure what to expect when I arrived and it turned out my father was this important guy who embraced me right away. It certainly made the transition easier. Life was good."

"And how long did the good times last?"

"About a month."

"What changed between you and the defendant?"

"The father-daughter boundary was eliminated."

"How so?"

"He made inappropriate physical contact with me."

"Could you describe when this contact first took place?"

Nina took a deep breath. *Once you get through this part, it gets easier,* she told herself. "He came to my room one night with a belated birthday gift, a series of children's books he knew I liked. I was thrilled with the gift and kissed him on the cheek. After that, things went downhill."

"What happened next?"

Nina relived for the court the first time her father raped her in her bedroom when she was ten years old: the brute force he used to keep her pinned down, his hands over her mouth to muffle her screams, the excruciating pain she felt when he penetrated her, the fear and confusion that followed, and the threat of abandonment if she told anyone.

> *My daddy is a bad man. Mr. Tibbs thinks so, too.*
>
> *Daddy says I'm not supposed to talk about it. He says I can't tell anyone because they would take him away and send Cassie and me to live in foster care. Cassie is only two years old and I'm not sure what foster care is but it doesn't sound good. I love my daddy ... but Mr. Tibbs and I wished he wouldn't come to my room at night because he always brings big trouble.*
>
> *It all started when daddy missed my tenth birthday last month because I was still on the island with Trevor and Mom. Daddy decided to surprise me with what he said grown-ups call a "bee*

lated" birthday present. I said I didn't know what bee lated meant, but Daddy said that was okay because he knew what it meant, and so long as I kept it a secret, he would show me. After Mr. Tibbs and I said our prayers, before we shut off the lights, there was a knock at the door. It was Daddy with a present. The box was so big, it almost didn't fit through my bedroom door.

"I have something special for my beautiful Gazella," Daddy said.

My name isn't really Gazella, but that's what Daddy always calls me. He says it's because I'm graceful and beautiful like a gazelle, which I looked up and which looks something like a cross between a deer and a ballerina. It's a silly nickname because I don't have four legs, but I don't want to make Daddy mad, so I pretend I like it.

"What is it?"

"Why don't you open it up and see?"

He put the box on my bed and sat down. I ripped the ribbons off and took the top off, too. Inside were a lot of books. I love books. I took one from the box and it was called *Five Get Into Trouble,* one of my favorites about the adventures of Juliana, Dick, Anne, Georgina and their dog, Timmy. I couldn't believe it.

"Look again," Daddy said with a big smile on his face.

I picked out another one. *Five on a Secret Trail.* I emptied the box on my bed and a ton of books cam tumbling out, all *Famous Five* novels. I counted them. Twenty-one. My daddy had bought me the entire series of *Famous Five* books.

"This is the best birthday present ever," I said. I wrapped my arms around Daddy's neck and hugged him so tight he almost choked. "Thank you, thank you, thank you infinity."

"You're welcome. You deserve it because you're special. You're smart and beautiful and Daddy needs you to be a good girl. That means you listen to Daddy and no one else. Okay?"

"Okay. How did you know I liked *Famous Five*?"

"Your mother told me you used to spend hours under a mango tree reading those books. She couldn't get you away from them."

"There are *Secret Sevens* too, but I like *Famous Five* better."

"I'm glad I could make you happy. Now it's your turn to make Daddy happy." He leaned down and tapped his cheek twice, looking sideways at me like he expected something, which of course he did.

I gave daddy a kiss on the cheek like usual, but he did the strangest thing. He pulled my face around and kissed me on the mouth, like grown-ups. I didn't know daddies were supposed to do that. Only mommies and daddies did that I thought, and princes and princesses, like on TV and in the movies.

"Can I go to bed now? I'm really tired."

"In a minute," he said. He threw all my brand new books on the floor and I saw one of the covers bend back in a way that I knew would leave a white scar across the glossy picture. I wanted to pick up the books but Daddy said I could pick them up tomorrow.

I wouldn't stop crying and that made Daddy mad.

"Someone is going to hear you if you don't shut up," Daddy said. "Do you want me to get in trouble? This is our secret, only special daddies and daughters do this so you have to keep it a secret. Can you keep a secret? It only hurts the first time, but it will get better, Gazella, you'll see."

After daddy left, I was scared to turn the lights back on. Mr. Tibbs and I decided to be brave. There was blood on my bed and pajamas. Yuck!

Daddy said it would only hurt the first time but he lied. My daddy lies a lot. Even Mr. Tibbs thinks so.

A spine-chilling silence enveloped the courtroom. Nina's emotions were in tatters, as she struggled to stop herself from a full on breakdown. But she had to hang on until the verdict was read. The little girl who wrote that diary entry was depending on her to see it through to the end. The little girl who endured that trauma waited twenty-six years for someone to stand up for her. Nina owed her.

Nina looked at the defense table. His face was expressionless. She wondered what he was thinking.

He was having difficulty controlling his emotions but outwardly, he refused to react. He knew all eyes from the jury were looking at him at various times during Nina's story and he had to force himself to stay focused, return their stares. He was fighting for his dignity as much as his freedom. He remembered the episode she described but it didn't happen that way. If he had any inkling she was so disturbed, he would have hauled her off to a psychiatrist when she was a kid and insisted she needed to be heavily medicated. How was he supposed to know a little affection from him would have unleashed her inner craziness, a craziness which went untreated for so long that he was now in a court of law fighting for his life?

McCloud fussed with his tie then readjusted his glasses for the umpteenth time, a gesture Nina realized was a nervous one.

"How often would the abuse take place?"

"Often enough. It depended on whether or not he was around. If he was traveling on business like he frequently did, nothing happened. If he was around, it was almost every day."

"Wasn't he afraid you would tell someone?"

"He made sure he was in control at all times."

"How did he accomplish that?"

"He needed to know where I was and who I was with at all times. He would tell me there were people who wanted to take him down and they would try to use me to do it, so it was critical that I remain loyal to him. Otherwise, if anything happened to him, I would be alone and possibly become a ward of the state. Charlene was the only person he didn't consider a threat."

"Could you elaborate?"

"As I said, he needed to keep me reined in at all times and I wasn't allowed to get close to anyone he didn't approve of. That included potential boyfriends."

Can you recall any specific incidents to demonstrate what you just testified to?"

"He once followed me to a classmate's house because he suspected the boy I was interested in would be present. About fifteen minutes into the visit, my classmate told me my father was outside and wanted to see me."

"How would you characterize his demeanor at the time?"

"He was breathing fire," she said, trying to lighten the mood.

"Nina, was the defendant ever physically violent towards you?"

Bosch angrily rose to her feet. "Your Honor, this is a travesty. First my client is portrayed a child molester, an accusation I have yet to see any concrete evidence of. Now he's been accused of being a physically abusive parent. How long will Your Honor allow this mockery of the rules of evidence and law to continue?"

Judge Sokoff didn't take kindly to being ridiculed in his own courtroom.

"Ms. Bosch, this is my courtroom and I decide what's admissible and what is not. The next time you want to challenge the way I run my courtroom, I'll hold you in contempt. Objection overruled."

The judge directed Nina to answer the question.

"Yes, the defendant did get violent."

"Could you describe what kind of violence took place?"

"It started out as a slap here or there for 'being disrespectful' as he put it, which meant I said something he didn't like, or challenged him."

"Where did he slap you?"

"Across the face."

"Were there other instances of physical abuse?"

"Yes." Nina closed her eyes as she struggled to suppress one particularly bad memory. She steadied her voice.

"The worst beating I ever got was because Constance told him I was monopolizing her boyfriend's attention. I announced his arrival and without thinking, went back to the living room where I had been listening to music. Her boyfriend sat down and asked me questions about what I was listening to."

"And for the record, what were you listening to?"

"Prince's *Purple Rain* album."

"Continue."

"Constance seemed to take a really long time to come over and greet him. Anyway, she eventually did, and I made myself scarce."

"But that wasn't the end, was it?"

"No. My father confronted me the next day."

"And what did the defendant do?"

"He got out the belt."

"The belt?"

"Yes, a regular belt, leather, as I recall. He hit me a couple of times with it and I decided it wasn't fair. I hadn't done anything wrong. I ran. He chased me around the house."

"How did this abusive incident end?"

"He won," she said flatly. "I have the scars to prove it."

"Nina, how old were you when this incident took place?"

"Fifteen."

"Wasn't there anyone who could help you?"

"My stepmother was out with my sister, and Constance was the only person in the house."

"She made no effort to help you?"

"No."

"Tell the court about your relationship with Constance."

"Things were fine at first, but soon that changed."

"When did things begin to change?"

"When I suspected she knew what was going on. She became a little hostile. We would argue about the silliest things. She became critical of everything I did."

"You mentioned her attitude changed when you suspected she knew what was going on. What made you think that?"

"She told me herself. One day we were arguing about something and her response was, 'at least I'm not sleeping with my father.'"

"Objection—"

"Overruled. I want to hear this," Judge Sokoff said.

Nina glanced at her section of the courtroom. Her mother looked like she was slowly dying. Marc was trying hard to be strong for the both of them, a battle Nina wasn't sure he was winning. She hated to see her loved ones in pain, and the only thing that kept her going was the fact they were at the halfway point. Once she made it through cross-examination, she would be home free.

"How did you react?"

"I was ashamed and humiliated because I thought nobody knew."

"Nina, let's go back to the sexual abuse. Where would it take place?"

"He would mostly come to my room at night when everyone else was asleep."

"Did you ever ask him why he did it, or try to get him to stop?"

"Numerous times. I kept telling him it was wrong. His response was 'lots of fathers and daughters do this.'"

"This next question is critical and I want you to be honest and truthful. Why didn't you ever tell anyone what was happening to you?"

This was the question that had plagued Nina from the very beginning and the answer, if she were to be honest, came down to two things: shame and revulsion.

"There were other people to consider. There was always the threat of foster care, the guilt of dismantling a family. And I couldn't handle the shame."

"That's a lot for a young girl to carry around. What changed your mind? What brought us to this point?"

"The defendant himself." It was true. If her father had never shown up at her office that day, she would have continued to live her life the way she had prior to his visit.

"Can you expand on that?"

"It all started when he paid me a visit a year ago. He still thought of me as the little girl he could manipulate and dominate. When I wouldn't bend to his will as I had in the past, things got ugly. He wanted me to pay for daring to defy him, so he kept pushing and pushing until I finally broke. I decided to do what I should have done a long time ago: let justice take its course."

"That must have been a gut-wrenching decision. Not many people would file criminal charges against a parent."

"It was."

"How did coming forward affect your family?"

"It was difficult. My sister Cassie has refused to speak to me since. In fact, she says we're no longer sisters."

"Thank you Nina. Your witness," McCloud said to the defense.

CHAPTER THIRTY-FOUR

osch approached Nina with steely calm.

"Did you tell your father you were going to get him, that you would make him pay?"

"I did."

"Can you explain what you meant by that?"

"He needed to be held accountable for his actions."

"So you didn't concoct this story of sexual abuse to, as you said, *get him*?"

"No."

"Nina, would you say my client was a responsible father?"

"In what sense?"

"I mean, he provided for you, he educated you, loved you, and wanted the very best for you."

"He provided for me and educated me throughout high school. As for the second part of your question, you'll have to ask a shrink. I don't know if it's possible to love your child and destroy her at the same time. The two seem incompatible to me, but I'm no psychiatrist."

Maybe if she had done what he asked years ago, she could have saved herself a lot of misery and she would be anywhere but sitting in a courtroom, being made to look like a liar in front of a bunch of strangers who had no idea what it was like to have walked in the shoes of a molested child. She should have done it, and no psychiatrist or court of law would have blamed her.

I decided to talk to him about the trouble he brings to my room at night. I have to try, even if I know what will probably follow. I'm sick of staying up, too afraid to go to sleep because he might show up. I'm tired all the time. Mrs. Walsh yelled at me for nodding off in her Spanish class the other day. I can't be falling asleep if I want to ace my AP exams. If I fail any of my classes, I won't get into a good college and then my plan …

Maybe if I tell Dad how it's affecting me at school during the day, he'll listen. I went to the kitchen and found him peeling an orange. Luckily, Cassie was at piano lessons with Theresa. I have to get it all out, really fast, otherwise, Dad will make me nervous and I won't be able to say what I need to.

"I just want you to know I got yelled at for almost falling asleep in Spanish class last week. I don't know if Mrs. Walsh called you, but I have a good reason."

Dad gave me the 'what are you talking about?' look, so I knew Mrs. Walsh hadn't called. He continued peeling the orange. That knife looked really scary. Maybe this wasn't a good time, like I thought it would be.

"Why are you telling me this?"

"Because … because … I was hoping you could help me."

"And how would I do that?"

I never really talked to him about the trouble before. I never told him how it made me feel because he acted like he didn't care. If he cared, he wouldn't do it, right? He knows it upsets me and he does it anyway, but sometimes you have to say stuff out loud, and then maybe the other person will hear you and understand you.

"Maybe … perhaps if … you wouldn't come to my room anymore, I wouldn't be so tired during school."

Dad didn't say anything, just started walking toward me with that knife. There were bits of white still stuck to it and I was scared, scared, scared that I was about to find out just how sharp it was. I wanted to run but my legs wouldn't move, like they were made of iron or something.

Dad lifted the knife hilt-first and handed it to me. "Keep this knife. If I ever bother you again, plunge it into my chest," he said.

I looked at him wide-eyed, like he was some mad scientist or something. He was really serious, I could tell by his eyes, how scary they got. I didn't move, I didn't say anything.

"Take it!" he screamed.

My legs suddenly didn't feel heavy anymore. "I'm sorry," I said. "I'm really sorry."

Then I ran to my bedroom and drowned my sorrows with Mr. Tibbs. Two days later, he was back. My dad lies a lot. Even Mr. Tibbs thinks so.

"Your Honor, I request permission to treat this witness as hostile."

"Request denied."

"You testified earlier that this alleged abuse took place mostly when my client was not traveling. Can you give us a more specific idea of the frequency of these alleged events?"

The prosecution objected. "The witness already answered that question in earlier testimony."

"Not to my satisfaction," the judge said. "Objection overruled."

Nina searched her mind to put her finger on the exact frequency. She knew where the defense was going with this and she had to tread carefully.

"To the best of my recollection, four to five times a week when he wasn't traveling. As his ex-wife testified, he often worked late into the night at home. That meant I was up late, too."

"Mrs. Kasai, who is Sonny Alvarez?"

"A friend."

"How did the two of you meet?"

"We met at Stanford. We kept in touch over the years."

"What exactly is the nature your relationship with Mr. Alvarez?"

"We're friends."

"Is that all, Mrs. Kasai?"

"Your Honor," McCloud objected, his patience wearing thin. "Is there a point to this? The witness has already answered the question."

"Move it along, Ms. Bosch."

"Isn't it true that you were involved in an extramarital affair with Mr. Alvarez last year?"

"No, I was not."

"Are you sure you don't want to change your answer?"

"I'm sure."

"Your honor, I'd like to enter copies of Mrs. Kasai's airline tickets to Baltimore as Exhibit B, and photographs of her with Mr. Alvarez as Exhibit C. Her cell phone records will be entered as Exhibit D."

The photographs were the same ones her father used to blackmail her. They were open to interpretation. There was nothing overtly sexual about them, but their smiling faces and physical contact could be interpreted numerous ways.

"So how do you explain these photographs, multiple calls to your cell phone from Mr. Alvarez and vice versa?"

"Mr. Alvarez works for a research firm and I needed his help to find out what my father was up to."

"So you wanted his help in spying on my client?"

"I had to protect myself and last time I checked, accessing public information wasn't a crime."

Bosch moved on. "When your father came to visit your office last year, what did he ask you?"

"He wanted me to retain my services as a communications consultant."

"Why would he ask you that?"

"He's your client, why don't you ask him?"

"Answer the question, young lady," the judge admonished.

"I was featured on the cover of *Executive Insider*, which got his attention. He thought I would be the right person for the job."

"Was that all?"

"He asked me to dinner as a way of apologizing for trying to force me to give him an answer quickly."

"What was your response?"

"I went to the dinner and in the end, still declined his offer. He got angry and sent the photographs you've been parading around to my husband."

"You testified earlier that you didn't tell anyone about the abuse because you didn't want to end up a ward of the state and destroy your family. But isn't it true that you had family on your mother's side you could have gone to if, as you say, my client were to be incarcerated?"

"Yes, my mother had family, but no, I couldn't stay with them."

"I'm sorry, I don't understand." Bosch made a spectacle of pretending to be confused.

"The few relatives my mother had were not in a position to take in a teenage girl and provide for her."

"Did you ask them?"

"No."

"Did you hint to any of them that you might be in trouble and needed their help?"

"No."

"Then how would you know they weren't in a position to take you in?"

"The relatives in question were an uncle and cousin. My cousin had a roommate, and they shared a one-bedroom apartment. My uncle had a live-in girlfriend and no place in his life for a teenage girl."

"Did you ever consider telling your stepmother that your father was abusing you, as you claim?"

"No."

"What about your biological mother?"

"No. For reasons I've already explained. I was too ashamed. And there was the burden of keeping the family together by remaining secretive."

"Did you tell a teacher or counselor at school?"

"No."

"Over the past decade or more, there was plenty of opportunity to come forward. You were no longer in your father's house. Everybody had grown up and moved on. You were on your own. Why didn't you come forward then?"

"I wanted to be free of my father and put that whole sordid chapter of my life behind me. In order to function and live a decent life, I had to file it away in my memory and hoped I would never have a reason to revisit the past."

"What changed?"

"He was determined to break me. I had the audacity to go on and live a happy life without him in it."

Bosch walked over to the defense table and picked up a notepad. "Please help us gain some perspective, Nina. You had dinner with my client and his wife at the Bristol Lounge at the Four Seasons Hotel last summer, and you had lunch with him at the Top of the Hub restaurant in the spring. You had dinner with him at your home at the invitation of your husband. It sounds like you wanted this man—the man you claim you wanted to escape—in your life. In fact, it sounds like you went out of your way to make him part of it."

"Then you heard wrong, Ms. Bosch."

She ignored the response and moved on. "You also testified that if my client had gone to prison, it would mean the end of your ambition. Is that right?"

"Yes."

"Can you explain what you meant?"

"I meant that if I exposed him, the future I wanted for myself would have been a huge question mark."

"Are you saying that one of the reasons you didn't come forward is because you didn't want to lose the lifestyle you had become accustomed to?"

"I'm saying I was too young and ill-prepared to deal with the consequences of coming forward. Staying quiet seemed a good idea at the time."

Bosch wasn't convinced. "Let me see if I understand this. You claimed you were molested by my client. You told no one, including your best friend, who by her own testimony was like a sister to you. You didn't tell your husband of several years, you didn't tell your own mother, though you had ample opportunity over the years to come forward. And you expect this court to believe my client is guilty?"

"I do," Nina said boldly.

"No further questions for this witness."

The State asked for a redirect.

"Nina, did you ever discuss the abuse with the defendant?"

"I did."

"When?"

Nina recapped the episode leading up to the miscarriage and the conversation she had with Phillip when he brought her the diamond cross as a gift.

"What was the defendant's response?"

"He wouldn't acknowledge any of it happened. Either that or he would sidestep the issue entirely. He claimed he loved me and he was devastated when I left home and cut off all communication with him."

"How did that make you feel?"

"Like trash. As if I weren't worthy of his consideration or deserving of an answer."

"Why did you invite him to your home after you went to great lengths to keep him at bay all these years?"

"My husband invited him to thank him for coming to my rescue when I had the miscarriage. At the time, my husband didn't know the whole story."

"Can you tell us what happened?"

Nina took a deep breath then exhaled slowly. "I went to his office at MIT because I discovered he was having an affair with my best friend. While we were there, I developed terrible cramping. I knew something was wrong with the baby. I tried to reach for my purse to call for help. He told me he would call, but kicked my purse out of reach. As the pain worsened, he just stood there."

"He didn't call?"

"Not while I was conscious and begging him to help me. I passed out. When I came to, I was in a hospital room."

"Your own father watched you have a miscarriage and didn't help you until it was too late?"

The defense objected. "My client called for help and got Mrs. Kasai the medical attention she needed. Anything else is pure conjecture."

"Sustained."

Nina was glad her testimony was over. She had made it through but wasn't sure if it was the slam-dunk the DA wanted. Bosch made a compelling argument. Why hadn't she told anyone? It was the very question Nina imagined must weigh heavy on the jurors' minds.

CHAPTER THIRTY-FIVE

"The defense calls Casselia Copeland to the stand."

Cassie shot daggers at Nina as she made her way to the witness box.

"I know you're testifying under very trying circumstances," Bosch said sweetly. "Tell us about your relationship with your father?"

Cassie smiled and looked at him. "I feel lucky that he's my dad. That's why it's so hard for me to be here. The man my sister describes doesn't exist."

"Why is that?"

"Because he has been nothing but a great father to both of us. But Dad and Nina have always had a difficult relationship as long as I can remember."

"Did your sister or father ever tell you why their relationship was so rocky?"

"They had a falling out years ago."

"About what?"

"Nina's boyfriend at the time was part of a group of people looking to start up a software company. Nina asked Dad to invest and he refused. The whole thing fell apart after that and she never forgave him."

Nina was livid. That incident was completely fabricated. Cassie knew better than to spit out that lie.

"Did your father explain why he wouldn't invest?"

"He said it was too risky and he thought the guy was just using Nina."

"So he was looking out for your sister's best interest?"

"Exactly."

"What happened after the falling out?"

"Nina wouldn't return Dad's calls. He tried to explain that he was protecting her, but she wouldn't budge. Things got worse when she got married."

Cassie was prodded for further details.

"My sister never told our father she was engaged. She begged me not to breathe a word to him. I couldn't take the guilt, so he eventually heard it from me just before the wedding."

"So your sister asked you to withhold the truth?"

"Yes."

"What was your father's reaction when he heard she was engaged?"

"He was really happy. He thought a pending marriage was just what the two of them needed to make up. He was excited at the possibility of becoming a grandfather."

"What was your father's reaction when you told him his eldest daughter was about to be married and neither informed nor invited him?"

"He broke down. I'd never seen Dad cry before."

Bosch handed Cassie a box of tissues.

"He just kept saying he didn't understand why she wouldn't want him at her wedding. He still bought her a wedding gift, though."

"Did she accept it?"

"No. She asked me to return it to him."

"What did he say when the gift was returned?"

"He was hurt."

"Has your attitude toward your sister changed in light of the allegations she's made?"

"Yes. Before she was my big sister, but now ..."

"But now?" Bosch asked expectantly.

"Now I think she's a liar and a manipulator."

Nina felt sorry for her younger sibling. Their father had brainwashed her to the point where she sounded like his hired mouthpiece. In a way, she was as much his victim as Nina.

"Why do you characterize your sister as a liar and manipulator?"

"Because she's got everyone fooled. She comes across as Miss Goody two-shoes, but she'll do and say anything to get her way."

"You seem very hurt by her actions."

"The things she's accusing Dad of are disgusting. Dad would destroy anyone who tried to hurt his children. He wouldn't turn around and hurt either one of us. He would constantly brag about how well Nina did in school."

"Were there any other instances where your sister asked you to hide the truth?"

"Yes. She asked me not to tell her husband that our father was here in Boston. I wasn't allowed to talk about Dad when Marc was around."

"Thank you, Cassie."

McCloud got straight to the point. "Ms. Copeland, isn't it possible that your sister rejected the defendant's attempts at reconciliation because of what she has been saying all along, that he molested her and she wanted no part of him?"

Cassie was dumbfounded. That line of reasoning had obviously never occurred to her. She looked at Phillip, as if searching for guidance, but no answer came. "I never thought about it that way. But I still don't believe what she says."

"Do you believe everything your father tells you?"

"Of course. Dad always tells me the truth."

"Would it surprise you to learn that there was no boyfriend, no software company to invest in, and this story was completely fabricated by the defendant because he didn't have the guts to tell you the real reason your sister wanted him to stay away from her?"

"Yes, he did."

"What was the boy's name?"

"I don't know."

The DA rattled off a series of rapid-fire questions that wilted Cassie's resolve. "Where was he from? Where did he live? What kind of software did they want your dad to invest in? Where was the company going to be located?"

Bosch was outraged. "Objection! He's badgering the witness."

Before the judge could rule, McCloud withdrew the questions but the point had already been made.

"Are you jealous of your sister, Cassie?"

"No, I'm not jealous of my sister," she said, as if insulted by the very idea. "Why would I be jealous of somebody like that?"

"But you already told us that you were."

Cassie looked confused. "I did not!"

"You said the defendant bragged about her. I wonder if there's a bit of sibling rivalry going on here?"

"No. I'm here because—"

He wouldn't let her finish. "Are you here testifying because you believe the defendant is innocent or because it's a way for you to stick it to your sister for taking away your meal ticket?"

The defense complained that the prosecution was overzealous and badgering the witness, yet again.

"Sustained."

"That's not true," Cassie responded.

Dan McCloud had no sympathy. "Cassie, when did you graduate from college?"

"I didn't," she said softly, lowering her head.

"So you lived under the same roof as you sister, were afforded the same opportunities, yet you're a college drop-out while your sister went to Stanford on a full academic scholarship, and later graduated top of her MBA class at Harvard. How does that happen?"

An exasperated defense objected. "Your Honor, I fail to see what any of this has to do with the facts of this case."

The judge ordered the DA to move on.

"Where do you work, Ms. Copeland?"

Bosch couldn't yell objection fast enough. "This is beyond ridiculous."

"My patience is wearing thin, Mr. McCloud. Where is this going?"

"Your Honor, I promise there is relevance to this line of questioning."

"I don't have a job right now," Cassie answered sheepishly.

"Isn't it true that your sister Nina encouraged you to go back to school to get your degree?"

"Yes."

"Did she offer to help you with tuition?"

"Yes."

"Why didn't you take her up on her offer?"

"Nina and I are very different people. Climbing the corporate ladder wasn't that important to me."

"What is important to you then?"

Cassie couldn't answer and McCloud moved on. "You lived in a pretty nice apartment in Boston, you travel, drive a nice car and wear designer clothes. That's not bad for someone with no degree and no job. Who pays for your expensive lifestyle?"

"My father is very generous."

"So it is your testimony that your sister has been loving and supportive, and wanted the best for you. She has volunteered to help you gain your independance. It is also your testimony that your quality of life is dependent on your father's generosity. Who's the liar and manipulator now?" he asked as he walked away.

Elizabeth Copeland, Nina and Cassie's bossy paternal aunt who lived in Minnesota was up next. She was a confident woman who was used to being in charge. She described her brother's relationship with his daughters as idyllic and went on about how Phillip felt guilty for missing eight years of Nina's life, and tried to compensate for it by spoiling her. She described her relationship with Nina as a happy one. She claimed she was unaware of any problems between Nina and her father.

Dan McCloud wasted no time with his cross-examination.

"You just testified that you live and work Minneapolis, so how would you know if there were any problems between the defendant and his daughter?"

"Phillip would have told me," she answered indignantly.

"Really? Your brother would have told you he was molesting his own daughter?"

"Objection!" Bosch squawked.

McCloud withdrew the question. "What was your reaction when your niece told you she was molested by the defendant?"

"I didn't believe her."

"Why not?"

"I think my niece is punishing her father for not being around during her early years."

Ms. Copeland, are you a doctor of mental health, a Psychologist or Psychiatrist?"

"No."

"So how did you come to that conclusion?"

"I love Nina, but she's a very insecure person. She told me on numerous occasions that growing up, she felt rejected by her father since he barely acknowledged her existence. I think these accusations are her way of getting back at him for what she considers a grave injustice."

"Do you have any evidence to back up this theory?"

"No."

Dr. Benjamin Obasanjo, Jenny's ex-husband and destroyer of the allegedly incriminating voice recording, testified next. His testimony was another dose of hero worship for Phillip's parenting skills and proclamations that his friend would never hurt his daughter. After his heartfelt speech about knocking sense into Phillip if he ever suspected he was molesting his own child, he was questioned about Jenny's claim of evidence to the contrary.

"But your ex-wife testified that you destroyed evidence proving otherwise," Bosch said.

"Jenny has remained bitter since the divorce. She'll say anything to disparage me.

"This tape that she speaks of never existed?"

"There was a tape. But many years have passed. It's possible her memory is distorted."

"Why did you destroy it?"

"There was no need to hang on to it. I had what I needed and Gloria was dismissed from our employ."

Nina could see Benjamin really believed what he was saying. Her father had everyone fooled, and Ben had just perjured himself to protect his friend.

Dan McCloud kept his cross-examination brief. "You said if there had been any inkling that something like this was going on someone would have said something. But witnesses testified earlier that they suspected something *was* wrong. Could you explain the discrepancy?"

Ben couldn't.

The defense saved its most powerful witness for last: State Senator Joanna Warren Smith. A rising political star with buzz of a US Senate run surrounding her, the pint-sized lawmaker with deep blue eyes and delicate features was a tigress in the state house, especially when it came to legislation regarding women's issues.

"Senator, we thank you for taking time from your extremely busy schedule to tell the truth on behalf of your friend and collaborator," Bosch said, obviously sucking up.

"I'm here to see that justice is served."

"Senator, how long have you known my client?"

"Over ten years."

"In what capacity?"

"Phillip and I served on the committees of several organizations together. Eventually, he became an ardent supporter of my efforts to strengthen the laws to prevent violence against women."

"Could you expand on that, Senator?"

"The Dare to Dream Foundation is one of the largest contributors to battered women's shelters and rape crisis centers across the state. There's no question he's dedicated and has put his money where his mouth is. A lot of politicians and community leaders specialize in rhetoric, but not Phillip. He's down in the trenches with those of us who feel strongly about these issues and are prepared to do the hard work to see change happen."

"What were your thoughts when you heard such an outstanding citizen was being accused of a sex crime?"

"I thought someone was playing a practical joke on me. It seemed so preposterous."

"How would you characterize your friend, Senator?"

The senator looked at Phillip warmly.

"He is one of the few men whom I deeply admire. He's a man of integrity and high moral fiber."

"Thank you, Senator."

"Senator, did you know the defendant had an older daughter?" McCloud asked.

"Not until recently."

"Did you also know he had an illegitimate son, fathered with a young woman who was only seventeen at the time of the child's conception?"

Bosch was on her feet. "The senator is not here to comment on my client's personal life."

"Your Honor, the senator has testified to the high moral fiber of the defendant, whom she's known for over a decade. This question is completely relevant."

The judge overruled the objection.

"Well … this is the first I've heard about that."

The DA thanked the senator for her testimony.

CHAPTER THIRTY-SIX

Forensic document examiner Fred Gilson testified to the authenticity of the diary pages found at Phillip's house, confirming that the content was indeed written by Nina. While the new evidence was great news for the prosecution, Nina dreaded what was to come next. She had to read out the contents of the pages out loud for the record. She had thought the worst was over after her testimony. She was wrong.

Nina was reminded she was still under oath and wearily sat in the witness stand for the second time.

"Nina, I know this is painful, but please read for the court what you wrote on March 18th 1989," McCloud directed. "Please speak clearly."

"He was in my room again last night," she read. *"I told him I wasn't feeling well but it didn't matter. He said he had a tough day at work and it would make him feel better. He said Theresa didn't understand him the way I did. It was the same old story. I don't know if he thinks I actually believe that crap. He asked me to undress slowly but then he must have gotten impatient because he started kissing me while he caressed my breast. It hurt because he was rough.*

I thought someone would hear him but no one did. I went to my happy place, although I could feel my tears spilling onto the pillow. When he was finished, he rolled off me. I lay there still, willing him to just disappear and never come back. He walked out without saying a word. When the coast was clear, I went to the bathroom to wash off his stench, like I have dozens of times before. No one ever notices. No one cares."

Nina wanted to collapse under the weight of her shame, but she resolved to hold her head high. First, she looked directly at the jurors, making eye contact with each and every one of them. Then she looked at her father. The silence in the courtroom had become a spectator, too. For the longest of seconds, Nina and Phillip were the only two people in the room, like two prized fighters sizing each other up, each willing their opponent to blink first. And then she did the one thing she hadn't been able to do in twenty-six years. She mouthed the words, *I forgive you.*

A subdued Bosch approached Nina. "Throughout this trial, it's been established that you have been less than truthful about a variety of important matters. Why should we believe you now? Why should we believe what's written in those pages is any truer than the lies you've told?"

"You shouldn't. But the sixteen-year-old girl who documented this crime never lied to you."

District Attorney Dan McCloud was presenting his closing argument to the jury.

"Ladies and gentlemen, this case is about one thing and one thing only: a horrific crime committed by a defendant who went unpunished for years. As if traumatizing his young daughter wasn't enough, the defendant deliberately sought her out years later so he could continue his reign of terror over her life. Nina Kasai simply wanted to put the anguish of her painful childhood behind her, and she had largely succeeded. But the defendant had other ideas. Mrs. Kasai finally had the courage to come forward and do what many victims of sexual assault cannot do. Nina Kasai couldn't stop her father as a young girl. She endured this hellish abuse beginning at age ten, ladies and gentlemen. Have you taken a look at a ten-year-old lately?"

A photo of Nina at age ten was blown up and pinned to an easel for all could see. She looked small and frail and afraid. Her eyes were not quite vacant, the innocence of childhood still struggling to hold on.

"It took guts for Nina Kasai to sit before you, ladies and gentlemen. You've heard from Lieutenant O'Reilly, who testified to the fact the adults around her cared more about protecting the abuser than the abused. And the victim herself told you everything you needed to know in graphic detail. The defense will have you believe this case is about revenge, an angry woman wanting to destroy a decent man. There is nothing decent about a man who would repeatedly and viciously violate his own child, then hunt her down after she managed to escape with the intention of victimizing her all over again. It is an irrefutable fact that Phillip Copeland broke the law. Don't let him go unpunished. Give Nina the justice she has been denied for years. Find the defendant guilty."

"Beyond the shadow of a doubt," Bosch said, facing the jury. "This is what the state has failed to prove in this case. You've heard a lot of testimony depicting my client as a monster, how he physically and sexually abused his daughter, how he manipulated her. But the evidence also shows a plaintiff who has a history of misrepresenting the truth. In fact, at times, she was deliberately deceptive—by her own admission. The state's entire case rests on this woman's flawed testimony. The plaintiff had years to come forward, but did she? No. Did she reveal this alleged abuse to her most trusted circle, her mother, her husband, her best friend? No, she did not. Did she spend time with my client, the man she claimed brutally abused her? The man she claimed she wanted to escape? She absolutely did.

"You've also heard testimony about who my client truly is: a committed and loving parent, philanthropist, and community leader. Ladies and gentlemen of the jury, justice can only be served if Dr. Copeland is allowed to return to the community that so desperately needs him, and the university that depends on him to train our future leaders. The only just verdict is not guilty."

*   *   *

NINA AND MARC WERE FINISHING up packing for their trip to Los Angeles when they got the call that the jury was back with a verdict after two days of deliberation. As they walked up the steps of the courthouse, Nina turned to Marc. "No matter what the verdict is, I want you to know I wouldn't have had the courage to make it this far if it weren't for your unwavering support. Thank you for loving me so completely and unconditionally. I know now we can survive anything."

His only response was to kiss her on the forehead, as he had a million times before, letting her know much he adored her.

The twelve men and women filed into the jury box, their expressions solemn.

"Before we get to the verdict, I would like to remind everyone to conduct themselves with the utmost sense of decorum and remain quiet when the verdict is read," said Judge Sokoff. He instructed defense council to rise along with the defendant.

"Has the jury reached a verdict?"

The jury foreman answered affirmatively and the judge directed him to read the verdict.

"As to the charge of aggravated child molestation, count one in the indictment, we the jury find the defendant guilty. As to the charge of aggravated sexual battery, count two in the indictment, we the jury find the defendant guilty."

Nina was oddly calm as the rest of the verdict was read and her father was found guilty on all counts. She could hear Marc asking if she was okay, but her lips wouldn't form a response. Her father sat with his shoulders slouched forward and Cassie was silently weeping. Nina got up from her seat and walked out of the courtroom. Her first stop was the ladies' room, where she threw up all over the porcelain sink. After splashing her face with cold water, her weakened knees carried her to the steps of the courthouse, where she sat in the forty-degree temperature with no coat on. She felt nothing. As voices in the distance got closer, she identified them as belonging to Marc and her mother. Charlene was not too far behind. Her mother was telling her she would catch pneumonia and a worried Marc tried to convince her to get back inside. When she didn't move, he scooped her up in his arms and took her somewhere warm.

Phillip sat at the defense table in a haze. His entire body felt like someone had injected him with a massive dose of Novocain. Guilty! On all counts. What the hell happened? How could they find him guilty? His lawyer was saying something about appealing but he wasn't paying attention. He would be sent to prison like a common criminal, all evidence of his prior life buried. The only thing people would remember about him was that he was a convicted rapist. He couldn't stand it. It wasn't fair! He wanted to scream it wasn't fair and the whole trial had been a mistake. He wanted to wake up and find himself in his den sipping a drink. Then out of nowhere or maybe because his defenses were down and his conscience was finally able to surface, he heard a voice taunting him. *Was she worth it? Was your obsession with her worth your freedom? But you're even now. You destroyed her childhood. Now she's taken what's left of your life.*

He shook off the voice. This was all a mistake wasn't it? What would happen to him in prison? Could he survive? He looked behind him and saw Cassie weeping. What would happen to her? She couldn't make it on her own. Why didn't somebody stop Nina before it got too far? He had failed to stop her and this was the end result. He was babbling in his own mind. His thoughts were all running up against each other and after a while, nothing made sense. His head started hammering. He just wanted the pain to end.

CHAPTER THIRTY-SEVEN

One month later, John-Phillip Copeland was sentenced to ten years in prison with the possibility of parole in five. Nina skipped the sentencing. She couldn't bear to see him that way. After the guilty verdict, she took a trip out to Worcester, to visit her baby brother, Alexander. The reception from his mother Tracey was cool at best but she struck Nina as a realist. The reality was that the hefty child support payments would no longer be flooding her bank account. The reality was her little boy would grow up without a father, a too common occurrence in black households.

Nina explained how she came to find out about Alexander's existence and no one in the Copeland family knew of him as far as she could tell, but Nina would make sure Alexander knew who his family was. She also promised to pay the boy's tuition and help out financially as much as she could. As for Cassie, she had no choice now but to go back to college and get a degree that would qualify her to do something she could earn a decent living from. She and Nina had been spending a lot of time together lately, mostly because they were the ones who felt the fallout from the verdict the most acutely.

"Take it all off," Nina told Charlene. She sat at the edge of the bed while a nervous-looking Charlene toyed with a pair of scissors.

"Are you sure you want to do this? Does Marc know you're doing this?"

Nina grabbed the scissors from her and started chopping off her hair.

A stunned Charlene retrieved the scissors quickly. "Have you lost your mind? Did that trial push you over the edge?"

"It's a new beginning, Char. Do you know he refused for me to get it cut and all throughout my adult life I just … well, I guess I subconsciously did what he wanted. I'm free now. I want my first official haircut. And make it a real one. Not the one or two-inch trims you've given me in the past."

"Really, Nina?"

"Yes, really," Nina said, shaking her head as the idea appealed to her more and more. "Eminem isn't the only one who had to clean out his closet."

The two women howled with laughter as Charlene snipped and snapped and Nina watched long clumps of her hair fall to the floor. When Charlene was finished, she gave Nina a mirror.

"Well?" Charlene asked expectantly.

"I love it, Char," Nina said, moving the mirror from side to side. "I look a little different, like a real grown up. My eyes look bigger, though. I don't know if that's a good thing."

"You're as gorgeous as ever, girl. That will never change."

Marc entered the bedroom and did a double take when he saw his wife's short bob, just shy of the jawline.

"What did you do?"

Nina offered a weak smile and Charlene looked guilty then disappeared from the bedroom in a flash.

"You hate it," Nina declared.

He sat next to Nina on the bed. "No. It's just a different you. A new you."

"If all goes well, I won't have time to worry about the latest hair style. A shorter cut seemed more practical."

He placed his hands on her stomach. "Your practicality will serve us well in the coming months and years."

*   *   *

IT'S STILL ME, MR. TIBBS. Don't be afraid. Why did I cut my hair? You ask a lot of questions for a bear, tough questions. And my answer is, I had to. I realize now my hair held me as much of a prisoner as my father did.

You know he wouldn't let me cut it, no matter how long it got. So I had Charlene cut it off. I started a new diary, too. I can't shake the habit. No, I'm through with secrets, Mr. Tibbs. This time around, it will be filled with laughter, not tears. And it won't be hidden in the attic. The same applies to you, Mr. Tibbs. I do know where the new you should be. You're coming downstairs. Your new home is going to be in the family room. At least until we finish constructing the playroom.

*   *   *

TWO YEARS LATER, NINA FOUND herself taking an hour-long drive to a state-of-the-art prison, one of the most secure in the nation and the only one to sit on a major highway. She arrived at one of the eight modules used to house prisoners and went through the usual security checkpoints. She was ushered into the visitors' room. She took a seat and nervously awaited his arrival.

She felt a sudden jolt when he walked into the visiting area. A slight man to begin with, he had aged, his head now completely grey. His face was gaunt, his cheeks sunken from massive weight loss. She bit down hard on her lips to stop the tears from forming. As she expected, he was less than pleased to see her.

"What are you doing here?"

She didn't respond.

"If you're looking for forgiveness, you're in the wrong place. But the prison chapel isn't too far from here."

She finally found her voice. "Forgiveness for what?"

"Sending you own father to prison is unforgivable."

"Then why did you do it?"

Sadness crept into his face, but it was quickly replaced by the familiar stubbornness and lack of empathy that had defined their relationship.

"I was a good daughter. You didn't deserve me."

Nina opened her pocketbook and took out her wallet. She removed a photo and pushed it across the table toward him. He glanced at it then looked back at her. He wanted to ask her something but was too proud.

"Grace and Faith Kasai. A year old today," she explained.

"Why did you come to see me? You've destroyed what was left of my life."

"No dad. You did that all on your own. All I wanted was a stinking apology, some acknowledgement that I wasn't some piece of property you could use and dispose of when you felt like it. You weren't sorry at all. I was living in a hell you sent me to. This was the only way I knew to get out. You had to answer to someone you couldn't bully or buy off or manipulate."

"I gave you everything."

"You gave me the best of what money could buy. What I needed from you didn't have a price tag."

Maybe she was right Phillip thought. There were some things his money couldn't buy, like Constance Buckwell's silence. The security he thought it would bring him failed to materialize and he had to take care of her himself by slipping something in her drink when they had dinner. That induced the heart attack that killed her. That should have been the end of his troubles combined with the diary he stole but it was all for naught. Now, he could honestly say it wasn't worth it. None of it was.

"Congratulations on the twins Nina. I know you'll make an outstanding mother. You're excellent at everything you do. I have no doubt that will extend to motherhood."

With that, Phillip Copeland signaled to be taken back to his cell.

As Nina made her way back to her car, she realized how lucky she was. A big, happy contented smile spread across her face. She had a life beyond anything she could have imagined. And this time, she knew she deserved it.

The End

Acknowledgements

I owe a debt of gratitude to many people who made this book possible. To my beta readers, thank you for taking the time to read the manuscript while it was still rough around the edges.

My husband Donat, your love, support, and advice mean more to me than I can ever express.

My boys Amini and Maximillian, thanks for being patient whenever Mama went into her writing zone. I love you both very much.

My mother Leonora gave me one of the greatest gifts a parent can give a child: the love of books.

Michaela Hamilton at Kensington Books, you fought for an unknown author. I'll always be grateful.

Karlai Brooks, what you did took courage. You know what I mean.

Dr. Desmond McCarthy, my journalism professor at Framingham State University, you believed in me. You have no idea what it means to me that you thought I had talent as a writer, even when I was still so very green.

To family and friends who have been supportive in various ways, much love.

About The Author

Gledé Browne Kabongo began writing at the age of 14 when she covered soccer matches for the newspaper in her hometown of Milton, MA. She has also written for the *Patriot Ledger* and *Metrowest Daily News,* two Massachusetts based metropolitan newspapers. She earned a master's degree in communications from Clark University, and once had dreams of winning a Pulitzer Prize for journalism. These days her dreams have shifted to winning the Pulitzer for fiction, and a Best Screenplay Academy Award. Gledé has worked in marketing management for more than 10 years for companies in the Information Technology, publishing and non-profit sectors. She lives in Massachusetts with her husband and two sons.

You can email her at glede@gledebrownekabongo.com. She wants to hear from you.